Satisfaction

Also by Karrine Steffans

The Vixen Diaries
The Vixen Manual

SatisFaction

Erotic Fantasies for the Advanced & Adventurous Couple

Karrine Steffans

GRAND CENTRAL
PUBLISHING

NEW YORK   BOSTON

Grand Central Publishing
Hachette Book Group
237 Park Avenue
New York, NY 10017
www.HachetteBookGroup.com

Printed in the United States of America
First Edition: August 2011
10 9 8 7 6 5 4 3 2 1

Grand Central Publishing is a division of Hachette Book Group, Inc. The Grand Central Publishing name and logo is a trademark of Hachette Book Group, Inc.

The publisher is not responsible for websites (or their content) that are not owned by the publisher.

Library of Congress Cataloging-in-Publication Data
Steffans, Karrine
    SatisFaction : erotic fantasies for the advanced & adventurous couple / by Karrine Steffans.
        p. cm.
    ISBN 978-0-446-55320-9
  1. Sexual fantasies.   2. Sexual excitement.   I. Title.
    HQ31.S788 2011
    306.7—dc22

                                                                2010049216

Contents

SatisFaction

Prologue

Ready...Set...Fuck!

Well, wouldn't you know it...here we are again! Back for another round of frank and meaningful discourse, contemplative advice, and what I hope will be, for you, page-after-page of nonstop hot-and-sexy fun, as much fun as it has been for me to pen. *SatisFaction: Erotic Fantasies for the Advanced & Adventurous Couple* promises to be just that, and more. What's most exciting for me about this, my fourth book, is that it's a hybrid work combining erotic fiction with advice and instructions on how to incorporate these fictional erotic adventures into your committed relationship.

When I first began outlining *SatisFaction*, I was unsure just how much I could lend myself to the subject of erotic fantasies. While many may consider me quite worldly when it comes to sex, at my core I've always been monogamous and traditional, preferring to operate within the realms of what most would define as traditional one-on-one, male-to-female interaction. Sure, I love role-playing, but that's not an uncommon practice in conventional relationships. This little foray into the range of possibilities for keeping your relationship fresh and exciting proved just as much an eye-opener for me as I'm sure it will be for you. Through intensive research, I began to delve into worlds that were wildly fascinating and exotic, far beyond what I now realize has been my relatively limited scope of experience.

I can't begin to recount how many different types of sexual fantasies I came across while conducting my carnal investigations. Just when I thought I had reached the limit of things to do, I would stumble upon a nugget of information that led to a mother lode of sexual fantasia, the likes of which would take at least ten more *SatisFaction*s to even scratch the surface.

I initially began this quest for knowledge by doing what any self-respecting, hard-nosed investigative author would: I Googled "free porn" and hit the Internet jackpot, finding 71,900,000 links. That's right, there are *millions* of sites on the Internet offering free pornography and/or sex-related material. And that's just as of the writing of this book.

Now, most women don't begin their days scouring the Internet for porn. We're usually busy with lives sometimes bigger than we planned or for which we bargained. We are mothers and daughters, sisters and wives, aunts and grandmothers. We are all things to all the people in our orbit, and more often than not we get lost in the shuffle of such an existence, forgetting to take care of ourselves. What we have to realize is that when we do this, we are also, by default, neglecting the people we work so hard to take care of, like our husbands. **When we're not up to par, neither is our marriage.**

If we're overtaxed and overwhelmed, sex is usually the first thing to fall by the wayside, creating an Achilles' heel of vulnerability we can ill afford. The sexual health of our marriages should be something we fight to strengthen, not leave weakened and exposed. This is the area where outside forces, which can cause a breach in your bond, are most likely to get in. Show me a sexually unhappy, unsatisfied, and unchallenged husband or wife, and I'll show you the potential for a wandering eye.

And yes, while it is true that marriage—whether spiritual, civil, or legal—is dependent on much more than sex, all the parts must work together to benefit the whole. Sex without love and trust can never lead to real intimacy. And while it's also true that I'm not a professional, I am a real woman with real experiences. I'm a mom, a wife, and a businesswoman doing all that I can to keep my family happy, my husband entertained, and my career thriving. It is one helluva juggling act, but I'm all-in—100 percent. With everything that I have on my plate, I do my best not to lose focus. The last thing I want is for the man I have chosen to spend the rest of my life with to wake up one morning, look me in the face, and say, "I'm bored."

Remember: A man will either marry the woman who will fulfill all his sexual fantasies or cheat on his wife with her.

Harsh? Perhaps. True? Probably. Does this mean every man and woman on the planet wants wild, exotic sex from his or her lover? *Of course not.* There are plenty of couples thrilled with their all-missionary-all-the-time sex lives and wouldn't have it any other way. If you and your partner are one of those couples, please, give this book to your mother. Seriously. She's probably having better, more adventurous sex than you.

With all the exhaustive research I undertook for this book, I have learned that there are more than seventy-four million ways to skin your cat. Husbands and wives alike are looking for new and exciting things to do to add a spark to their relationship. Most of us, however, feel as if those sparks and the fantasies that are intertwined with them are far-off ideas, too complicated and tedious to undertake. Many women feel as if being a wife is something completely different from being a mistress, a liaison, or even a whore. The surprising truth in all of this is that **marriage is the only institution that morally condones you being all those things and more to your spouse** without feeling compromised, dirty, embarrassed, or judged.

Ladies, you want to be and do as much as your husbands desire, as well as all the things you've wanted to do yourselves, but were afraid to try in less significant relationships. I mean, seriously, you can't just do this sort of stuff with some guy you're dating. **The fantasies and acts we discuss in this book should be shared with a life partner,** someone with whom you are exploring and building the utmost levels of intimacy and trust. If, in fact, you are not in a marriage of some sort, please stop reading right now and give this book to someone who is. The last thing I want is to be responsible for thousands of women following the advice inside these pages with some random dude who will sexually exploit them, encouraging an exploration of every single fantasy herein and never calling back after the last chapter. As fun and lighthearted as it may seem on the surface, this book is a serious matter. Used responsibly, it can be your marriage's secret weapon. In the hands of the uncommitted and reckless, however, it is dangerous—emotionally, spiritually, even physically—to engage in some of these fantasies with anyone who doesn't care about your well-being.

Don't rush the ready. If you must have this book, put it away for safekeeping until you're married, preferably to someone who is fully deserving of you. Until then, peek at the pages, take note, but reserve this kind of stuff for your life mate, not some waffling wankster who's not sure if he's ready to even call you his girlfriend.

As for you men, maybe you've been afraid to tell your wife about your fantasies, thinking she'll be repulsed, angry, judgmental, or all three. This usually happens because when women hear the word *fantasy*, we automatically assume you're talking about something that doesn't involve us. **Let your wife know that *she* is your fantasy.** Include her in your every whim. Having this trusty how-to on your nightstand is just the way to make that happen.

And because I believe in seeing a thing all the way through to its most logical—or in this case, illogical—conclusion, each chapter is followed by what I call a *V-Log*, short for *Vixen Log*, a hypothetical cautionary scenario, if you will. These fictitious examples detail what could happen if the fantasy in the prior chapter goes horribly awry. I include them to reinforce that you should read every chapter in this book with a close eye and thoroughly investigate beforehand just what it means to implement these fantasies. Erotic role-playing is an excellent way to increase intimacy and stoke the heat in your love life, but must be handled with absolute care. When you know better, you do better.

Chapter One

Domination

Fantasy

Sex with a married man, to me, was the best sex in the world. The thrill of being a mistress and knowing he was fucking me better, harder, and more adventurously than he fucked his wife got me excited in ways nothing else could. Sexual encounters with married men allow them to be assertive and in control in ways they might never have attempted with their spouses. Husbands often found themselves in power struggles at home, browbeaten over every little thing. It could make a man understandably tense. With a mistress, someone like me, they could release some of that pent-up tension and be in control of everything—when they see me, where they see me, how long they see me, and with whom I can interact. A mistress is a woman in a box, constrained, completely subject to her married lover's will.

As restrictive as that kind of arrangement sounds, I loved being the other woman ... savored it, even. And although my relationship with my married lover was limited to a specific place at a specific time, I was privy to a view of him that his wife would never see, a side that would disturb her if she ever did. I knew the real him, unmasked. I knew the man who loved to indulge in edgy things, sadistic things—things that weren't always conventional or socially acceptable. Within the four walls of our motel, he was my overlord and master, able to manipulate me with his brutal touch and the promise of his superior cock.

I relished the sway my married lover held over me, and in time my need to be sexually dominated by him became a narcotic and as necessary as the air I breathed.

It was late in the evening and I was waiting for him at our usual spot—a dingy, dirty motel steps away from the highway and a truck stop. When I wasn't with him in this sleazy lair, I was an upscale, professional woman who enjoyed the finer things in life. I preferred plush hotels like the Four Seasons and The Peninsula, liveried valets, and Michelin-starred room service to some low-class dive like this. I would have never chosen it on my own, but for him I was willing to be downmarket. For him, I would get in the gutter.

This location, from the very beginning, had been his idea. We needed a spot, he said, where dark deeds could go unnoticed, a room where he could "put me in my place." This place delivered just that, with its cheap curtains, seldom-laundered bedspread, and threadbare sheets, all spattered with mysterious stains.

I waited, geared in knee-high leather boots, a body-hugging black vinyl dress, and a red cape. I glanced at the clock radio next to the bed, anxious, eager, nervous, and a little afraid. I never knew how he would come at me, how he would leave me; the battle scars he left me with were different each time. They became a road map to our couplings, bruises that spanned my body in odd patterns, each revealing everything and nothing about who we were. I paced back and forth, around and around, like a feral animal, trying to still my mind in anticipation of his arrival.

I dug into my overnight bag, checking my supplies, rustling through the body wash, vibrators, lotions, and handcuffs. I searched and took count, double-checking I hadn't forgotten the things he liked. Suddenly a firm hand wrapped around the right side of my throat and squeezed as another hand clasped the left side. My heart raced, my body electrified by the thrill of surprise. Even though I'd expected him, he'd caught me unaware. His body pressed into my back as his hands slid down to my shoulders and shoved me facedown onto the bed.

He flipped me over and loomed above, a dark scowl on his face. I whimpered with fear, even though I was aroused. He leaned down, close to my face.

"I'm late," he growled, "and it's all your fault."

"I'm sorry," I squeaked. It was always my fault. It always would be. Without fault, there could be no punishment, and I needed to be punished. I was a bad, bad girl.

"So what are we going to do about it?" he asked, his dark eyes piercing mine. "Do you think I should cut you a break?"

"No, master."

"Then what should I do?"

His finger trailed up the inside of my thigh, over my moistening slit, resting on my fleshy mound.

"Hmmm?" he asked again.

I trembled beneath him. He gripped my crotch, squeezing it tight. My pussy throbbed at his violent touch.

"Tell me, you cunt. What should I do?"

"Show me no mercy," I whispered.

"What? I can't hear you."

"Show me no mercy!" I shouted.

He released his grip and mounted me, his legs pressed tightly against the sides of my hips. He grabbed my throat with both hands, first choking me, then slapping my face as he grunted with anger. My cheeks went numb, and my body was on fire.

He ripped my cape open.

"I brought..."

"Shut up!" he barked, slapping my face once again.

He grabbed my shoulders and shook me like a rag doll, then flung me back down with disgust.

"If I hadn't been late, we'd be fucking by now."

"I know," I cried, my cheeks burning with pain.

"Maybe you did it on purpose," he sneered. "Were you fucking someone else?"

"Never," I said, reaching between his legs. "I only want you."

He slapped my hand away.

"Say it again," he demanded with another slap to my face.

"I only want you."

"Say no one fucks you better."

"No one fucks me better."

"Louder!" he ordered.

"No one fucks me better than you!" I screamed at the ceiling.

He wrapped his hands around my throat, wringing it tight.

"Now say it."

I could barely breathe, let alone speak. I mouthed the words, my face flushed, my eyes stinging with tears. He released me, flinging my head back. I exploded in a fit of coughs and gasped for air. His smile was sinister as he watched with indifference.

"Prove it," he said.

I reached up, running my hand over his shirt, searching for his nipple. I pinched it as hard as I could, twisting it cruelly, enough to break the skin. A tiny dot of blood appeared.

"You bitch!" he cried as I took advantage of the moment and shoved him away. I rushed from the bed, away from him, across the room, cowering in the corner near the window. My cape had fallen onto the floor. He stepped over it as he came toward me, kicking off his shoes, removing his tie, peeling out of his shirt and pants with quiet seething. His dick was a knife inside his briefs, aimed at me, ready to kill.

"Come here," he demanded.

Nervously, I did.

He circled me, slow, deliberate, deciding his next move. He stopped behind me, his arm across my throat, pulling my head back. He squeezed my breast with his free hand, squeezed it hard enough to make me spill tears.

"No one can save you, you know," he whispered.

His hand slid down the black vinyl dress, past my stomach, stopping at my loins. He cupped my hot wetness, gently at first, then hard and vicious, lifting me up by my pussy. I moaned in delicious agony.

"I don't want to be saved," I said in reply.

He bent me over with a harsh shove and delivered a series of slaps to my ass that radiated through my wet hole all the way to my clit.

"You're a whore," he barked as he slapped me again.

"Yes," I whispered. "I'm a whore."

"You're a fucking slut."

"I'm a fucking slut."

He lifted my dress, his angry hands gripping my fleshy bottom.

"I love this fat ass, you fucking slut."

"Then fuck it," I begged. "Fuck my fat ass."

He pulled out his cock, bending me farther, putting my ass in the air. He crammed into my sphincter. It resisted at first, and then bloomed like a lotus, letting him inside. He grabbed a fistful of my hair and snatched my head back, thrusting deep inside me over and over.

"Take it, you bitch!"

I wriggled and writhed against his evil fuck stick. He pumped a few more times, then pushed me away, onto the floor, his dick snapping out of my ass with a pop.

I tried to crawl forward, but he grabbed me by the hair again and hauled me backward toward the bed.

"Get up there and lie down with your feet facing the headboard."

I climbed weakly onto the bed, my asshole, ass, and face stinging raw.

"Lower. I want your head hanging off."

I scooted a few inches, eager to please him. He was upside down as I watched him now, blood rushing to my head, making me dizzy.

He shoved his dirty cock in my mouth.

"Now suck it."

I grabbed it with both hands, pulling it in, tasting my body's discarded remains.

"Suck my dick, you shitty-mouthed whore!"

I twirled my tongue around the head of his meat, and then pulled the shaft deeper inside. He began pumping, slow at first, then faster, harder, beating my mouth with his monster. He groaned in ecstasy as he fucked my face, my saliva bubbling around his cock, out of my mouth, onto the soiled carpet.

I began to gag, but he continued pumping, demanding I service him despite all else. I kept on sucking, my pussy dripping with hot desire. I held on to him with one hand, touching my aching clit with the other.

"Leave it alone," he said. "Your pussy belongs to me."

He pushed my face away, removing his dick, then grabbed me by the hair and neck and pulled me onto the floor.

"On your knees!"

I crawled forward, onto my knees.

He lifted the back of my dress, grabbed the back of my red thong, and ripped it off. The sensation of the material being pulled quickly against my clit sent a spasm of pleasure through my body. He ran his index and middle fingers down the crack of my ass, stopping at my very wet pussy. He was on his knees behind me now, his cock toying at the entrance to my love tunnel. He moved it up and down against the wet slit, torturing me with the promise of more.

"Put it in," I begged. "Please fuck me right now."

He positioned himself with exact precision, and then plunged his steel rod as deep as it could go. He hit the bottom, awakening the entire length of me inside. My walls quivered, their juices fully unleashed, as he did a slow grind against me, stirring his dick around inside. He pushed in hard. He pulled out slow, stopping right at the edge of my tunnel, close to the exit, the most sensitive area inside my walls. He lingered there, his dick rubbing slowly against the floor of my pussy. I was dying inside, on the verge of explosion. He pulled back a little bit farther, then plunged back in, all the way to the balls. The dam burst inside me.

"I'm cumming!" I cried.

He slapped my ass, and the sting resonated, making me cum harder.

"Do it again!"

He slapped the other cheek as he pounded me with his cock. My body buckled beneath him as my hole gushed and gushed. He held on to me, pulling me back into place, pumping with renewed vigor, raising his thigh so he could maneuver his thrust even more.

I shook violently against him from the intensity of my orgasm. He pulled out and picked me up, placing me on my back at the edge of the bed.

He rammed his cock deep inside me, thrusting with desperation. I gazed up at him as my throbbing clit pulsed anew. He slapped my face and squeezed my breasts, staining the soft flesh with bruises. I raised my hips to meet his thrusts, but he didn't like that. He wanted to be in control. He always had to be the one in charge.

"Bad girl," he grunted, pulling out of me. "I run this show."

"Then run it," I said, daring to be bold.

Angered by my flippant remark, he lifted me up by my pussy with his right hand and grabbed me by the back of my head. He flung me higher on the bed. I landed with a flop, terrified and turned on. He climbed on over me and shoved two fingers inside my pussy, fucking me hard, so hard that it hurt. My eyes filled with tears, but I didn't speak. I didn't want to. The pain was delicious. My clit was engorged to capacity, throbbing with fury. My walls trembled as I neared release. He pulled his two fingers out, balled his hand up into a fist, and shoved it inside me. I came with a jolt, my body rocked so violently, it caused me to sit up. That didn't stop him. He fisted my pussy, all the way up to his wrist, working his closed hand inside me, setting me off even more. I reeled with ecstasy, collapsing back onto the bed, dizzy, delirious. I felt like I would faint.

He removed his fist and placed his hand, drenched with my pussy juices, open-palmed on my face. He stuck his fingers inside my mouth.

"Open wider," he said.

I widened my jaws, sticking my tongue out. He put his whole hand inside. I licked and sucked his fingers, savoring my taste.

"Good girl," he whispered.

He patted me on the cheek and got up from the bed.

I watched him, wondering what would come next. He gathered his clothes from the floor and began to get dressed.

"Wait!" I exclaimed. "What are you doing?"

He stared at me plainly.

"I have to go home."

I rushed over to him, my body fully alive from the thrashing it had just taken.

"But I thought..."

"Sorry, honey. I just needed to get some aggression out. I could never do this at home. You don't know how valuable you are to me."

He touched my cheek, and then finished dressing.

I sat on the edge of the bed, watching him, knowing this drill.

"Till next time," he said as he stood at the door.

His eyes lingered on mine for a moment, and then he was gone.

I grabbed my clothes from the closet and got dressed, giving him time to get in his car and leave. I followed behind a few minutes later.

He got home first. I arrived ten minutes later. I could hear him in the shower as I walked into our bedroom and tossed my bag of goodies into the back of the closet. His shirt hung halfway out of the hamper, stained with a tiny dot of blood. I pushed it all the way down and tossed in my soiled clothing. I took a fresh nightgown and underwear from my dresser and showered in the bathroom down the hall.

He was already in bed when I returned to our room smelling clean and wholesome. I slid in next to him. We watched Conan's monologue, our usual routine, and then he reached robotically for me, climbing on top, in our usual, boring missionary fuck.

Reality

In all marital relationships, someone assumes a dominant position. That position, ideally, should be shared between the two of you, alternating depending upon the circumstance. Perhaps your husband is the dominant voice when it comes to making repairs around the house. Maybe you play a more dominant role when it comes to caring for the children. Whatever the case, there should be a balance of power. **Neither of you should exclusively be the dominant person in every area of your lives together.** Such a scenario is not conducive to a healthy relationship.

A woman or man who is dominated by a mate often experiences diminished self-esteem, lack of confidence, and, in many cases, a fear of making decisions, lest the repercussions of those decisions create additional duress. Such relationships also prove rife with resentment, in both parties. The more dominant person may resent the fact that the mate doesn't speak up more or take the initiative, thus causing him or her to lose respect for that mate. Where there is an absence of respect, the door opens for all manner of infidelity and betrayal. Conversely, the more submissive person may despise feeling as if he or she is being controlled or suppressed, and may also seek comfort and solace outside the marriage. Both partners must wholly encourage each other and play a positive, active part in maintaining a balanced relationship. Only then can you thrive together.

Vixen Tip

For those of you who are deep into your sexual fantasies and consider it a lifestyle, consider seeing a sex therapist now and again to be sure that what you're doing and how you're doing it is in the best sexual spirit and not a result of deep-rooted angst or anger. Also, seeing a sex therapist regularly may safeguard against these sorts of fantasies causing more harm than good.

That said, however, in the bedroom—or whatever setting you choose for your sexual encounter—**role-play involving dominant and submissive partners can, if properly executed, lead to extremely fulfilling and explosive sex.**

While not everyone is into domination, it can be a fun and exciting way to add variety to your relationship. I must emphatically state again that it's imperative there be mutual consent beforehand. This is not the type of thing to spring on someone in the middle of intimacy. Everyone doesn't always respond the same to an unexpected slap in the face or a nipple pinched hard enough to draw blood. Your mate could easily misinterpret it as you taking out your anger under the guise of engaging in sexual play and sour on the whole experience. **Things like this can turn ugly very quickly unless you clearly define what is and isn't allowed.**

Vixen Tip

It's Supposed to Hurt So Good!

Just as with defilement, make sure you and your partner are physically prepared and capable of taking the smacks and blows that come with the domination experience. Ladies, don't use this opportunity to give your man a fat lip for that sarcastic comment he made to you in mixed company last month. Similarly, gentlemen, don't see this as a chance to check your lady for some slight she has long forgotten.

If, however, the two you of agree ahead of time to incorporate "punishment" into this experience for minor perceived wrongs and elect to work out said wrongs in the bedroom rather than over dinner, this could be the perfect way to do so. Save them up for just this occasion, agreeing to let this moment put them to rest.

Talk dirty! Hurl agreed-upon epithets! And yes, it is important that you both agree about which coarse words you're free to use on each other. Now is not the time to call your wife a "stank bitch" without having cleared it first. Make a list, if you have to, of words that are a go. Otherwise, you risk being misconstrued or, heaven forbid, perceived as expressing how you really feel about your mate!

The key is to punish your spouse with an endurable amount of painful pleasure, not to beat and berate anyone silly. Implementing domination should be done in a way that enhances your sexual

Vixen Tip

encounter without opening literal and figurative wounds that cause irretrievable damage to your relationship.

Fear not. This isn't as difficult as you think. Pain and ecstasy are separated by a thin wall, and in this kind of experience it's very easy to teeter on the brink of either. But with the proper amount of foreplay, a stinging blow to the face or buttocks, followed by an approved aspersion, can cause that wall to drop and make the two merge into something truly extraordinary!

Now that you've agreed this is going to happen, know your boundaries and limitations. Agree upon and employ the use of a safe word—we like *buttons* because it has a nice, harmless ring to it, but feel free to come up with your own—for when things have gone beyond adventurous play for either of you and made you feel physically threatened, genuinely humiliated, and/or afraid.

Where you choose to have your encounter take place is just as important. Will it be at home, and, if so, **can you clearly separate the marital bed where you make sweet, gentle love from the place where you smack each other around and call each other less-than-flattering names?** If you have no problem doing so, by all means, proceed! If, however, using the same place for all your sexual experiences blurs the lines too much, consider a location outside your bedroom. In the case of domination, a seedy motel might add to the atmosphere of simulated humiliation you're trying to create.

While there are plenty of local stores and places on the Internet to purchase the necessary costumes and accessories, you may already have a store in mind where you plan to go for everything you need.

Vixen Tip

Dress to Impress

Whether you're the dominator or the dominated, the appropriate garb, accessories, and toys can help you set the proper tone.

- Vinyl or leather catsuits and dresses make for ideal dominatrix gear for women. It should fit you well, not too loose or too tight, or you'll lose the desired effect. You should look sexy and inviting enough to arouse his desire and faux ire. Without his arousal, this whole exercise is moot.

- Matching boots and fishnet hose are essential.

- Masks, gloves, handcuffs, chokers, riding crops, cat-o'-nine-tails, bullwhips, oh my! Mix-and-match to create a complete look that is sure to turn your partner on.

Wherever you choose to shop for your goodies, make sure that on the big night you look the part. For this particular fantasy, Coco de Mer is the perfect high-end fantasy supply store. Trashy Lingerie is moderately priced. Feel free to Google sex shops in your local area. All such stores have back entrances, so don't feel strange about visiting. Or visit any one of these shops online!

If executed correctly, the domination theme is a certified winner. With the perfect cocktail of pleasure and pain, the hits—and you—should keep on cumming!

Recap

- Neither of you should exclusively be the dominant person in every area of your lives together.

- Role-play involving dominant and submissive partners can, if properly executed, lead to extremely fulfilling and explosive sex.

- Things like this can turn ugly very quickly unless you clearly define what is and isn't allowed.

- Talk dirty! Hurl agreed-upon epithets!

- Can you clearly separate the marital bed where you make sweet, gentle love from the place where you smack each other around and call each other less-than-flattering names?

- Wherever you choose to shop for your goodies, make sure that on the big night you look the part.

V-Log #1
So, Now You're in Jail...

Not unlike other fantasies, a faultily implemented domination fantasy can have ugly repercussions. The dynamic with this particular fantasy is a tricky one, because it involves the abandonment of any power struggles. One of you chooses to be clearly submissive and the other, clearly dominant. There's no fence straddling here. If you and your husband have power-struggle issues in your relationship, especially unaddressed and/or unresolved ones, the moment when those issues will rear their beastly heads is now.

So here the two of you are, role-playing. In fact, you're reenacting the very scene from the Domination chapter. Cheap motel, cape, knee-high leather boots, black vinyl dress, the whole thing, all the way down to pretending he is married. There's the slapping, the degradation. You've already been getting heated over the things he's been saying. *"Dirty slut!" "Fat, nasty whore!"* And the one that really got to you as you were still reeling from being called fat... *"Shut up, you stupid bitch, and suck my cock!"* Stupid? He called you *stupid*? And with those words, he broke the fourth wall and what was supposed to be a fantasy suddenly began to feel, for you, very real.

As you can see, these words sound all cute, fun, and edgy when you're reading them on the page and imagining your man saying them, but it can be a different story when they're actually said as you're being smacked around during an intense, experimental act of sexual role-playing.

That's right, ladies. Saying you want to participate in a fantasy is one thing; actually going all the way and immersing yourself in that specific fantasy is another. A domination fantasy means one party having power over another—physically, sexually, emotionally, and mentally. If you're the one who acts as the submissive partner in this scenario, that calls for letting yourself be overtaken in all ways. As noted in other chapters, this kind of fantasy should not be approached lightly. It has the potential to tap into really sensitive areas in relationships. You and your partner, depending on which of you will be the dominant force in the fantasy, may find yourselves saying things that you really mean, but haven't otherwise broached. The things being said and done under the supposed cloak of indulging in a fantasy can get downright nasty vicious.

So you're in the moment, as we noted, and your husband is the dominant one. He's slapping and cursing and calling you everything except a child of God, including, as we already mentioned, the dreaded terms *slut*, *fat*, *whore*, and *stupid bitch*. He has even gone on to throw in a few choice words about your mother. Things you've suspected deep in your heart that he really felt about her, but dared not say aloud partially out of deference to her and partially from fear of repercussions from you. But now—well, now the gloves are off and he's saying all manner of things about your dear mother. He's casting even more despicable aspersions at you, her hell-bred spawn (his words, not mine). All that aspersion casting has him majorly aroused, harder than string theory, but you're not turned on in the slightest anymore. When the night first began, you were into things, but then, as he became more aggressive and derogatory, you began to grow uncomfortable. You even used your safe word, and—silly forgetful man—he totally failed to recognize it and kept on going. Now you're long past the *I'm uncomfortable* stage and find yourself full-on seething. Him smacking you around isn't helping. In fact, nothing about this moment is feeling the way that you imagined it would.

And then, he is suddenly choking you. *Hard*. He has his two big strong hands encircled tightly around your neck to the point that they're cutting off your ability to breathe. You thrash and sputter as your face runs the gamut of the rainbow, but he is so caught up in this moment of permitted sexual domination that he is oblivious to your genuine plight. Remember, this is still a fantasy for him, and he is all in it, sexually intoxicated, drunk with power. So his hands clench tighter. You can't even utter your safe word again because, well, you can barely even breathe! His hands—the same hands that lovingly hold you at night, cradle your babies when they wake up crying, mow the lawn, finger paint with his daughters, and help him earn a living to take care of you and your family—are now strangling you as he simultaneously pumps, thrusts, and denigrates you and your mother. It's hard for any woman to not become furious in a moment like this, and you are beyond furious.

He finally notices, releases your neck, but is unaware of the gravity of the moment and slaps you one more time for good measure. That last slap—that's the one that finally ends the game. You shove him off you, the fantasy over. Your vinyl outfit squeaks as you rush toward the bathroom in a coughing fit, clamoring for a glass of water to help you catch your breath. You're livid beyond words. He stands there with a rock-hard penis, thinking you're still in character, but you're not. This fantasy is done. With outrage and unwavering intent, you walk over to the phone in your seedy motel room, and without even thinking you call the police. This fool just tried to kill you. He talked about your mother like she was a dog, he talked about you in ways you never even knew were possible, he called you *fat*, he beat your ass way beyond what you feel are the boundaries of sexual role-playing, and then he almost strangled you to death!

Or did he? This is the love of your life. Perhaps you're being a bit irrational because you're so caught up in your rage.

Who cares? You're calling the cops!

Your husband tries to explain himself, but you don't want to hear it. He obviously has deep-seated issues going on that have unexpectedly been set free. What was supposed to be a loving journey to the land of intimate adventure suddenly took a right turn and landed you smack dab in questionable territory, and you're not happy about it. Not one bit.

Cut to: Ten minutes later, the police show up, and there you are in a black vinyl suit with a cutaway crotch—a cutaway crotch that you've forgotten all about, thus giving the police officers a nice eyeful of your peeper—black high-heeled boots, and gloves up to your elbows. A cat-o'-nine-tails is on the floor. He never got to use it on you because he was too busy choking you out. The cops can tell that something really heavy went down, but they can't get the details clearly because you're too busy screaming, *"Get this motherfucker out of here NOW! He tried to kill me! Look at the marks around my neck!"*

Amid your beloved hubby's cries of panic and pleas for you to explain what was really taking place, the police restrain him. Meanwhile, a second set of officers arrives to assess the situation.

You've got a black eye, handprints across your face, thighs, arms, and, of course, your neck. You're a mosaic of bruises, a real punched-out Picasso. It is not pretty, not one bit. The first cops put your husband's big, strong, strapping hands in handcuffs, escort him from the motel room, and whisk him off to county jail. Why? Because assault is assault, and this definitely looks like domestic abuse, albeit a freaky example, so it's *Book 'em, Danno!* Kiss your man good-bye for the night. Of course, you want his ass to spend a night in jail. It will teach him the lesson of a lifetime.

But what's this? The second set of police is taking you to the hospital. "Wait, no, that's not necess...oh, it's procedure? And they have to take pictures?" *Riiiiiiiight.* So now you've got to deal with *that*. Here come a million questions, Polaroids of your black eye, handprinted throat, and black-and-blue body. Plus, there'll be questions about the state of your marriage, the safety of your children, a possible history of domestic abuse in your marriage. Then you can look forward to counselors and a handful of pamphlets—all because you and your husband wanted to add a little adventure to your relationship.

Not exactly what you pictured when you decided to do this, eh? That's because you didn't follow my instructions! Know your boundaries and limitations. Use and acknowledge safe words. Discuss, at length, just exactly what the word *domination* will entail. This is not the kind of thing you want to figure out after the fact.

A good fantasy shouldn't have to involve a night in jail and a visit to the hospital. That's how rumors get started. All you need is for someone you barely know to see you in the emergency room of a local hospital wearing a crotchless, black vinyl catsuit and knee-high boots, plus a black eye and a fingerprint necklace. That's a pretty decent setup. The acquaintance and the rumor mill will take it from there. Who knows how the story will spin before it makes its way around to you again? But you can trust that it won't be pretty and it will definitely be far-fetched.

Chapter Two

The One-Man Gangbang

Fantasy

I knew there'd be more than one, but there was no way I could be prepared for what was going to happen. So I closed my eyes and waited. I was helpless, lying naked on my stomach with several pillows propped under my pelvis, my sex exposed and vulnerable. I can't lie: I was very nervous. The idea of the looming inevitable—dick after dick pounding my pussy, me drowning in an ocean of creampies—crowded my mind. I closed my eyes tightly, trying to push the image away, lest I become paralyzed with panic from too much thought.

Surely, though, my mind whispered, it would be an onslaught of dicks. It was the stuff of dreams, something every woman has imagined at least once. To be sated limp, pounded silly, a guilt-free gangbang with no consequences. I was scared, apprehensive, but at the same time I couldn't wait. I was already hot, growing wet with anticipation.

"Fuck the fear," I said aloud to the empty room.

Bring on the dicks!

I couldn't see who was first, but in short order he was on me, mounting my backside with bravado and intent. His cock was warm and solid as it slid into my wet canal. The girth took me by surprise, exciting me even more. He wasted no time getting down to business, pulling my hips back against him as he plunged farther inside. He was fully cocked, ramming me with long, hard strokes as he went deeper than I had ever experienced.

He pounded harder still, pressing my face against the bed, pinning my wrists with his own. I screamed in pain as his pelvis rammed mercilessly against my swollen lips, exhilarated by the agony of his vicious dick.

And then the dam broke, as waves of throbs unleashed from deep within me and I found myself cumming and cumming, in unstoppable squirts, thoroughly soaking his cock and balls.

He responded in kind with a deep and satisfying groan, convulsing against me as he filled my throbbing pussy with his thick white jizz. He emptied what felt like a tsunami of cum, and then thrust one last time, as if making sure he'd drained himself completely. He pulled out without ceremony. His rapid exit caused my hole to make a suctioning sound that both surprised and embarrassed me. I glanced back apologetically, but he was already gone, his warm essence oozing out of my bruised pussy like primordial goo, past my engorged clit, onto the sheets.

Before I could adjust myself, a different shaft—long, curved, and slender—slid effortlessly inside me. He pulled me back to the edge of the bed as he hunched primitively over my tiny frame, pounding my pussy with a sidewinding motion to maximize the sickle shape of his member. His curved dick found my G-spot in record time, four pumps in, as I began to buckle and shake from the intensity of what was a powerful, instant orgasm. He kept pounding, spurred on by my tremors, this time with downward strokes, as his shaft hit nerves within my walls I didn't even know existed. My body had never felt pleasure like this as I came again and again, each spasm more racking than the last. My body was overwhelmed, and my right side grew numb. This second man pulled out, his wet shaft thumping against my back. Just as I began to catch my breath, he plunged in anew, thrusting over and over, in and out. My body synced with his rhythm so perfectly that I began to go absolutely wild.

"More! More! Keep fucking me more!"

And he did, happily, obligingly, grinding against me in a corkscrew motion, going deeper and deeper, sparking more undiscovered nerves along the way.

"I'm cumming!" I screamed. "I can't stop! Don't stop!"

I pressed my backside deeper onto his cock, trying to swallow it whole and him along with it. I could barely breathe as my pussy drenched him with every throb within my walls. My chest felt constricted, my lungs tight, my head swimming. It was too much. If I kept cumming like this without pause, I was going to faint.

"Cum for me, baby," I begged. "I need you to cum."

I reached back, far beneath me for his balls, massaging them with gentle aggression. He came with a roar as his load spewed, hot and plentiful, mixing with the juices already basting inside me. His nectar was thinner and wetter than the last, running out of me like a spilled glass of milk. He had barely pulled out before another turgid cock barged in. I looked back, alarmed at the speed at which this was all taking place. A large, strong hand gently pressed my face toward the wall.

"Don't watch," he said softly. "Just feel."

I obeyed, my breath still coming quickly, bracing myself for the next round of violent thrusts.

But this man was different.

Though he'd entered me with force, once inside my cum-soaked cunt he was gentle and romantic. He took his time with slow, shallow strokes while caressing my lower back and massaging my tight round bottom. He leaned against my ear, whispering sweet words with each thrust.

"Your pussy is so wet," he cooed.

Well, yes, my pussy *was* wet. Very wet. I was holding the cum of two men inside me plus my uncounted squirts.

Just the thought of him back there, balls-deep in the juices of two others, turned me on even more. I raised my hips higher, grinding against his slow-stirring dick.

"Yeah, baby," he whispered. "You like that? You like that dick?"

I liked that dick.

"Mmm-hmmm," I moaned, grinding harder.

"Keep doing that," he said, "and you're gonna make me cum."

I kept doing it. He began to groan.

"You're trying to make me cum," he said. "Slow down."

I kept grinding.

"Wait…wait…," he pleaded. "Slow down. I'm not ready yet."

I didn't.

I could feel the swelling build in his cock. I began to grind harder, faster and faster.

Just as I could feel that he was about to blow, he removed his wet rod from my pussy and brought it around to my face, plunging it deep into my mouth. As I hungrily sucked the cum of two other men off his cock, he came on my tongue in soft, gentle spurts while gripping my shoulders, eyes closed, head thrown back, moaning in pleasure.

"Mmmmmm." I smiled, gulping him down.

He smiled in return as he pulled out of my mouth.

"Thank you," he said, bending down and kissing me on the forehead. "That was nice. Very nice."

Just as I was marveling at his politeness, the soft warmth of a man's mouth sucking at my love hole distracted me. I looked down to see a fourth man between my legs, savoring the remaining cum of his bang partners. His hot tongue darted in and out, lapping up all the cream he could find. I watched in amazement, having never experienced anything this deviant before. This man had no shame, no boundaries. He wanted that cum, dove in for it like it was gold, and was getting me hot all over again in the process. I couldn't take my eyes off him as he spread my legs wider, pushing his face deeper into my beaten labia, plunging his tongue into me like a sword.

My cunt was throbbing anew, and, as good as his tongue felt, I needed more. I had to have more.

"Fuck me," I demanded. "Fuck me now."

He emerged from between my legs and climbed into the bed, lying on his back. He pulled me on top of him. I eagerly slid onto his rock-hard dick.

"Mmmmmm," I moaned as I sank down to the base. "That's better."

I gripped his chest and began slow, gyrating my hips with a burning hunger. He felt so good inside me. I couldn't take it. My gyrating increased, faster, faster, and I began riding him hard, desperate to cum again. I sensed another presence looming behind me. A hand pressed me forward onto the chest of the man beneath me. A finger probed at my anus in brief introduction, quickly followed by the massive cock of a fifth man shoved into my ass. He thrust in deep, all the way to his balls.

"*Owwwwww!*" I cried in excruciating pleasure.

I came immediately, savagely, completely blown away by the sensation of being double-penetrated and beast-fucked by two men at once. It was the most incredible thing I'd ever felt in my life, so wonderfully degrading, I wasn't sure I ever wanted to experience it again. I felt like an animal, lower than a dog. I loved it and despised myself at the same time.

Both men kept going as I writhed between them, two distinct strokes beating my body into oblivion—one was shallow and quick, the other slow and deep—both working together. I eagerly responded to each thrust, front and back, until the three of us, moving in unison, became one big fuck monster . . . a double-breasted, four-balled, six-legged beast on the verge of what was going to be the biggest orgasm the world had ever seen.

I opened my mouth to scream. It was immediately filled with cock number six.

Whoever he was, he must have been watching for a while, because the moment his rigid cock was cradled in my moist mouth he blasted, his hot load cascading against the back of my throat. My body was in sensory overload as the other men simultaneously erupted inside me.

The nerves in my ass and pussy exploded in a nuclear thunderclap of pleasure that raced through my body. I couldn't stop shaking. Every wire within me was crossed and confused, but vibrantly alive.

It was too much to process. I began to cry.

Cum and cry.

Even as the men pulled out of my ravaged pussy, ass, and mouth, I was still cumming, balled up and crying, completely overwhelmed by the uncontrollable bolts of lightning raging through my loins.

The men abandoned me without even a good-bye as I lay there, exhausted, sweating, my eyes closed, cum draining from every hole.

"You all right, baby?" a voice softly asked.

I nodded weakly, opening my eyes. He was fuzzy through the veil of tears clouding my sight, but he was there. My husband, sweaty and spent—lying at the foot of our bed among a heap of toys that included my favorite strap-on, vibrators, and an assortment of dildos—as soaked with my cum as I was with his.

"How do you feel?" he asked.

"Magnificent," I said breathlessly. "How do *you* feel?"

"Like I did my job."

"Times six." I smiled.

"Very good. Then my work here is done."

He climbed up toward me, pulling me into his arms, the two of us bound together in life and mutual stickiness.

I was never more in love with him than I was in that moment.

He was more than just the man of my dreams.

He was all of them.

Reality

I can already hear the wheels turning in your head as you think, *Vixen, how in the hell are my husband and I supposed to simulate a gangbang! That's impossible!* Well, let me stop you right there. In the world of fantasy, *nothing* is impossible. As long as you both believe, anything is a go.

All that any relationship needs to pull off any fantasy is a little imagination and a reasonable amount of effort. If you're creative and have a willing body and partner, making this fantasy a reality in your marital bed is just a few steps away!

For you, the woman, this fantasy is easy. Your only job is to lie there, ready to get served. **For your guy, this exercise is going to**

Vixen Tip

Research! Research! Research!

Everyone has their way of going about things—tried-and-true moves that have worked for them since college. And even though your man's signature strokes may have wowed the ladies over the years and were smooth enough to permanently win you, this gangbang thing is a whole new ball game.

Your man has to become more than one man—preferably, at least three—for the two of you to fully experience this fantasy. That means he's going to have to do some research on how to assume the sexual personas of other men, men unlike himself, so he can bring this scenario to life. Maybe you're lucky enough to have a guy with a talent for taking on different personalities. If so, you're almost ready to go! For most men, however, some homework will be necessary.

But my man isn't too keen on research, you say. *He's already got a lot on his plate.* Fear not. He'll love this kind of research. It's everybody's favorite: porn, porn, and more porn!

I bet he'll make room on his plate for that!

take quite a bit of stamina and dedication. He may need to eat his Wheaties for the week leading up to things, pop some extra vitamins, or maybe get a B12 shot. Of course, if necessary, he can also take advantage of one of the many quasi-pharmaceutical assists constantly being offered on television. And if that's what it's going to take, I can only recommend your husband obtain a prescription from his doctor and not pick up a pack of those nondescript pills placed between the lighters and the incense at the corner market. Just make sure your man is prepared . . . and while you're at it, you'd better fasten your seat belt as well. It's definitely going to be a bumpy night!

Since this will be such an intense and potentially exhausting experience, the two of you may want to begin with the Starter Gangbang Kit: three sexual personalities. Once your man becomes comfortable with three, he can always work in more personalities, as many as he feels he can seamlessly switch into.

Vixen Tip

No Matter the Number, Diversity Is Key

Make sure each member of your gangbang is different. Some examples:

- Soft and sweet.
- Rough and indifferent.
- Fast and eager.
- Young and inexperienced.
- Extremely experienced and eager to teach.

Now that the hard part is out of the way for your man, here's where your imagination comes into play. For you, the key to pretending there's more than one man in the room is to **allow yourself to be dominated and absolutely helpless.** In my opinion, doggy-style is best suited for this. It makes an excellent position of vulnerability and unimpeded entry. Oh, and feel free to close your eyes. Or wear a blindfold, if that helps your imagination even more. Above all, **it's important that your man actually dismounts and remounts each time he switches identities.** This allows him to come back with a whole new stroke and disposition, while creating the effect of being a new person entering the scenario and you!

Want the thrill of double penetration? **Implement toys and gadgets to enhance the experience.** Doing so also gives your husband the ability to extend the moment so that he isn't relying on just his own penis to do the job. Penises can only do so much, and they do tend to get very excited during a scenario like this. It can be an incredible amount of pressure to maintain control while pretending to be at least three men. You, definitely, don't want him to cum too quickly and have the party end before the second man even has a chance to show up. By using vibrators, dildos, and other available gadgets, your guy can provide multiple simultaneous penetrations, giving you the illusion that many men are besetting you.

And for those lucky ones whose mates are capable of having more than one orgasm in a short window of time—ladies, you are going to be in gangbang heaven!

Recap

- All that any relationship needs to pull off any fantasy is a little imagination and a reasonable amount of effort.

- For your guy, this exercise is going to take quite a bit of stamina and dedication.

- Allow yourself to be dominated and absolutely helpless.

- It's important that your man actually dismounts and remounts each time he switches identities.

- Implement toys and gadgets to enhance the experience.

V-Log #2
Hey, Where're All Your Friends?

So your man just ravaged you with the smackdown of all smackdowns. You've had more orgasms tonight than you usually have in a year! Dear husband employed all manner of toys, plugs, teases, and touches, filling every welcoming hole in your body to create an evening rich with electric explosion after electric explosion after electric explosion. It was the most incredible thing you ever experienced and now, um ... you'd like to have it again. Actually, you'd like this every night, because anything after this is, well—not *this*.

That's the über-tricky tightrope you walk by trying this fantasy. You are being pleasured in a lot of places, simultaneously, and the resulting sensations are so spectacular, so mind-blowingly delicious, your whole universe shifts. Now that you know he can transform into a sleek, many-armed, multiple-orifice-plugging, orgasm-slinging machine, you want it like this *all* the time. If conventional missionary sex is considered a gateway drug, the One-Man Gangbang could very well be considered crack. And now that you've had a taste of it, you've got it bad. You're hardcore strung out and good ol' straight one-pole-in-one-hole sex just isn't going to cut it for you anymore.

It is very much akin to Cinderella being swept up from her ragtag existence, taken on an extravagant whirl with the prince, shown the time of her life—then watching her carriage turn back into a friggin' pumpkin. In this case, sadly, your husband in his normal state is that pumpkin. You were fine with him before this fantasy, but now that you've been exposed to more, he's a bore unless he brings along all his accoutrements. Vibrators, plugs, gewgaws, doodads, and assorted kinky tchotchkes, all in the name of keeping the peace and keeping you happy.

Oh my! What a dilemma we have on our hands. Actually, the dilemma is your husband's, because now that he has opened your sexual Pandora's box he's going to have to deliver on a regular basis or figure out a way to talk you down off that gimme-more ledge. Ten-to-one he is going for the latter. What man with a reasonably full and busy life can be expected to play octopussy with his wife all the time—unless, of course, he loves the idea of such a thing? If that's the case, then move along, folks. There's nothing here to see. You two have tapped into something that truly works for you and there's peace in the valley.

But that's not what we're discussing right now. This V-Log is about what happens when keeping it fantasy gets horribly real, and a man who's not in perfect shape—as well as on Viagra, Cialis, Levitra, ExtenZe, Enzyte, or using a penis pump and a kickstand—is going to have a helluva time keeping this kind of thing going. It is important that we remember exactly what a fantasy is. Merriam-Webster, in one of its definitions, describes it as *the power or process of creating especially unrealistic or improbable mental images in response to psychological need*. That's exactly what's happening when you and your husband act out the One-Man Gangbang. Via the use of multiple gadgets, he creates the unrealistic and improbable mental image of a group of men servicing you, instead of just one. His doing so meets your psychological need for adventure. The key words, however, in that Merriam-Webster definition are *unrealistic* and *improbable*. This is not the reality of your life. It is an escape. A fantasy is supposed to be a treat, like a decadent dessert that you allow yourself every once in a while, but don't eat every day because it would be bad for your health. Any woman who demands that her husband One-Man Gangbang her every time they have sex is a selfish, inconsiderate bitch. Yeah, I said it. The OMG (the perfect acronym, because that's exactly how it makes you feel) is that most decadent of treats. Day-to-day sex should be a give-and-take experience. The OMG is all about him servicing you. Do not demand that your husband do this every time you make love because then it becomes a job, and an exhausting one at that.

And let's be honest, ladies . . . we all know how men's penises react when we place extraordinary expectations upon them. Despite how hard they get and the way they pound us when they're excited, penises are sensitive, fragile, independent entities prone to defying the intent of their owners. Your man may want to service you, but his peen may be downright disgusted with how demanding you've become. It may start to retreat on occasion. Eventually, it might stop rising altogether. Your husband will have no choice but to use all his gewgaws and tchotchkes to service you because his penis will have completely bailed. That would be horrible for all parties involved. Your man's ego will suffer immensely. After all, you broke his dick. And with no dick and a sad hubby, you'll be even less satisfied than you were before implementing the fantasy.

All this drama will open the door for legions of marital problems, with infidelity leading the pack. You'll be so pissed at your man's broken peen and so hungry for more OMG that you may start sneaking off with his doodads, gewgaws, plugs, and whatnot to service yourself! But since none of that can replace the feel of a real penis, you might find yourself starting to look outside the marriage for excitement, something you would have never thought yourself capable of doing. But hey, getting turned out by multiple faux cocks, then being faced with a broken one, can make a lot of women do things they never thought they would.

In the meantime, your poor, dear husband might start looking for outside validation . . . someone who can prove that his peen is not, in fact, broken, but just doesn't like *you*. It doesn't matter who she is. More than likely she will be some chick who is so beneath you on every level that you'll be baffled by the attraction. Her looks and station in life are irrelevant. What is relevant is that she'll make him feel like a man again, and we all know that a woman, any woman, who can make a man feel like a man can make that same man do whatever she wants, including leave you—especially if he isn't feeling appreciated at home and *especially* if you broke his dick.

Imagine that ugly scenario: you out there hunting down gangbangs and him thrilled out of his mind because he's found a woman who's just grateful for missionary. Is that what you want? Hmmm? I didn't think so.

So dial back on the pressure already. Give the deejay a break. Yes, the One-Man Gangbang is spectacular. It's supposed to be. It's a fantasy, dammit! The fact that it feels so amazing means your husband did it right. Give him credit for that. Just don't demand that the OMG be put on the daily menu. Even the weekly menu might be too much. The fantasy OMG should be savored slowly, sweetly, wallowed in with sheer delight. Enjoy the moment. Stretch it out for as long as you can. Then hold off until the next time. Why? Because. If you demand regular OMGs from your husband, it will kill you *and* your marriage. Learn the meaning of moderation and, in turn, you will have a healthy appreciation for your husband when he shows up with his armload of toys. Return the favor with a fantasy that completely services him. There are plenty in this book to choose from. Make it a party. Make it fun. Then hold him close and tell him you love him because it is all about reciprocation, ladies. That's what marriage is supposed to be.

Be a lady about all this and, for heaven's sake, don't break his dick.

Chapter Three

Paid Escort

Fantasy

It was a sickness—this tossing and turning, this wanting. It had been so long since a man was here in the way that I needed, even though it had been just seconds since I'd been inside myself. For all my efforts, I still wasn't satisfied. They say no one knows better than a woman how to pleasure herself, but no amount of self-indulgence could soothe this ache. The telltale stickiness of my middle and index fingers were just further proof that I kept coming up short. My bed seemed cold, even though I was hot and the sheets were damp with sweat. My home had become a cave, a dark and lonely place of my own making where I'd taken refuge—restless, hopeless, loveless, alone. There was an entire world beyond these four walls, and a deeper, warmer, wetter world within mine. Only by my hand would the twain meet, and only the hand of the right man could douse this fire.

I wasn't beyond whoring myself out. I'd done it before, in the distant past, for adventure and excitement. In time, I'd decided to wait for the passion that comes with love, but that passion couldn't be found, and my quaking desire had become all-consuming. Desperate times, as they say, call for desperate measures, such as this, and nothing was going to stop me. I would have my man tonight, even if it meant selling myself to get him.

I wore a formfitting dress, pumps, stockings attached to a silk garter with a matching bustier, no panties, and the perfect perfume—all necessary to lure my prey. I was determined to introduce my scent to someone just as needy as me, determined to place my pulp upon his lips and have him drink of its juices. He would feast on my flesh throughout the night, into the dawn. Tonight, this night, I would be my own procuress.

In the lobby of the hotel, the piano man played over the chatter of patrons and the clinking of wineglasses. The redolence of star lilies followed my every step, as did the eyes of every man in the room who lacked female companionship, and even a few who didn't. I could smell them beyond the lilies. I could feel their breath upon me. Perfume was no competition for the savor of lust. A sudden, Pavlovian dampness formed between my thighs, a conditioned response to the presence of fresh meat. I wanted them all, part and parcel, but tonight I would only take one.

I found my place on the edge of a stool along the bar and rubbed my naked, moist, sensitive flesh along its corner before sitting. I did my best not to whimper as my swollen clitoris became painfully engorged. I needed to be entered, to be ravished—torn, piece by piece, from myself. I wanted to be left used and worthless, dripping with and drowned in his nectar. Sweet and rich, I wanted to taste it, to swallow and quench this never-ending thirst. The thought left me parched. I signaled for the barkeep.

"What would you like, ma'am?"

He was handsome and my thoughts traveled immediately from his face to his loins, though I made certain my eyes didn't give it away. What if he was the one? Maybe *he* would be my warrior tonight.

"A glass of Syrah, please. The best vintage you carry." I wanted to revel in decadence.

"Coming right up."

I watched his firm backside as he walked away. Hmmm. Perhaps.

In a matter of seconds he was back with my drink.

"This first one's on the house," he said.

Were his eyes searching mine? My clit throbbed in response. Maybe he'd be it; or maybe the man pulling up a seat to my right would. This new stranger's eyes met mine for a fleeting moment as yet another man breezed past, leaving his scent upon my memory. He smelled like an oceanfront bonfire, evoking images of things wet and warm, airy and inviting. My eyes followed him as he disappeared around the corner and out of my life and scheme. If not him, then who? Where was he, the man I came for—the man I will cum for?

I sipped my Syrah. I looked into my glass, my hot breath steaming the inside, releasing the woodsy aroma of the wine. As I inhaled, I took it all in, and as I exhaled he finally touched me. As he squeezed himself into the seat to my left, he brushed against my yearning form, spilling some of my wine on the bar. I leaned closer, smelling him, knowing he was meant for me.

"Excuse me," he said apologetically. "I'm so clumsy. Let me get you another drink," he insisted while beckoning the barkeep.

We struck up a conversation, but I wasn't half as interested in what he was saying as I was in the prospect of his naked body ramming into mine. I squirmed in my seat as we went through the formality of small talk.

"Did you come here with anyone?" he asked.

"No. I came alone."

He droned on, his words running on with no form or meaning.

"Right," I replied with an empty nod. Who cared what he was saying?

Why were we even still talking? He should be fucking me by now. Let's make a deal!

I could feel the oozing from my desperate cavity. I listened to his rambling until I couldn't any longer and interrupted with a brazen, "Fuck me."

For a moment, he was silent, taken aback, his mouth frozen in midsentence. His eyes widened. His succulent, parted lips were driving me mad. Not waiting for him to respond, I leaned forward and began to suck his mouth and tongue, forcing his submission to my demand, intruding his space with this one last plea. He tasted like the maraschinos in his cocktail, surrendering to my audacious entry as I begged him for his.

"Take me upstairs," I whispered close to his ear. "Ravage my mouth. Fuck my sweet, hot pussy. Do whatever you like. I'll be worth every minute."

He paused, and then, as if on cue . . .

"How much?" His eyes scanned the room furtively to see who was watching.

"Five hundred," I answered. "The whole night. You can do anything. Everything. Stuff your hard cock in every hole in my body."

I waited, but he never replied.

Instead he just took my hand and led me away. The barkeep watched us with knowing disinterest.

His suite was cold and dimly lit, but I was hot, glowing with desire, ready to be taken. We entered the room locked at the lips as he fumbled to remove my clothing. I stopped him before he could go any farther.

"Let's get the business out of the way."

"Of course," he said, embarrassed. "I almost forgot."

He pulled out his wallet and opened it. The aroma of rich leather seamlessly blended with the smell of crisp, new money. He lifted out five hundred-dollar bills. I went over to my purse and placed them inside. I turned to him, motioning.

"Get over here," I said.

He rushed toward me, our bodies banging against the walls and furniture. We tore at each other's clothes, ripping them off in record time, two strangers in the dark, hot and naked, desperate for pleasure. We crashed onto the down duvet as he covered my face, neck, and chest with a thousand sensuous kisses. It was nice, but kisses weren't what I needed.

"Touch my pussy," I begged.

He lowered his head, following the aroma of endless nights of yearning. I lay on my back as his mouth soothed that yearning with tender kisses and the relentless stroking of his tongue. I opened wide, every nerve in my body aware of his presence. As his tongue worked faster, I could feel the ball of ecstasy building inside me, anxious for release. I clamped my thighs around his face, locking him in. He burrowed deeper, alternately plunging his tongue in and out of my pussy and sucking my clit. The ball inside me grew bigger and bigger, until I could no longer hold it inside. I exploded with cries of pleasure, my hips thrashing wildly, as I came upon his tongue.

I flipped over and on top of him, sitting on his face, grinding, smothering him, and screaming with delight as I continued to cum. The beast was set free and in need of flesh.

I was a man-eating animal hunting for meat and was relieved to have found it as we switched positions and I became his receptacle. He unleashed a live, massive serpent and shoved his girth into my mouth with explosive force. I gagged. I spit. I couldn't breathe. It was everything I wanted and more.

We wrestled back and forth, in and out, giving and taking. My garter, dangling from the bedside lamp, rocked with the rhythm of our movements and slipped from the nightstand onto the floor. We battled on, his body just as desperate for mine as I was for his. He choked. I bit. He spanked and, like the dirty girl I was, I took it. Happily. I raised my ass higher. He spanked me again. We fucked and fucked, all over the room, in ways I remembered, in ways I'd never known.

My mouth, my slutty cunt, and my filthiest hole—he filled them all with his most mannish extremity, then filled each with his abundant, gushing cum. And then he was gone, leaving me leaking and loving it. I curled into a ball and fell into an exhausted, blissful sleep. Abandoned. Used. Worthless and happy.

I awakened with the sun, wrapped in the once-crisp white sheets, now sullied with my fantasy realized. Pleased, I made my way through the lobby of the five-star hotel, my head hung low, knowing I looked just like a woman who had been fucked and fucked good. My makeup smeared, my hair mussed, reamed stockings in hand, I dashed to my car as the valet brought it around. At first, I couldn't bear to look at myself in the rearview mirror, but when I did, I smiled—a devilish grin oozing with mischief and a clear absence of guilt.

Where was he now, I wondered, this man I let use me up, a man whose name I never even asked? Where was he now, as I leaked traces of his fluid onto the seat of my car, thinking of him?

When I arrived home, I could still smell him on me. I could smell him all around, in the air, intoxicating me all over again. I dropped my purse at the door as I made my way through the house. I stepped out of my wrinkled dress at the foot of the bed and slipped beneath my own fresh sheets. It would be improper to shower, to erase his presence so soon after he had done so much to stoke my libido, so much to sate me.

Even in my bed, I could still feel him. I could smell myself on his lips. I touched his chest and felt his heart racing within it, his bulge growing between my thighs, his breath heavy on my neck, as he eagerly mounted me again. He was here with me. He always would be. In the bright morning light, we made tender, passionate love. But last night, under the cover of darkness, my husband fucked me like a whore.

Reality

There is a long-standing urban myth that states, "You can't turn a hoe into a housewife." Geez, people, give me a break! That's one of those statements you just *know* came from some bitter little man who didn't know how to satisfy his woman, so he blamed his inadequacy on her perfectly functioning libido. Oy! It's all her fault because he's not skilled enough to keep her.

And while that hoe/housewife phrase, as sexist and disconcerting as it may be, seems to wittily roll off the tongue and sounds oh-so-clever among your most pea-brained acquaintances, it (or its reverse) couldn't be more absurd and incorrect in practical application.

Stick with me here, ladies. It is about to get really real.

While asking his woman to sell herself for sex is a bit much, **any man would be lucky to find a woman who will toe the line like a whore.**

Vixen! you gasp. *How could you say such a thing? Who wants to be like a whore? Certainly not me!*

Calm down. No one's calling you a whore, and I'm definitely not telling you to hit the streets to make money for your man. What we're exploring now are the dynamics surrounding what it *takes* to be a whore—the level of commitment, focus, and blind loyalty, typically at the expense of all else. It is the ultimate example of taking one for the team, literally. If a man were able to get a woman with that kind of stick-to-itiveness, he'd be hard-pressed to lose her. She'd be an ideal housewife.

There are plenty of men out there mocking others for trying to "turn a hoe into a housewife," yet those same men secretly long for their own housewife to behave like a hoe—namely, their hoe. Discreetly, of course. (Oh, and before I go any further, let me say right now that I am perfectly aware that the term *hoe* is incorrect as a slang term for "whore." Yes, I know that a *hoe* is a garden tool. Really, people, that line is so overused. I'm strictly using the word *hoe* colloquially. I've never liked the look of the word I'm supposed to use as the slang for "whore," which is *ho'*, with an apostrophe, indicating that the *w, r,* and *e* have been dropped. In that case, shouldn't it be *'ho''*, with apostrophes for each missing letter? Anyway, it just looks all kinds of wrong, like you're talking about Santa or something. I like my hoe-for-whore spelled like the garden tool, so for the purposes of this book and for right now, our slang for "whore" will be *hoe*. Deal with it. Now, back to the main event.)

The truth is, **almost every man wants his housewife to be *his* escort; they find sexually liberated and exploratory women fascinating on many levels,** often enough so to make them a permanent part of their lives. For centuries, society's strict morals and stereotypical judgments have sometimes prevented people—men and women alike—from coupling with the person who can most fulfill their sexual fantasies. Instead, we find ourselves trapped in boring, loveless, even sexless relationships, all for the sake of decorum and propriety. During it all, we silently yearn for more, constantly seeking (read, *sneaking*) outside our relationships for that little something extra—something with bite. Something that can stoke the dying embers of passion.

Ladies, it is time that *you* become that little something extra. It's time for *you* to stoke that dying fire and turn the blaze all the way back up. **A man will either marry the sexually daring woman he fantasizes about, or cheat on his wife with her.** Choose your scenario, ladies.

Which would you prefer? If it's to become the former, to be the woman of his fantasies who gets the ring, then by all means…read on.

Many people think that fantasies are far-fetched and impractical. After all, who has time in their day to plan some elaborate sexual adventure? Fantasies are for *those* girls—you know, the freaky ones with no morals or home training, girls you've spent your whole life convincing others you've got nothing in common with. Well, honey, *those* girls are the ones your husband secretly masturbates to while trolling the Internet for porn. *Those* girls are the ones he spends his and your hard-earned money on at the local strip clubs, massage parlors, and street corners. Yes, you read that right. Street corners. Are you horrified at the thought that your man—your wholesome and upstanding man, the father of your children!—would pick up a woman off the street corner? Well, wrap your brain around it. It happens thousands, if not millions, of times a day, every day. Otherwise *those* women wouldn't be out there.

And don't just think the kinds of men who are picking up *those* women and enlisting their services are the durty mo's of the world, the scuzzy, skeevy, Skid-Row-bummy types. No, honey. Your man might indeed be lumped in there as well. Don't believe me? Got a Netflix account or access to cable or satellite TV? Check out some episodes of HBO's *Cathouse* reality series, where the men go to brothels to release the inner freak that's not being satisfied by their wives at home. Or maybe *Hookers at the Point* or *Pimps Up, Ho's Down* (even though the latter spells *hoes* in that fugly way that I don't particularly care for). The Hughes Brothers also have an excellent film called *American Pimp*. You're in for an eye-opening look at a world that you most likely frown upon, but is much more familiar to your man than you may want to believe. Pimps exist because hoes exist, and hoes exist because as long as there are women who won't do everything their man wants, there will be a slew of women waiting in the wings who will, for a price.

Still think your guy is exempt? Wake the hell up. He may not be frequenting that world now, but that doesn't mean he hasn't in the past and won't in the future. Like Eddie Murphy said in his stand-up classic *Raw*, "Yes, your man too!"

Ladies, it is high time we change our way of thinking and become more open to being just like *those* girls. Not out in public, but within the confines of our relationship with our man. It's time to turn your fantasies, and your partner's fantasies, into reality, and not just on birthdays and holidays or as a reward when your man finally paints the garage. **Fantasies should never be just for rare occasions.** They can and should play an active part in your sex life. You don't have to do them every day. That will just make it a new ordinary, replacing your old ordinary. They can, however, be a natural part of your romantic landscape; that special dessert that you partake of now and then that reminds the two of you of who you are and what you mean to each other. It's important to keep the passion alive in long-term relationships, and there's nothing like a fantasy thrown in here and there to remind the two of you of why you chose each other and why you remain together.

From this point forward, **choose to make fantasies and role-playing a part of your and your husband's sexual menu**. I guarantee that it will be one of the most liberating decisions of your life. Look, there's nothing wrong with being exactly who your mother and father raised you to be. Maybe you're an educated woman with a promising career, well respected in your field. Congratulations for that. What an achievement! Perhaps you've even found the love of your life, married him, and the two of you are raising a beautiful family in a fabulous home. Your life is like *Leave It to Beaver* meets *The Cosby Show,* and you're admired by friends and family alike. Kudos to you, girl! Looks like you've got it all!

But wait...there's a problem. Your husband is bored to tears in the bedroom and so are you, and if he climbs his ever-fattening ass on top of you once more with that *time to make the doughnuts* look on his face, you're going to go ape shit. You're at the intersection of *Get the fuck off me!* and *Why did I marry you, anyway?,* wondering if this is how you're doomed to spend the rest of your life. That's right, *doomed*, because you're stuck, you see. Not one of your friends or family members would understand or commiserate if you left. You've got the perfect life— remember? An enviable career, a committed husband, those beautiful kids, and girl, that house! Everyone would look at you as an ingrate. Besides, you don't want to leave anyway. You still love him very much. You're both just stuck in a very deep rut. All right, a valley. Okay, the Grand Canyon. That's really deep. How'd you get down there? Can you even hear me? Hello-hello-helloooooooooo!

Ladies, you are not alone. This same scenario is playing out by the thousands, perhaps millions, all over the world. Plenty of us have been exactly where you are right now, and plenty more will soon find themselves there, unless they choose to do something about it.

How's this for an idea: Maybe that good-girl persona you've been keeping up since junior high isn't what his loins yearn for anymore. Heck, *your* loins are even rebelling against it! After a while, the mother, the wife, the chauffeur, the launderer, and the dishwasher begin to lose their sexual allure. Day after day, your husband sees you in sweats with your hair tied up or unkempt, rushing from room to room, food stains on your clothes, chasing after kids, piling them into the minivan, throwing together dinner, mopping the floors. And wait, what's that smell? Is it...bleach? It's Pine-Sol! *Oh noes!* You've become the Pine-Sol lady! All you have to do is put your hand on your hip and wag your finger at him and your transition will be complete.

Now you're just like his mother. And, I'm sorry, people, I don't give a damn what Freud says, **men do *not* want to fuck their mothers**. They're polite to their mothers. They respect their mothers. Many of them are downright afraid of their mothers. Whatever the case, they don't want to fuck them. And if you've become his mother, he doesn't want to fuck you.

But wait. Not so fast. Before you start beating yourself up, let's not forget that your husband has become unfuckable, too. So now we've got two unfuckable people who fuck each other only because they're all they've got, till death do you part. That's if you can part, considering you've both gotten kind of heavy and it's not so easy for him to roll off the top of you once he's finished his business. Till death you don't part.

That's a long time to be with someone you no longer consider sexy.

One of you will eventually crack and break ranks for something better on the outside, by way of cheating or divorce. If that doesn't happen and the two of you choose to stick it out with no change, the sex will ultimately wither up altogether and you'll end up as just two married companions, repulsed by the thought of sex with each other, electing to forgo it altogether rather than travel down that disappointing road. Instead of sex, you'll opt for snacks and cuddling. You both love s'mores! You'll make s'mores together. Or you'll gather up the Cheez-Its, put on a good DVD, and watch movies on the couch in your matching Snuggies. Because that's what good companions do.

Congratulations. You're officially each other's pets. Lapdogs for life. Holy smokes, people. This is ridiculous.

Now would be a good time to be and do the exact opposite of whatever the hell it is that's gotten your sex life in a slump. Make a decision to do something that sounds drastic, but really isn't. Hey, I've got an idea. The two of you should have a fantasy. No, for real. Go wipe the chocolate and marshmallows from those s'mores off your face first. Done? Okay. You ready? Let's begin!

Slip into something your man could never imagine you wearing, and then wear it in public. When he sees you in that simple, yet sultry, little black dress, the hem about four inches higher than anything he's ever seen in your closet, and the neckline several inches lower than what you wear to work, your man will want to get you upstairs and out of plain sight as quickly as possible. Not because he is ashamed of you. Oh no! It will be because he can't wait to ravage you. By dressing like this,

Vixen Tip

Set the Date and Destination

• Choose a day or night when the two of you are alone at home and neither of you has been working all day.

• Call in reinforcements to babysit.

• Turn the ringers off on all your phones, both landlines and cells.

• Choose a place the two of you have always wanted to go, but never had the time. A chic, expensive hotel can set the tone for a decadent evening.

• Or you can select a place that has significant meaning to you both.

• It may be even more exciting to pick a random spot—a place that is unfamiliar.

purely for the purpose of provoking and exciting him, you've essentially just hit the RESET button on your relationship.

Once he's had enough of seeing you with your clothes on, be sure that what's waiting for him underneath is enough to jump-start his heart and cause an instant fire in his nether regions. You can never lose with thigh-high hosiery secured by a garter belt. Throw in a matching brassiere and panties and it's game on!

So now you're perfectly put together, ready to blow him away the moment he sees you. But wait…you're not done!

You not only have to act the part, but you absolutely have to look the part and be comfortable in your new role as your husband's every

Vixen Tip

Primp

- Now is the time for your sexy best. Put some serious effort into it!

- For around fifty dollars, there's always someone willing to do your makeup at the local department store's cosmetic counter.

- The same goes for your hair. To really kick things up a notch, purchase a pre-styled wig that changes your look completely!

- Search online or in current fashion magazines to find the latest trends and either try to duplicate the look, or have a friend or professional help out.

sexual fantasy. Here are a few components that will help you tie it all together:

Lingerie. Be as sexy and/or as whorish—*hoeish* even—as you want.

Vixen Tip

Come Prepared

Your mate may not be prepared for what's about to happen, but you certainly must be. Once you've chosen a sexy locale for your fantasy to take place, you're going to have to pack a goodie bag. Yes, a goodie bag! This bag will be filled with all sorts of naughty delights chosen especially for your tryst.

Traditional sophisticated lingerie, like stockings and garters, a corset, or a bustier, always creates a dramatic visual effect, but there are other more provocative types of lingerie available at erotic shops and websites.

Shoes. Some men have a fetish for a particular type of shoe. Your husband might be one of those men. Depending on the style of lingerie you have chosen, the shoes you select should complement what you're wearing, raising the excitement factor. Anything from clear plastic heels to thigh-high leather boots is fine; just be sure that whatever shoes you choose, they come with at least a five-inch heel. *Five inches, Vixen!* Yes, five inches. If you want to play the part, you have to play it all the way. And yes, I understand that there are plenty of you out there who have no experience whatsoever walking in a heel that high. Many of you eschew heels altogether, which may be how you wound up in a rut in the first place. Every woman should wear heels, at least on occasion. Even if you don't wear them at five-inch heights on a regular basis, you should at least wear a shoe that shows off the curve of your calf and the turn of your leg, and nothing does that like a shoe with a sleek, tapered heel. Unless there are medical or health factors preventing you from wearing them, you owe it to yourself to add some to your collection. You don't have to don them every day, but I can guarantee that your man will appreciate the times you do. Sexy legs in sexy shoes are always a good thing. You might even be surprised at the way you feel once you see yourself in them.

Now, back to those five-inch heels. Practice walking in them beforehand. It's important that you feel comfortable in them and walk with confidence and flair. The last thing we want is for you to create a hot, sexy look that brings a fantasy vividly to life for your man...only for you to take one step and topple over, clumsily killing the dream and possibly hurting yourself in the process. Of course, you both can just laugh about it and keep things moving, but the fantasy will have been irreversibly shattered. Strive for perfection, the full effect. That full effect requires that you be able to walk like a practiced whore in five-inch heels.

Lotions and potions. Lubricants come in a variety of styles, including flavored and self-heating. Depending on the scope of your plans, it might be a good idea to bring some along. Massages are an excellent way to pamper a man and get him in the mood. If your man likes these sorts of things, bring either lotions or massage oils, or both. What you bring may depend on the sort of escort you're planning on becoming for the night. As silly as it may seem, when it comes to fantasies, it is important to be specific to create the desired effect. Your appearance may vary from fantasy to fantasy. Tonight's tart might be tomorrow night's straitlaced schoolteacher, eager to dole out punishment. Be sure to get this one right in order to satisfy both you and your man.

Toys. Handcuffs, blindfolds, cat-o'-nine-tails, oh my! Be adventurous and add toys to your escort's-night-out fantasy. Don't be afraid to wear a sensuous mask that covers your eyes (but not your face) or brandish a whip, if your outfit calls for it. And don't think these accessories will exclusively be for you to please your man. He very well might want to use any or all of them on you. Be a willing subject. Submission is a vital part of your role-playing on this night!

Open up. More important than anything else in your goodie bag, be sure to pack an open mind. Be willing to shed your housewife shell and let your inhibitions go. Those same inhibitions are probably what helped create that rut in which the two of you have been stuck for so long.

The two of you should arrive separately and leave separately. You're a paid escort meeting a stranger for a wild, uninhibited tryst, and that's just the way you should treat it. When you get home, mention nothing of your evening together because, hey, it wasn't you! Part of the fantasy is keeping it all a secret from each other. He'll tell you he was watching a football game with his boys and you'll tell him you were at your sister's house, helping her do her hair. You both know the truth, but by leaving it unspoken, you keep the thrill of the liaison alive and leave room for lots more in the future.

Vixen Tip

Stay the Course

Whatever you do, do not break character! There is no faster way to ruin a wet dream or kill a fantasy than to wake up and realize you left the iron on before leaving the house. For one night—just one—do yourself and your mate a favor and forget about the bills, the house, the kids, the dog, everything! This is your night to make his and your fantasy come true. It would be a shame to have gone through all this trouble just to ruin it by announcing, in the middle of fantasy pillow talk, that your mother's coming to visit.

Remember, you're his escort—he doesn't even know your mother!

There's nothing wrong with wanting to be someone else, even if that means wanting to be the kind of person you've never understood or may have been intimidated by. There is also nothing wrong with your mate fantasizing about being with someone other than you. This only becomes problematic when that fantasy becomes a reality—without you. **Words like *whore* and *escort* and the descriptions that accompany them hold negative connotations only if you view them in a negative, stereotypical light.**

Being an escort may not be a career goal for you, but that doesn't mean it shouldn't be on the menu when looking to add some spice to your relationship.

Recap

⁊ Any man would be lucky to find a woman who will toe the line like a whore.

⁊ Almost every man wants his housewife to be *his* escort; they find sexually liberated and exploratory women fascinating on many levels.

⁊ A man will either marry the sexually daring woman he fantasizes about, or cheat on his wife with her.

⁊ Fantasies should never be just for rare occasions.

⁊ Choose to make fantasies and role-playing a part of your and your husband's sexual menu.

⁊ Men do *not* want to fuck their mothers.

⁊ Now would be a good time to be and do the exact opposite of whatever the hell it is that's gotten your sex life in a slump.

⁊ Whatever you do, do not break character!

⁊ The two of you should arrive separately and leave separately.

⁊ Words like *whore* and *escort* and the descriptions that accompany them hold negative connotations only if you view them in a negative, stereotypical light.

V-Log #3
You Do This Like You've Done It Before, Part 1

Isn't it rich? Aren't you a pair? The two of you just took a textbook sex fantasy and, because you didn't examine beforehand the potential negatives that might come with all the fun parts, you're now at odds. You're sad. He's mad—furious, even. What went wrong?

Everything.

Let's start with the one positive we can root out of this whole debacle: you played a damn good escort. *Bravo!* You did it, girl. In fact, you did it so well, he bought the whole bit—hook, line, and did-you-do-this-on-the-side-or-something sinker. And what a sinker it was. So much so that now you're sunk. You walked, talked, dressed, smelled, and sexed like premium paid-for poon. You knew just the right things to say when you seduced him at the bar. When you led him up to your hotel room, told him your fee, took the money, and proceeded to work him over with a zeal unlike any you've ever exhibited at home, he was simultaneously turned on and painfully confused. He loved what you were doing, but you were so fluid in the way you did it. It was all so rote and automatic. It felt like something you were accustomed to. Were you tricking on the side? he wondered. You had been showing up with things that hadn't been factored into the household budget. Where were you getting the money to do that? And the super-hot La Perla underwear you wore during the fantasy. How did you pay for that? He didn't recall "fancy draws" (*sic*) being allotted in this month's expenses. No matter. They were on the floor now and, as he'd just declared, he never wanted to see you wearing those "fancy draws" (*sic*) again.

And so he is hot as fish grease, as they say in the South, and I'm not talking about in the loins. Sure, he went through with the paid escort fantasy. What man is going to deny a gift horse like that? His wife decked out like a top-shelf call girl, doing all manner of things for a price. But the more you got into it, the more you excited and pleasured him with your supposedly put-on professional wiles, the more you failed to break character, the more he wondered—nay, feared—that the woman he'd married, the mother of his children, might have some secret past or present that she hadn't exactly been forthright about. He wanted a fantasy about being with a whore, but he didn't want to learn, or come to think, that his wife was a prostitute for real! He is pacing in the hotel room now, his rage so extreme that he can barely squeeze out words. You're in the bed, covers pulled up to your neck, the opposite of sexy, afraid to show any skin whatsoever now that he has branded you a pro-hoe.

Oh, and those aren't just my words. He did, in fact, brand you that very thing. He did it right after he came. Following a moment of prolonged silence, he very quietly, very calmly stated, "So, you're a pro-hoe. Is this the way you wanted to tell me?" You're shocked, appalled; it never occurred to you that something as thrilling as a role-playing fantasy would turn into a nightmare like this. You protest, deny, proclaim, exclaim, but he is not having it. You were good, really good—good enough to get *real* money, if you wanted it, for what you just did. His words, not mine. And now he wants to know how you got that good. He wants an explanation that makes sense, too, not some coy "I got skills" comeback meant to evoke a laugh.

You suddenly find yourself in that scene from *Four Weddings and a Funeral*, ticking off, one by one, every man you've ever slept with. The number is kind of high. Okay, it's really high. And like Andie MacDowell's character in the movie, your list of lovers is so long, you've begun identifying them by number. "Forty-seven had big, big teeth and hated blow jobs. Forty-eight always came before I finished. Forty-nine had this lumpy thing on his back that used to freak me out..." Your crazed, wild-eyed husband demands to know them all, right then and there, in the nuclear afterglow of what should have been a loving postcoital moment, so you recount them, one by one, as he grows more and more agitated and furious at your seemingly miles-long road map of literal fuckery.

You whore—you filthy, dirty damn-good-at-what-you-do whore.

Sidebar, girl: Um, why haven't you and your husband had this conversation before? This is the kind of thing people talk about when they're dating. How old you were when you first had sex, your first crush, your first love, people you thought you would marry, how many men you've been with, how many women he has been with. Sure, you might fudge the numbers a bit. You may subtract some if the number sounds too epic. You may add some to make yourself seem worldlier. However you do it, these are things that are talked out during courtship, and if you continue to date the person and, ultimately, marry him or her, it is with the understanding that you are the sum of all those experiences. They come with the territory of you.

But now here you are, freshly sexed, but unable even to enjoy what just happened. You've opened the proverbial can of worms by being all you can be for your husband. You do your best to explain that it was all play-acting. Stuff you've seen on TV on that Showtime series *Secret Diary of a Call Girl*. He is not buying it. You guys don't even *have* Showtime! How do you get out of this? Is there any getting out of this? He doesn't want to hear any apologies and on the way home, all you're getting from him is angry side-eye as he mulls over the fact that maybe he never really knew you at all.

So now we've got to clean up this mess, and we can't do it by having you sex him some more. Let's face it: You've just scared the sex clean out of your husband. He thinks you're a seasoned pro. A pro-hoe. Now every time he looks at you, he imagines you doing what you did to him to someone else—several, dozens, hundreds of people! That's the thing with men. When they love us, they own us. We're their property. I'm sure most men don't mean that in a *you're my chattel* kind of way, but they do see us as under their watch, protection, and care. That kind of devoted immersion means that anything ever done by and to us, if discussed or referred to, will be turned over in their heads, sometimes keeping them awake deep into the night. Describe to him the way you wore your hair in second grade, and he'll find himself picturing you as a kid in pigtails jumping rope. Describe to him the way your college boyfriend used to make your head bang against the headboard during sex and that's why you have that hardened spot on the top of your head, and you may as well just stick him in the heart with a knife. Oh, and he is never coming anywhere near that hard spot again. You can forget about that. He wouldn't touch it with a Hazmat glove now that he knows how you got it. That place on your head is now *hard spotta non grata*.

Our partners don't want to think about us with men that we once loved or liked or even had drive-by sex with, which is why they don't like it when we tell our little anecdotes about sexual things we used to do "back in the day." Yes, some men can take it. Some men want to know. For many, however, it's just too much. They'll wonder how they stacked up to those past lovers. They'll wonder why those past lovers linger in your mind to the point that you feel like candidly sharing happy and/or humorous remembrances of your adventures with them. Heaven forbid you choose to delineate for him a string of lovers too long to recall each one by name. You've just placed the poor guy in the lowest chamber of his own personal hell. He'll envision a nonstop slew of men running an infinite train on you, for money, because you're a whore—remember? A pro-hoe.

His words. Not mine.

This is why you have to discuss things with men in advance, not just spring things on them. Like us, they need time to adjust. Tell your man about your past experiences as you're dating him, especially if those past experiences involve an extensive sexual pedigree or what might be viewed from a mainstream perspective as promiscuity. Give him a chance to take it all in. Let him ask questions. If you're reading this book, however, you're more than likely already committed, and he should know all that stuff by now. If he doesn't, sit him down and tell him everything. Wait, wait, wait! Don't just blurt it out and scare the bejeezus out of the guy. Pick your moments, preferably calm and pleasant ones. Make it gradual. Allow him to absorb what it means, all while reassuring him that because of your past experiences, you have evolved into the woman that you are, the woman he fell in love with and chose to marry.

Whenever you decide to tell him, make sure it's long before you even think about delving into adventurous sexual role-play. You can't just slip into the part of a paid escort and claim you threw yourself into the role and were winging it and that's why you managed to do it so well. Women learn sexual skills firsthand, through practical application, and men are smart enough to know that. Your mate should know the breadth and width of your sexual savvy by the time he marries you, but definitely before the two of you elect to dive wholeheartedly into a fantasy.

The male imagination is both vivid and concrete, so the last thing we want to do is give them visuals of things that will stick around forever, haunting them down to the very marrow of their bones. You'll never be able to have any fun living like that. Fantasies, at least the kind where you get to strut your stuff, won't even be on the agenda, and that would suck—majorly. What makes it extra unfortunate is that, unlike the One-Man Gangbang, which requires far too much stamina on your husband's part to be included in your day-to-day sexual repertoire, this one could fit that bill, if only your husband wasn't so skittish. If only you had warned him ahead of time that you really had skills—skills, by the way, that you've obviously been holding back in your regular sex life with your husband. Tsk, tsk, tsk! You know what they say. If you don't use it...

No worries! Let's make lemonade out of this big ol' sourpuss and his bag full of lemons. Take that money he paid you in the hotel room and go shopping! Shopping fixes everything! Besides, it'll give him a chance to get over his sulking. Take your time. Take all day! Blame it on your hurt feelings. Let him think about how mean-spirited his words

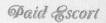

were. When you get back, if he asks about the money, tell him you spent it.

What? He accused you of being a whore. You may as well take the payday that comes along with it.

That'll teach him to call people names. Hmph!

Chapter Four

Self-Pleasure

Fantasy

Flying from the East Coast to the West has never been as enjoyable as it was on my last trip. Normally, I hate sitting in the rear of the plane next to the restroom, but this time was a welcome exception.

He sat in the window seat as I plopped myself next to him in the middle, leaving the aisle seat open; I was glad it remained that way. Once we were airborne, I happily lifted the arm, swung my legs onto the empty seat, covered myself with a blanket, and settled into a well-needed nap during the five-hour red-eye flight.

Within moments of stretching across both seats, I was fast asleep and dreaming of my favorite spa back in LA. I was naked, my body being scrubbed clean by what felt like thousands of hands. Fingers were shampooing my hair. More fingers began to bathe my body. They moved across my legs and thighs, my freshly exfoliated skin zinging from the aromatic body wash then soothed with warm milk. I was lost in bliss, supremely relaxed and pampered, when the hands moved to my breasts. I was too embarrassed to confront my attendants, so I lay still on the table, my eyes squeezed tight.

The hand on my breasts massaged with a bold vigor, encircling my nipple with a finger, then cupping it, full palm. As my lower half began to awaken, I realized that I was no longer dreaming. My eyes sprang open. A large muscular hand was actually under my blanket, fondling me without permission or remorse.

I followed the arm attached to it, all the way up to the face of the handsome man in the window seat next to me. Our eyes met for a lingering moment and, without a word, he clearly understood what I wanted, more so, *needed* him to do.

I adjusted myself into a more upright position, my feet back on the floor, with the blanket still covering me. I turned slightly toward him as his hand roamed across both my breasts, stirring my nipples from a semi-distracted state to full-on hardness. He leaned into my neck, raining hot, gentle kisses against my skin. I craned my chin upward, allowing more access, as his kisses made their way down to the swell of my bosom. He followed the path he'd made back up my neck to my waiting lips, his tongue searching softly at first, then pushing its way into my mouth, sucking, tasting, pulling me in.

Beneath the blanket, I lifted my skirt, pushing my panties down to expose my bare strip of pulsating flesh. I raised a corner of the blanket, allowing him to peek.

"Beautiful," he whispered, his deep voice sending a pulse of pleasure all the way through me. I reached down, spread my pussy lips, and began fingering myself while rubbing my clit. Both of his hands were on me now, caressing my body as I slid my fingers deeper inside my juicy canal.

He slid both hands under his blanket, furiously jerking up and down, exposing himself to me so I could see him rubbing his magnificent, engorged cock. Just seeing it almost made me cum. I rubbed my clit with aching desperation, my sticky fingers plunging deep inside my hole. We both moaned in unison, the pressure growing and growing until it was too much to bear. His eyes were on my hands between my legs as his dick began to twitch, and then spurt his creaminess into the blanket. I came instantly, my pussy racked with spasms, fluids raining from my walls, covering my fingers. Spent, we glanced at each other with embarrassed disbelief, and then burst into a fit of giggles.

"Ssssh," I whispered. "We'll wake everyone."

"You were the noisy one," he replied.

"I was not!"

A flight attendant standing in the aisle several rows up turned in our direction. My seatmate pulled me into his chest, pretending to sleep.

"My panties are still pulled down," I snickered.

"So what?" He laughed. "My cock is still out."

I reached under his blanket, taking it in my hand.

"This is mine now," I said close to his ear.

"But I still get to jerk it from time to time, right?"

"Only if you let me watch."

"Do I get to watch you rub your pussy?" he asked.

"Anytime you want."

Panties down, dick out, covered in blankets, we snuggled close for the rest of the flight. Our honeymoon had officially begun.

Reality

All right, before we go any further, let's drop the pretenses, shall we? Everyone masturbates—everyone, without exception. That means *you*, honey. You masturbate, and you probably do it a whole lot more than you'd like to let on.

So what if you don't refer to it by that name? I don't care what you choose to call it—that thing you do with your hand absently stuck inside your pants as you watch TV, or those toys you keep in the nightstand next to the bed. Maybe you think that if you don't use the actual word *masturbate*, it means you don't indulge in it, right? Wrong! The bottom line is, if you've ever touched your genitals for comfort, pleasure, or just fondled your clitoris and labia out of unconscious habit, you're masturbating! Own it.

You're a big girl now, someone who is not afraid to expand and explore the boundaries of her sexual self within her marriage. If that weren't true, you wouldn't be reading this book. **It's time to get over the guilt and shame that come from admitting to an act that is as natural and common as eating and breathing.** The fact that you do it isn't something you should be hiding from your mate. If there was ever an act that could spice up your love life with minimal threat to your comfort zones, it's a little autoeroticism, baby!

Vixen, I don't have to masturbate, some of you insist. *My man gives it to me on a regular basis, so I'm pretty satisfied.*

Poppycock! **Masturbation and the frequency with which you do it aren't always a measure of whether you are sexually satisfied, or dissatisfied, by your mate.** Sometimes you just need to get one off on your own. You may be having a rough day or a rough moment and just feel the need to release some tension. Masturbation accomplishes a whole lot in a little bit of time—expeditiously, effectively, and, most important, correctly. You know exactly what turns you on, exactly the way your clitoris, vagina, breasts, and other highly sensitive areas need to be touched to stimulate you to the point of orgasm. Armed with such knowledge, you can bring yourself to climax quickly and efficiently. **It is only through exploring our bodies firsthand that we can best direct others as to what pleases us most.**

However, too much masturbation, especially while using battery-operated tools and gadgets, runs the risk of setting a bar too high to be reached by your husband, or any human, for that matter. I mean, who can compete with the kind of orgasm a vibrator can deliver? Besides, buzzing your clitoris into oblivion on a hyper-regular basis isn't exactly the way to go. When it comes to your marriage, however, by introducing self-pleasuring as an active part of your sex lives, you can not only turn the heat up on your romance, but learn a lot more about yourself and your partner as well.

Vixen Tip

Do as I Do

Masturbation is one of the best ways to learn about your partner's erogenous zones while also visually exciting each other as a prelude to intercourse. Use the opportunity to show your mate exactly what you like.

• **Be vocal.** This is one time when show-and-tell is a must. As you touch yourself, be your body's tour guide for your partner. Tell him why you are touching a particular body part. Tell him how it makes you feel.

• **Touch your body the way you would like your husband to touch you.** If your nipples are a particular hot spot in getting you aroused, show him the exact way to tweak, stroke, or lick them for maximum effect. If your clitoris responds to your own stroke better than that of your husband, explain why. You've had that clitoris for years. Of course you know it better than anyone else. Let him see you touch it "the right way." Don't be afraid or ashamed to become completely aroused by your own hand in front of him.

Vixen Tip

- **Lose yourself in the moment.** Orgasm the same way you would if you were doing this alone. If you normally masturbate with slow and gentle motions, do so now. If your technique is fast and furious, full of harried rubbing as you burn to an intense finish, don't hold back. Let him see you unedited. A wise husband will want his wife to climax just as intensely by his touch, so he'll be sure to incorporate what you do into his own moves the next time you make love.

- **Your man should masturbate** for you with the same lack of inhibition as when he does it alone.

- **Watch how he strokes his penis.** Pay close attention to whether he starts at the base and works his way up to the head, or focuses his stroke just at the head or the base. The way your man jerks himself off is directly related to how he likes to be fellated, stroked, and/or ridden by you. Watch how he touches his nipples or rubs his testicles. Take notes with your eyes and listen to what he says.

- **Use toys!** Vibrators, massagers, and assorted goodies are an excellent way to demonstrate exactly what turns you on.

- **Use your partner's hands** to demonstrate where and how you like to be touched; let his hands bring you to orgasm.

- **Eye contact is crucial.** Hold your partner's gaze as you stimulate yourself to orgasm—unless, of course, your head is thrown back in ecstasy. Eye contact strengthens your bond during this type of intimacy. You are sharing with your mate the secret ways you touch yourself. This is the ultimate form of trust. You are saying, "I'm not ashamed to let you see me. I'm not afraid to show you who I am."

Just as stimulating, intimacy strengthening, and informative as masturbating *for* each other is the act of masturbating each other, simultaneously. Remember, mutual masturbation is not the same as sexual intercourse. You're not engaging in the usual penis-in-vagina action. You are, however, using your hands and toys to do what your mate would normally do for him- or herself. Ladies, hold your husband's penis the same way he does when he masturbates himself; simultaneously, he should massage your clitoris just as you would. Be extensions of each other. If you've been doing your homework as you watched him pleasure himself, you know exactly how he likes it done. He should touch your erogenous zones just as he witnessed you touching yourself. **Being each other's hands as you bring yourselves to explosive climaxes can open the two of you to a level of honesty, sharing, and trust you never dreamed you were capable of reaching.**

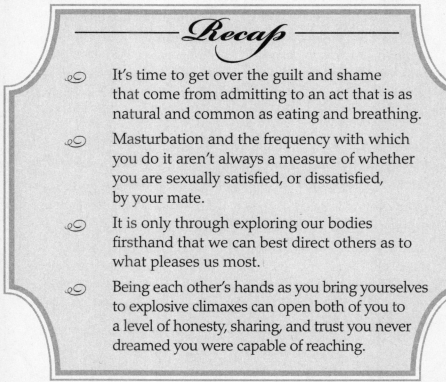

Recap

- It's time to get over the guilt and shame that come from admitting to an act that is as natural and common as eating and breathing.

- Masturbation and the frequency with which you do it aren't always a measure of whether you are sexually satisfied, or dissatisfied, by your mate.

- It is only through exploring our bodies firsthand that we can best direct others as to what pleases us most.

- Being each other's hands as you bring yourselves to explosive climaxes can open both of you to a level of honesty, sharing, and trust you never dreamed you were capable of reaching.

V-Log #4
If I Have to Show You What to Do, Why Are You Here?

How cute! You and your husband chose the self-pleasure fantasy. More than any other, this particular form of role-playing is an excellent way to deepen the intimacy between the two of you. By masturbating using each other's hands to demonstrate what gets you aroused, you break down barriers of resistance and vulnerability, opening yourselves up to a whole new horizon of closeness and trust.

I'm so excited just thinking about how it must have been for you guys—the expressiveness, the tender moments, stroking each other to beautiful simultaneous org...huh? Wait. You mean it didn't happen like that? Oh, it sort of happened like that. Wait. It happened like that for him but not you? How's that even possible? I see. You were able to successfully bring him to climax, but when it was your turn, he didn't exactly follow your instructions. Hmmm, that's not good.

First of all, the selection of this fantasy was your idea. After all these years with your husband, he still doesn't make love to you in a way that successfully and consistently brings you to orgasm. And although it seems obvious that you should have been able to tell him how to pleasure you by now, you've always stepped lightly, not wanting to upset what can sometimes be the fragile male ego. Men like to think they know exactly what we want, and if we take too long to point them in the right direction, we may find ourselves relegated to a life of faking it and using alone time to get ourselves off.

You were exactly this type of woman until you came across this book and saw my helpful chapter about having a fantasy that involves mutual masturbation. You became so excited. Here was your chance! You could say everything you've never known how to express under the auspices of engaging in a marital fantasy, and finally, *finally*, your husband could be told all the places you wanted him to touch, not just the places he chose based on the style of lovemaking he'd employed since losing his virginity two decades ago. Hurray!

Or not.

So there you both are, all alone. The kids are spending the night with your parents. You've got takeout, wine, soft ambient lighting, seductive music. You're sitting on the bed naked, facing each other, an assortment of vibrators and flavored massage oils at your side. You ask your husband to show you how he wants to be touched, and he does. He grabs his penis and holds it, closing his eyes and jerking himself. What he is doing is nothing you don't already know. You've stroked him exactly this way for years because, unlike him, you've always paid attention to just the way he likes to be touched. You squeeze some massage oil into your palm, and then reach out for him, replacing his hand on his penis with your own. You stroke slowly, then quickly, and then slowly again, not wanting to bring him to completion without deriving some pleasure of your own. This is, after all, supposed to be a mutual moment, right? With your free hand, you tweak his nipples, knowing they are among the most sensitive parts of his body. He takes it all in, letting you service him as you've always done. During all this, you sweetly remind him that he is supposed to be doing the same thing to you, and before you can release him from your grasp and show him the way you want him to touch you, he already has his hands on your tits, squeezing much too hard, the way he has for years.

"A little softer," you say.

"Like this?" he asks, barely easing up the pressure. You take your own hands and place them on his, showing him just the way it should be done. He does it like that for a few moments as you resume stroking his penis, and then fondling his balls. Within moments he is back to his old ways, pressing hard on your breasts once again. He is growing more excited from your touch, but for you, this isn't exactly going the way you'd hoped. To top it off, now he's twisting your nipples like they're dials on a radio. You hate that. You've always hated it. Well, here's your chance to put the kibosh on it.

"That hurts," you say, careful with your tone. "Can you be a little gentler?"

"But that always makes you scream!" he exclaims. "Whenever I do it, you cum right away."

You fake-cum, that is, and you scream because it doesn't feel good. The way he squeezes your nipples is so uncomfortable, you pretend to be excited when what you really want is for the damn thing to be over. So tell him that. Go on, tell him now.

"Let me massage your back," you say instead.

What a wuss you are! How is he ever going to know? This is a mutual masturbation fantasy. This is where you're supposed to tell your husband what sets you afire. Open your mouth. He is not nearly as fragile as you think.

Your husband lies down on his stomach and you drizzle chocolate-raspberry oil onto his back, gently rubbing it into his skin. He moans in pleasure at your measured, knowing touch, his penis hard beneath him as he revels in this most awesome of fantasies. You lick his skin with your hot obliging tongue, tasting the chocolate-raspberry deliciousness. You massage and kiss his buttocks, his thighs, pressing your face between his legs as you flick your tongue across his balls. You flip him over and take him in your mouth, sucking him with sublime perfection. He groans with delight. You know him so well.

But hold on a minute. He's not touching you! This is supposed to be *mutual*. What gives here?

Wait, I spoke too soon. He just pulled you on top of him. Whew! I was really worried. Okay, and now he is massaging your breasts, still hard the way you hate, but remind him not to do it like that. Remind him now. Say something. It's a self-pleasuring fantasy, not a self-martyring one. Open your freakin' mouth!

Oops, too late, he is already inside you, pumping and thrusting, just like he always does. You sit there and take it, not even guiding his hand to touch your clitoris the way you like, the way you touch it when you masturbate to climax alone. Hell, he didn't even give you head! What kind of crazy, one-sided, masochistic fantasy *is* this? If one of you was supposed to be abused and neglected in this fantasy, you would have just skipped over to the Domination chapter!

Now he's done. Out of habit, you fake an orgasm along with him, choosing to continue protecting what you believe is his very fragile ego. He glances up at you lovingly, pulling you down onto his warm, chocolate-raspberry-flavored body, holding you and your unsatisfied, uninspired loins in a loving embrace.

Now, whose fault is this? Be honest when you answer. That's right, it's yours. You chose this fantasy as a way to let your man, your life mate, know what pleases you, and before the whole thing could even get started correctly, you chickened out and fell back into your everyday pattern of letting him think he's getting you off when he really isn't. Sure, men's feelings can be delicate. They like to think they know our bodies and how to satisfy a woman without us having to give them a road map. That's all great in theory, but it is an untruth that needs to be quashed right out of the gate.

For starters, shame on you for going all these years without letting your husband know where and how to touch you to bring you to satisfaction. You aren't just throwing yourself under the bus when you do such a thing; you're throwing him under there right along with you. Men can no more read our minds than we can read theirs. Yes, he may be taken aback when you point out that he is nibbling on your clitoris too roughly or the way he thrusts when he's inside you does nothing whatsoever to stimulate you. Better to fix it early than wait too late and make him feel like a jerk for doing something for years that you've never enjoyed.

Imagine how mortifying that would be for him. Remember, men think about everything, especially when it comes to the women they love. He'll probably stay awake deep into the night thinking about all the times the two of you made love and you seemed to enjoy it. He'll realize that you were faking it, time after time. He might even conclude that you've faked it every time you've done it with him, and that could really affect his self-esteem, much worse than telling him what you need from him ever could. The poor guy might even lose the ability to get aroused out of fear that he is unable to please you at all!

If this is you, please, do not pick this fantasy. In fact, don't choose any fantasy, not just yet. You're not ready, girlfriend—no way, no how. If you haven't already, read my last book, *The Vixen Book: How to Find, Seduce & Keep the Man You Want*. You may have found your man already, but it wouldn't hurt to brush up on some key points, not just for him, but also for you.

As of right now, you're apparently not willing to be truly honest with yourself, let alone your man, having placed the onus exclusively on him to know what it takes to please you and choosing to pretend that he is good at it, rather than opening your mouth and setting things right when he is clumsily flailing. The way you went about this fantasy was all wrong. This wasn't a self-pleasuring/mutual masturbation extravaganza; this was the anti-fantasy, an exercise in static behavior. And once again, your poor husband has been misled. He thinks he just had his first real role-playing moment with you and that he knows exactly how to get you off. That's why he's snoring right now, lost in a chocolate-raspberry fog, still holding you close to his naked bosom. You're trapped in this mess . . . a mess of your own making. It didn't have to be this way.

Oh well, why waste a tender moment? You may as well go to sleep along with him. Maybe you'll dream about how this fantasy should have turned out.

Here's to knotted loins, chocolate snores, and raspberry dreams!

Chapter Five

Defilement

Fantasy

It was business as usual at our house that morning. The children were upstairs bustling around, the oldest one on his way to school. I watched him and my husband pull out of the driveway as I waved good-bye from the front door wearing a short, white terry robe and nothing more. My hair in a bun, glasses perched on my nose, I headed to the kitchen to start breakfast. I rustled through the refrigerator and then the pantry, looking for something to ignite my appetite. Nothing. I searched again.

After a few minutes, I heard the front door open and the alarm chime, announcing that someone had come into the house. I headed toward the foyer to greet my husband, eager to pick his brain for breakfast ideas. I was met by an imposing figure in a gray sweatshirt rushing toward me, the hood cloaking his face.

"Oh...!" I cried, startled, backing away.

Before I could say or do anything more, he was already upon me, lifting me off my feet. I thrashed in his arms as he carried me into the kitchen and slammed me on top of the kitchen counter.

I struggled to free myself, but I was weak with hunger and gripped by fear.

"Please," I cried. "Don't do this! I have children upstairs."

"Then maybe if you shut up," he muttered, pinning me tight, "they won't have to hear."

His hands were enormous, able to wrap around my forearms and hold me down with ease. I wriggled and grunted as I attempted to pry myself loose from his numbing grip. I wriggled and I grunted to no avail. The beast stood fixed between my legs as I began to tire and give up my fight. With one hand still pinning me, he unfastened his jeans, pushing them down past his muscular butt. No underwear in sight, his rigid shaft jutted angrily forward as he pressed himself between my thighs, resting against my vulva. Though the muscle was hard and solid, the skin was supple, possessing a softness that belied its aggression. I attempted to struggle further, only to be filled by his engorged, throbbing member. I couldn't fight. I could barely breathe. It was as if, when he entered, all the air was pushed out of my body.

He pumped and he pumped, this wild man above me, once, twice, thrice, and whatever comes after, in a flurry of thrusts as he hastened to quench what was apparently a desperate thirst. He freed my hair from the lone pin holding it in a bun.

"Shake it loose," he commanded.

I obediently did, tossing my head until my hair fell around my shoulders.

He thrust harder, deeper, the heat from his body radiating through mine. Spurred on by the panicked thrill of this most unexpected situation, my loins responded with a succession of throbs that began to build into a fiery knot of intensity. I was in it now, feverishly wet, drunk on a cocktail of lust and fear. Just as I attempted to muster the strength to grind against him, it was over. He was done.

"*Unnnnhhhh,*" he groaned, releasing himself inside me, his eyes boldly locked with mine.

I oozed with his hot abundant essence, and even though he remained inside me, his semi-swollen member still tight against my walls, a few drops of our mingled love juices managed to escape and hit the hardwood floor. He pulled out and backed away, breathing heavily as he removed the hood from his head, a look of accomplishment and utter satisfaction on his face.

"Wow." I giggled, my breath coming quick as I touched my sticky wet crevice. "How long have you been wanting to do *that*?"

"Too long," he said.

"Who knew? You should have said something."

He smiled.

"I figured actions would speak louder than words."

"*Mommyyyyyyyyy!*" came a cry from upstairs.

And suddenly the magic was broken.

"I guess that's the end of that," I said, about to get down from the counter. My husband stopped me.

"Is it?" he asked with a wry grin. "The way I see it, this is just the beginning."

His eyes danced with a devilish fire that made me even hotter.

"*Mommmmyyyyyyyyyyyyyyyyyyyyyyyyyyy!*"

He lifted me from the counter, pulling my robe together. He kissed me softly on the lips.

"Expect the unexpected," he whispered.

"Ooh, I like the sound of that!"

"Good," he says. "Because there's more to come."

He spanked me gently on the ass as I rushed off to the kids.

Reality

In a legal and moral context, rape is a menace, a criminal act of sexual aggression that psychological studies have found to be motivated more by a need to express violence and rage than the actual desire for sex. Beyond the defiling nature of the act itself, its impact upon the victim can be devastating and far reaching, especially if sufficient counseling is not sought, globally affecting the individual's ability to trust others, have healthy relationships, and interact socially on even on the most basic levels.

When viewed in the aforementioned context, rape is a reprehensible and horrific thing, a subject not to be made light of in any manner. The discussion to follow is in no way an endorsement of such a criminal and soul-damaging act—a crime of which I have been a victim. The topic addressed in this chapter, as with all other topics in this book, deals exclusively with mutually agreed-upon interactive role-playing between consenting adults.

Vixen Tip

If you have been a victim of or have witnessed a rape, please contact your local authorities immediately. Also, seek national support groups or those in your area. Visit websites like Rainn.org or search rape crisis centers and help lines online.

To that end, **in the fantasy realm, rape and defilement—figurative definitions based upon mutual agreement—can become exciting additions to a couple's sexual repertoire and adventures.** Please note that when I say *agreement*, I mean 100 percent, hands-down, irrefutable agreement. Put it in writing for yourselves, if you have to, setting both your signatures to it, should future reference become necessary. Being in a relationship with someone does not give you license to commit an unsolicited sexually violent act against that person. Charges can be brought against a man for raping his girlfriend/wife and, conversely, against a woman for raping her boyfriend/husband, if the partner is not a willing participant or submits to the act out of fear. The only time this sort of game is going to be fun—and legal—is if both parties involved agree to it in advance.

Okay, now that the disclaimer is out of the way, let's get down to the nitty-gritty of things, or what I'll henceforth refer to as: *How to Get Raped by Someone You Know After Planning It Together, Yet Still Be Genuinely Surprised When It Happens*. By Karrine Steffans. Yeah. Let's get down to that!

Vixen Tip

Choose the Proper Window of Opportunity

Set a series of guidelines by which to identify when it is the right time to engage in the fantasy. For example: Maybe the event should only occur in the mornings after your workout, but before your shower. Or during the evening after the kids are asleep, but before your favorite television show. Though you are determining the basic logistics of the event, you are not planning the event, per se, thus still making it possible for the element of surprise within set

Vixen Tip

parameters. This will simply **allow your partner to identify which window of opportunity is most convenient for the act to occur** in order to avoid possibly:

a. scarring the kids for life ("Mommy, is that masked man with the tent in his pants…*Daddy*?").

b. interrupting the inflexible parts of your day (work, school).

c. being confused with an actual attacker, so that no one ends up convulsing on the floor with a Taser connected to his or her neck.

Once you two have reached an agreement on when and where the fantasy is allowed to take place, then it is time for each of you to prepare, separately. Both of you have the task of preparing yourselves emotionally and physically for the big event and, because you have no idea of the exact date when your mate is going to burst through the door demanding that you give up the goods, you're going to have to stay prepared for as long as possible. Like any good game, however, the spoils are better snatched when the target of your search-and-seizure isn't expecting you at all! After the two of you have decided upon your window of opportunity, I highly recommend that you **give your partner plenty of time to relax and forget all about the possibility of being accosted** by the love of his or her life while in the bath listening to *The Best of Paul Anka*. Nobody expects to be faux-defiled relaxing in a tub of bubbles, humming "Puppy Love." Let the games begin!

Once you are of one mind and ready to proceed, you both must decide and make plain exactly what the fantasy details. Is it as simple as a voyeuristic rape or is it a compound fantasy, where two or more fantasies are represented at once? Maybe the assault includes some

---

Vixen Tip

Be Physically and Emotionally
Fortified for Your Fantasy

When agreeing to delve into the world of violent fantasies, **be sure to consider the possibilities of one or both of you getting physically hurt**. Be honest about how you feel about being dominated by or dominating your mate. Being a victim isn't an easy role to play, especially when you begin to see something in your partner's eyes that you've never seen before. Being an aggressor, conversely, could mean facing some hard truths about yourself regarding things of which you weren't even aware. Remember, you've basically given each other permission to go to the dark side, so to speak, and with that dark side might come the unleashing of traits neither of you knew you possessed.

From a physical standpoint, in rape fantasies, there's always the potential for strong touch and forceful play, including, but not limited to, spanking, slapping, bondage, and bruising. Consider and discuss these possibilities and more with your partner before you proceed with your plans.

The aftermath of this kind of fantasy and how you both individually and collectively deal with it are critical. It's important that everyone is on the same page so that no one will need a bail bondsman by the end of the night!

---

role-play and is happening to a sexy schoolteacher or an annoying silence-demanding librarian. Maybe you'd love to be "raped" by the mailman. Don't be afraid to get out the gear and suit up! The possibilities are endless for you advanced and adventurous couples.

Vixen Tip

Simplicity Makes It Real
and Creativity Makes It Really Hot

Because of the nature, or rather the unnatural nature, of a rape fantasy, it is best done when the intended "victim" least expects it and is lost in his or her usual routine. **Your job, when playing the victim, is to be at the ready without looking as if you've been waiting for this moment all your life.** Don't change a thing about your day-to-day routine if you want your fantasy to have an authentic voyeuristic feeling.

If your wish is to pleasantly complicate matters a bit, or if you're pressed for time and can only do this type of thing once in a while, combine your defilement fantasy with any one of the other fantasies discussed in this book, or whatever might be floating around in your head. As long as you know your mate is open to them, the sky—and the floor—is the limit!

Finally, before you get started, it is imperative that you implement a *safe word*, a signal that you are uncomfortable or afraid. Sure, screaming *"Get the fuck off me, you fucking creep!"* would work, but it may be a bit of a mood dampener—or a turn-on, for that matter. **Come up with a safe word that doesn't make your mate feel like a bad person and won't blemish your relationship and adventurous spirit.** Maybe it's something as forthright as, "Be easy, baby, I'm sensitive," or something as simple as saying, "Buttons," because no one is turned on by the word *buttons*. Whatever it is, agree upon it and stick to it. If you find yourself in a position of needing to use your safe word(s) and your partner still doesn't stop, feel free to go for the tried and true, *"Get the fuck off me, you fucking creep!"* scream. Nothing beats the naked truth bleated full-throat to get your point across.

Recap

- In the fantasy realm, rape and defilement—figurative definitions based upon mutual agreement—can become exciting additions to a couple's sexual repertoire and adventures.

- Allow your partner to identify which window of opportunity is most convenient for the act to occur.

- Give your partner plenty of time to relax and forget all about the possibility of being accosted.

- Be sure to consider the possibilities of one or both of you getting physically hurt.

- Your job, when playing the victim, is to be at the ready without looking as if you've been waiting for this moment all your life.

- Come up with a safe word that doesn't make your mate feel like a bad person and won't blemish your relationship and adventurous spirit.

V-Log #5
Methinks He Doth Defile Too Much

So you and your man have just indulged in your very first defilement fantasy. *Hurrrrayyyyyy!* Isn't it wonderful? Don't you feel amazing, awesome, and astonishingly liberated, as though a Berlin Wall in your relationship has just been torn down? Yes! No! Wait. No? That's not how you feel? All right, hold up, ladies. Let's discuss. If you followed my steps as directed, everything should be fine—but remember, I did warn of the possibility of things going horribly wrong, especially if the proper precautions are not undertaken.

Let's examine what happened. You and your husband decided to implement a defilement/rape fantasy like the one I presented. You sat down, read the chapter together, got turned on by the idea of it all, and said yes to taking that bold, adventurous step. Your loins were swelling just from the thought of how hot this was going to be. The consent was mutual. Check. The plan was solid, from the where on down to the how. Check. You agreed that he would take you at a time when you least expected it. Check. No check? You didn't agree on a window of time when this pseudo-assault would happen?

So this is where everything fell apart. Days passed. Weeks passed. Two whole months went by! Your husband, in his overly imaginative and focused intent to truly surprise you and make this fantasy feel as real as possible, waited too long and you forgot about the discussion altogether. Why wouldn't you? You're a wife, a mother, and a professional with a career, someone with a whole, full life going on around her. We are often creatures of the moment; the thing making the most noise at any given time becomes the one that garners our immediate attention. Previously made plans sometimes fall by the wayside without the benefit of reminders, but with this kind of fantasy, a reminder would ruin everything. Your husband can't say, "Don't forget, on Thursday morning at nine forty-five, I'll be bursting in to rape you!" That would make this whole fantasy moot.

It is all about the element of surprise. You're not supposed to remember that it's going to happen until it actually is happening. Heck, you have a hard enough time remembering things as it is. What adventure-craving, sexually vibrant, excitement-starved man in his right mind waits *that* long anyway, especially when he has been given permission to do it? What was your husband thinking? This is not supposed to be a theatrical production that requires intricate planning. It is a defilement/rape fantasy with a fragile shelf life, lest it be considered the real thing.

But yes, he took too long and you forgot. Dear husband, unwittingly, bursts through the bedroom door and into the master bathroom as you hurriedly shower, your head filled with thoughts of all the things you need to get done that day. His gloved hand covers your mouth and feels you up from behind as he pulls down his pants. He aggressively rams himself inside you, his fingers tight across your lips. You, in turn, have a full-on freak-out. Who can distinguish fake rape from real rape when you're thinking about work, your life, your children, what to eat for lunch, *whatever*, all while taking a shower? So you thrash, fight, kick, bite, cry, and scream, all to no avail.

Your husband—excited by it all, totally hyped at the fact that you're getting into this fantasy thing in an Oscar-worthy way—goes hog wild, tearing into you. He shoves you against the shower wall, busting your lip in the process, mashes your face into the cold, wet tile, then proceeds to slam, ram, and pound you, relentlessly. He is more turned on than he has ever been and can't believe how you're letting him violate you like this, can't believe that you *wanted* him to violate you like this! You, of course, don't realize this is your husband yet. He is tearing you to pieces, ignoring your screams, pleas, and the flood of panicked tears mixing with the shower water washing down your face.

He carries you to the bed, throws you down, and gives it to you hard and fast. You continue to plead for him to stop, and—*horror of horrors*—he slaps you across the face as he calls you all kinds of bitches and whores and tells you to shut the fuck up. You beg him to stop and he responds by slapping you again and demanding you *"shut your fucking pie hole!"* You don't know what a pie hole is, but he means business, so you shut the thing in your face that does, in fact, like pie. You shut up and let this masked, yet-unidentified rapist, have his way with you. He flips you over, grabs you by the hair, and takes you from behind. He *rapes* you. And yes, at this point, in your head it is real rape because you have no idea who this man is.

And just like that, it's over. He is on top of you, wet, spent, more in love with you than he has ever been. Why not? His life mate has just allowed him to ravage her, getting out all his aggression and sexual zeal without fear of penalty. But perhaps he should be afraid . . . very afraid. Why? Because you've just thrown him off and made a hysterical, desperate escape, grabbed your iPhone, run to the bathroom, locked yourself in, and dialed 911—or maybe there's an app for that.

And now the cops are on the way . . . but wait! Now this guy, this violent madman, is at the bathroom door banging loudly and calling your name, and your heart sinks as you, in your ravaged, shaking terror, realize that's your husband on the other side of the door.

What the hell? Why would he do something so ridi . . . oh wait . . . yeah . . . that thing—that rape fantasy thing. But that was months ago! Why is he just doing it now? Good grief. Men are so damn . . .

Sigh

But the cops are on the way. The worst part of it is that you're the one who called 911, and, well, you can't just un-call 911 now, can you? I mean, you *can*, but the police are still going to come. They are, by law, required to see a call made on an emergency line through to its completion, whether it's bogus or not, so brace yourselves, Lucy and Ricky. You two have got some *'splainin'* to do!

Odds are once the two of you confess to the cops that this was just some sexual role-play gone horribly awry, they'll leave you to yourselves with a grim warning and a few smirks. Or—depending on your race and the neighborhood you live in—your man might find himself getting his record checked while the two of you wait. Let's hope he doesn't have any outstanding warrants.

Rape is an extremely serious thing, and even though I may seem to be making light of it here, I'm not. A defilement/rape fantasy gone badly can have repercussions that make both you and your husband feel defiled for real, on multiple levels, and that would be awful.

What's the lesson in all this? Once this particular fantasy is agreed upon, don't wait too long to enact the damn thing. In fact, give this fantasy an expiration date! A good fantasy should end with both parties feeling loved, fulfilled, and closer than ever. The cops shouldn't factor into this scenario in any way, and neither should ridicule or embarrassment.

Don't let this happen to you, ladies. Plan appropriately. Make sure you and your man set a reasonable time frame within which to implement your fantasy of choice—especially a defilement fantasy that involves the presumption of danger and being attacked—and act within that time frame, while your memory is still fresh and alert. Know your safety zones and how far the violence, if any, can and should go. This should be a fun and wildly erotic experience, not a moment that leaves you and your husband more alienated from each other than ever.

Chapter Six

Streetwalker

Fantasy

This life is rough. Night after night, until just before daybreak, I am here on the street. I strut and peacock up and down this boulevard, waiting, looking, and hoping. Not for the right trick or some john to help me pay my rent, but for the perfect man, someone who will make me feel as I have never felt before. I desperately seek the man who will make me a lady, if only for one night. I walk. I look. For hours, there is no one. I look. I walk. And then...I see you.

You are perfect. Your face is kind and your hands are strong as they cover mine and pull me close. The streets are quiet tonight, and it feels as if you and I are the only two people in the world.

"How much?" you ask, but price doesn't matter. Not now. Not tonight. Tonight, I would go with you for free.

Tonight, I would go with you forever.

I ride with you on this damp fall morning as dew mists lightly on the windshield. I unzip your pants and lower my head, poised to taste your delicious manhood. My mouth agape, you stop me.

"No," you say.

I sit up, my face flush with embarrassment, although I'm unsure why. This is what I do for a living, but you, special you, have turned me away. I glance out the window, hiding my shame. You reach for my face, pulling it back in your direction. And then, you kiss me. A sweet, tender flutter against my lips that warms the surface of my skin and pushes away all shadow of doubt.

"I want you," you say, your eyes dividing between the road and me. "But let's do this right."

We drive away from the squalor of the world where I've desperately been earning my keep, to a place where the streets are free of potholes, the air is clean, and the moon shines directly, as if its glow is just for us. As the car pulls up at an upscale hotel, I am suddenly shy and self-conscious. This moment is out of my realm, bigger than my small hustle back on my own sordid streets. I am underdressed. No, poorly dressed. Certainly not done up in a way befitting a place such as this. A gorgeous woman in a stunning gown waits at the curb, her arm tucked into that of a man in a splendidly tailored tuxedo. I am mortified. A valet rushes to open my door.

"Welcome to The Crescent," he says, his smile wide, but his eyes giving him away as he takes in my tawdry appearance. I step out of the car, glancing up in awe at the dazzling building before me. It is a far cry from the strip and seedy motels I frequent nightly.

The chilled night air stiffens my shoulders and frosts my breath. I tremble from a mixture of cold and fear. In a moment you are beside me, sheltering me from judgment and the elements as you place your heavy woolen coat over my shivering frame. The woman in the gown glances at me with disdain, and I hang my head, cowed by the power of her gaze. On the strip, I am confident and empowered, bold in my endeavors. Here, I am a fish out of water, an ill-equipped interloper among others way out of my league. As if sensing my panic, you raise my chin high.

"Never be ashamed," you say, your eyes holding mine. "You are with me tonight. And that's all that matters."

You slip your arm around my waist and lead me through the grandiose lobby, past the front desk and the concierge station. The concierge nods his head at you in humble recognition. You smile as you guide me to the bank of elevators. With a solitary ding, a set of doors opens. We step inside as you slip a plastic card into a slot above the numbered buttons, and then push the highest number. It lights up. The doors close, and with a *swoosh* we are lifted away.

Your lips are on me now as the floors fly by, gently sucking at my neck, suddenly making me feel brand new.

The room is not just a room but a suite, luxurious and plush. Two couches, a chaise, a dining table for eight, and a fabulous view of the twinkling city. A wood-burning fireplace crackles in greeting. I take it all in with wonder as you lead me down the hall.

The bath has already been run in anticipation—as though you have been waiting for me all along—heat rising from beneath the bubbles, steaming the mirrors, the walls, and my skin. Your eyes are lovingly on mine as you remove the heavy coat and my worn, cheap clothing. You unclasp my bra and my nipples, exposed, instantly harden. I hold on to your shoulders as you pull off my panties. I am so wet for you, I almost feel faint.

You undress without ever taking your eyes off me, filling me with a warmth and desire unlike anything I've ever known.

We sink into the soothing depths of the whirlpool tub as I lie between your legs and you gently, sweetly wash away from my body and mind all traces of everything that has ever come before this moment. With tender circular motions you scrub, purifying every inch of me.

I am clean. I am reborn.

The king-size bed is an ocean of comfort as you lay me naked against the turned-down sheets. Soft music is playing, the lights are already dim, and I feel natural here, completely at ease. This is where I belong. This is where I've always wanted to be.

You straddle my body, looming over me, prepared for descent. Your hardened manhood is an eager sword. I spread my legs just enough, an invitation for entry, as you slowly lean into me, eyes on mine. We are skin-to-skin, chest-to-chest, your heart beating in unison with mine. I spread my legs wider. Your member throbs between them, but it doesn't slip inside. You want to take your time, so you reach down and touch my wetness. I ache inside. I need you to come in. I need you now.

"I want to love you slowly," you whisper close to my ear. "I want to feel every inch of you inside and out."

This is all so unfamiliar, I'm unsure what to do. With you, there is no tearing at my clothes, no grabbing or pushing, no dark corners in dank back alleys. You touch and caress my body with care and intent; this body that has been used without regard, again and again, a hollow receptacle for anyone who could afford to pay for a few detached moments of carnal heat, never giving me a second thought after release. Men never stay with a woman like me. They never come back for anything more than another tumble just like the last. My life, up to this point, has been a series of strangers and familiar johns, each one bringing me that much closer to a bill paid, a week's worth of food, clothing, shelter, heat for my meager home. But you . . . you make me believe all that is over. As your tongue trails down my belly toward my wanton womanhood, I feel as if I'll never see that dark, cold street again, as if you'll cherish me and never, ever let me go.

You stop at my clit, first breathing me in, and then covering it with your warm, wet mouth. I close my eyes in ecstasy, feeling sensations I had long abandoned as memories past, never to be experienced again. Your tongue slides into my glistening hole, tasting my sweet honey. I want you so badly I'm dying inside.

"Please," I utter.

In response, you rise from between my legs, moving your hips closer. I open my eyes in time to witness you planting yourself deep inside me, all the way to the bottom. I am overwhelmed with so much pleasure, I can barely breathe. Your member is strong, pulsating, sending shivers through my core. As you move in and out, out and in, I move in sync. Within moments, for the first time in many years, I achieve full, uncontrollable orgasm. I cling to you, tightly, as I shudder and quake, my tunnel and my eyes both glazed with joy.

"Please," I gasp, my arms tight around your back, "don't send me back. Please don't ever let me go."

You answer me with another round of thrusts, grinding against me and into me, renewing my pleasure once more. I arch beneath you, raising my love so you can plunge even deeper. I touch your chest, my fingers flickering across your hardened nipples, and with my touch you let out a great moan as I feel you twitching and throbbing within me, your cream filling my canal with its goodness. I shift my hips beneath you, cherishing this incredible feeling, the joy I have been able to give you in return, as I feel you slowly pull out. I panic, fearing the worst, not willing to accept abandonment once again. I am hopeless now, bracing myself for the inevitable, but instead you sink below the crisp white Egyptian cotton and I feel your warm, wet mouth upon my pink flesh. You taste me, and not only me, but the hundreds upon hundreds of men who have, quite literally, come before you. You taste the pain of a thousand nights spent parading alone on that desperate strip, in search of—in search of. You taste me with appreciation and delight, relishing all your palate encounters. You devour me. Tonight, I am loved.

"Take me home," I whimper, my eyes closed in pained ecstasy. Pain at the reality that soon this would have to come to an end. Ecstasy as you spread my legs wider, your tongue searching for more delicious treasures deep within.

"But you *are* home," you reply, your words a distant echo as I come even harder than before. I don't remember when sleep overtook me, but when I opened my eyes this morning, I realized he was right. I *am* home, those are the sounds of our children playing, that is the smell of my husband making breakfast, and last night was the kind of night only a man in love can truly deliver.

Reality

There are many instances—too many to count—when men and women meet, marry, and start families, all without ever really knowing each other. Women, especially, are prone to do this more than men. We are sometimes so intent on getting married, so focused on that endgame, that we have no idea what marriage actually means and what we need to do to maintain a healthy, enduring bond. I'm not saying I have all the answers, because I don't, but I do know this: Marrying a stranger is no way to make a marriage work.

Vixen Tip

For more on this subject, see "Getting Married vs. Being Married" in *The Vixen Book: How to Find, Seduce & Keep the Man You Want.*

Having said that, however, **playing a stranger can definitely help keep the ties that bind bound.** Acting out fantasies, as we've been establishing all along, does wonders for reinvigorating the marital bed and your overall intimacy. Pretending to bed a stranger is a surefire way to set off the sexual fireworks.

Ironically and hilariously, **being single is one of the most common fantasies married people have.** Now, ladies, it may be unnerving to those of you reading this to consider that, for even one millisecond, your man would rather be well rid of you. The nerve! Who does he think he is? If anybody would rather be rid of anybody, it would be you wanting to get rid of him!

Even though we both know that you couldn't imagine yourself in *real life* without him for a minute, in *fantasy life* all bets are off! You and he could both be living the single life—together—having some of the best sex ever as a result. It is the perfect case of having your cake and eating it, too!

When you spend day in and day out with the exact same person for years and years, it can become a little torturous at times. That's normal. Any two people, no matter how much in love, who are pushed upon each other along with children, if they have them, can't help but irritate each other on occasion. When real life sets in and the bloom is off the rose of your enthusiasm for each other, your partner can start to feel like an absolute bore and, in many cases, a downright nuisance. Life does that; as the adage states, "Familiarity breeds contempt." This is why things like Xbox, the Super Bowl, basketball games, and golf exist for men, while we have our *Sex and the City* DVDs, margarita night with the girls, shoe shopping, and spa days. If we don't get away from each other to de-stress when we're feeling contemptuous, that contempt runs the risk of devolving into something truly ugly. We can say things we don't really mean as a result of feeling too crowded or as though we're losing our identity inside the marriage. We all need a little time away now and again, but it is a pretty sound idea to also **learn how to get away from each other *together*, in a fantasy that allows us to get a fresh start.** After all, ladies, how many times can we watch Carrie Bradshaw break Aidan's heart? Seriously?

I can hear you already: *Vixen, how am I supposed to be with my husband without being* with *my husband?* Ladies, I hereby present, for your consideration, the strategy (rather, fantasy) of being a couple of perfect strangers in search of a good time.

Vixen Tip

Set the Stage

To pull off the quintessential streetwalker caper, try the following:

• Spend a few days apart. Whether sleeping over at a friend's or your mother's for two or three days, be bold enough to leave your man alone. **Make him miss you.** Make yourself miss him.

• **Send your hubby a message**—by mail, email, or messenger—telling him when and where you will be. *Rogers Park. 9:15 p.m.*

• **Post up in the specified location.** Be sure, however, that it is well lit and safe, and definitely not somewhere known for actual prostitution. Please. No one wants you to get harassed by real johns looking to get lucky—or get arrested for looking too much like the real thing.

• **Wear something alluring** but not outright whorish. You want your husband to be turned on, but you most certainly do not want to be arrested.

Now, while I know you would love to believe that your husband has never fantasized about being with anyone *but* you since you two have been together, the truth is you're only fooling yourself if that's what you think. Take heart, and whatever you do, don't take it personally. Be happy your man has a vivid imagination. As long as he isn't acting on his fantasies to be with someone new, all is well. The upside of all this is that if you are a chameleon in your own right, **your husband's fantasies of an extramarital affair with a completely different woman are just a wardrobe change away.** And even though you'll be playing a streetwalker, play it on the conservative side, giving your mate layers he can peel away. Everyday clothing with a hint of sultriness can make a much better impression than being done up like a stereotypical tawdry hooker.

Vixen Tip

Dress for Success

Here are a few ideas that'll make your man want to poke you without landing you in the pokey:

- Wear an erotic **bra** and **panty** set under your clothing.

- Dress up your everyday outfit with **stilettos,** four inches or higher.

- Don't leave your legs bare. Slip into a sexy pair of fishnets, or **hosiery,** preferably with a pattern running along the back.

- Be sure not to fix your **hair** and **makeup** the same way you've been doing for the past few years; reference photos, online or in magazines, for a newer, sultrier look.

Being a believable streetwalker is going to depend on your attitude more than anything else. Remember, this not the same as the sleek, impeccably attired and coiffed escort we've discussed in a prior chapter. No, ma'am. This chick is a gum-popping, fast-talking, money-hungry slut who's willing to do anything for a buck. She carries a roll of condoms and a canister of Mace in her purse (you may even find a switchblade in there as well). Now, that's not to say that you have to channel Charlize Theron in *Monster* and get all buck-wild on your hubby. Just **make sure you have the right attitude, and stay in character, in order to bring this fantasy to life.** Think *Pretty Woman*—the first twenty minutes. You, too, can be like Julia's character, Vivian, swept away on your very own streetwalker adventure!

Recap

- Playing a stranger can definitely help keep the ties that bind bound.

- Being single is one of the most common fantasies married people have.

- Learn how to get away from each other *together*, in a fantasy that allows you to get a fresh start.

- Your husband's fantasies of an extramarital affair with a completely different woman are just a wardrobe change away.

- Make sure you have the right attitude, and stay in character, in order to bring this fantasy to life.

V-Log #6
You Do This Like You've Done It Before, Part 2

Wasn't that amazing—that whole *Pretty Woman* streetwalking concept? It was so amazing, you and your husband decided to try it out right away, a version of it anyway, where you play a streetwalker and he picks you up. You run out to the store, gathering all the props and materials to doll yourself up—rather, down—in complete tawdry streetwalker fashion. You even know the perfect corner where you can pull this whole thing off. One edgy enough in appearance to create the proper illusion, but not so edgy that you'll get sliced, shot, or shanked the moment you step out on the curb. You get your hair done the next day, wild, big, and disheveled, to top off the look. You overdo your makeup, spritz on some gaudy, cheap perfume, and then post up at the designated spot. Your husband is just a few yards away in his car, so you won't be out there for long, even though you are a bit nervous.

The hoe-stroll experience is about as far from your life as Chicago is from China. Still, you definitely look the part with your torn fishnets and seven-dollar high heels. He pulls up to the curb and you saunter over to his window with a what's-your-pleasure swagger that catches the eye of those in the area. A few passing cars honk and slow down, checking out your wares. You're not sure whether to feel flattered or offended by that, but it's irrelevant. You're playing a hooker, so a hooker you'll be.

You husband slowly lowers the window, seductively drinking you in.

"You buying?" you flirtatiously ask.

Without answering, he opens the passenger door and you get in. He whisks you away from this dangerous street. To your surprise, there's folded money in the cup holder between the front seats, yours for the taking.

"It's all there," he tells you, looking straight ahead.

You pick it up, counting through it. Fifty dollars. Fifty dollars! Is this what streetwalkers make? It can't be. Maybe it is. You have no way of knowing. This whole world is foreign to you. *Oh well, it's a fantasy*, you think. *When in Rome...*

Before you can get to whatever mystery destination he has planned, he pulls onto the side of the road near a discreet wooded area. He stops the car, unzipping his pants, whipping out his already rock-hard meat.

"Blow me," he demands.

Wow, you think. *He is really getting into this. He has never talked like this to me before.* But wait, you're a tramp he just picked up off the street. Of course this would be how he'd talk to you. You're a cheap whore, not some high-class escort, and you are certainly not his wife! Decorum goes out the window for hookers. There is no kid-glove treatment for a woman who walks the streets. You're game. It is role-playing, after all.

You lower your head into his lap and he mashes down on your freshly coiffed hair, which sort of pisses you off because you did just get it done, even if it was precisely for this. He rudely presses your face onto his hardness. You barely have your hand around it as you bring it into your mouth before he begins thrusting upward, pushing you down, grunting, groaning, forcing himself down your throat. All the gentility and dignified touches that usually accompany his lovemaking are strikingly absent. In their place, harsh, rough handling and shockingly salty language. The things he is saying to you...my goodness!

"Suck it, bitch. Yeah, suck it like that."

You suck it like that, unsure about the bitch part, but you're play-acting, so you try to keep a straight face—a hooker's face—as you lick and lap and suck and do your best to breathe and he shoves your head down, down, down like he's working a jackhammer.

"Suck that dick, you stank-ass hoe!"

That did it. Game over. You raise your head, completely breaking character, outraged at the way he has been talking to you and jamming your head down into his lap. He is shocked by your response, rightfully thinking that the two of you were in the middle of a fantasy. You inform him that the fantasy's done and you want to go home... now. Apologetic, he starts up the car and the two of you ride home in silence, your mind spinning with a million and one thoughts about what you've just experienced.

The problem: You're upset that your man, without much prepping, seems not only familiar, but very comfortable with the care and treatment of streetwalkers. The leaving of the money in the cup holder, the cheap-ass fifty-dollar rate, the pulling over on the side of the road, and, most disgusting of all, the rough way he forced you to go down on him. But ladies, let's assess this fairly. This is, after all, a streetwalking *fantasy*. You did what he expected you to do—dressed up, or down, like a whore, worked the corner, came up to his car, and agreed to get in. He did what johns do once they've picked up a hooker: He pulled over onto the side of the road or into an alley and had you give him a blow job. Had you let him, he probably would have put you in the backseat and given it to you right there! It was a streetwalking fantasy, not a Disney movie.

Your husband wanted to add some adventure to your marriage by pretending his wife was a hooker he could use as he chose. You indicated you were okay with this fantasy by quickly rushing off to get all the materials required to create it, including getting your hair done. What the two of you *didn't* do is set the boundaries of what could and couldn't be included in this fantasy. You were so eager to play the part that you forgot about all the things that could seriously affect you regarding how your husband plays *his* part as a john.

It is important to realize that fantasies, by their very nature, mandate stepping out of your comfort zone. You are electing to do something edgy, something different, something daring, something so outside the realm of your world that the mere thought of it gets you excited, and maybe even frightened to your core. Because it requires you to do the uncomfortable and the unfamiliar, you have to decide upfront, with your spouse, that you are willing to go all the way. You can't be half-in. You can't start the fantasy, realize that your man is getting into it more than you expected, then shut down the party. It is the kind of thing that will make your husband unwilling to try a fantasy with you in the future. He won't be able to trust how you'll react and he might worry that it's all just a setup for you to browbeat him later.

Ladies, please, discuss, discuss, discuss! I cannot emphasize this enough. As you can see with each progressive V-Log, failure to discuss and clearly define the parameters of what might go right or wrong during the commission of your fantasy is a recurring issue. What results is usually more division between the two of you than ever, which foils the whole purpose of this book. This book was created to bring you closer, to help eliminate barriers, to heighten your mutual sexual pleasure and experiences, and to keep you together as a loving, committed couple. Having you become pissed because your husband treated you in a way that made you believe he has picked up hookers before is not the desired objective.

So please, whatever you do, don't spend the rest of the night screaming and interrogating him about whether he has been with hookers in the past. These are things you should know about him already, although I'm not sure how many men would actually own up to having trolled for prostitutes. It is a slippery slope. That's a secret many men would happily take to the grave. Maybe he has. Maybe he hasn't. Whatever the case, just pray that he isn't doing it now.

If you keep yelling at him, though, don't be surprised if he slips out while you're sleeping and finishes up this fantasy with a streetwalker for real. Choose your battles, girls. And for goodness' sake, make sure you're really prepared to do a fantasy—not just prop-wise, but mentally, emotionally, everything—before you decide to just jump into it. Now, don't spend that fifty dollars all in one place.

Chapter Seven

Swingers

Fantasy

I was searching for excitement—and anonymity—when I applied for a membership to this special club. Once a month, I eagerly awaited the invitation and address to a secret rendezvous, then donned a fantasy costume, wig, and masquerade mask. The costume varied from month to month. Once I was a brazen handmaiden of the British royal court. Another time, a 1970s-era action star, complete with bouncing Afro, heaving breasts, hip-hugging shorts, and patent-leather boots. Tonight I was cloaked in black: a Chantilly lace bra and crotchless panty set with matching garter belt, black nylon stockings, and a black feathered eye mask. I wrapped myself in a knee-length black trench coat and headed out into the night.

Following the invitation's directions, I found myself on a dark, winding road high above the city, circling up, up, higher and higher, finally terminating at ominous gates looming tall before a stone-walled mansion. Undaunted, I rang the buzzer.

"May I help you?" the man on the other end of the intercom inquired.

"Mayhem," I answered, using the password given in the invitation.

The gates yawned open with a slow, deliberate screech—a foreboding sound that, under any other circumstances, would instantly have sent me rushing away. I pressed my foot on the gas and proceeded forward, onto the property. Anxious. Eager. Ready for adventure.

I pulled up behind a host of other vehicles, most of them high-end. Maseratis, Aston Martins, Ferraris, Bugattis, Maybachs, Porsche Panameras. The fatter the wallet, the bigger the freak. I exited the car and passed my keys to a familiar valet who recognized me at once despite my mask. He always worked these monthly events and showed me special courtesies each time. One day, I promised, I would return the favor. He was very sexy and—from the conspicuous print in the front of his pants, visible even on this shadowy night—generously hung.

I walked toward the stately mansion. Two shirtless, strapping black men opened the double doors, revealing a steamy sexed-up soiree that looked to rival, maybe even surpass, the previous parties I'd attended. I stood in the foyer, surveying the lay (and laying) of the land. The house was sex incarnate. Literally every square inch of space was bursting with action.

The downstairs was a free-for-all. There were couples and groups going at it on the floor, on the furniture, in the lanai rooms that opened out onto patios, where even more sexing commenced. A symphony of groans, moans, tongues lapping, flesh slapping against flesh. The sounds and smells were simultaneously intoxicating and compelling.

I ventured farther into the house, glancing toward the second level. What on earth were they doing up there?

My hands hiding safely inside my coat pockets, my mask affixed tightly to my face, I proceeded upstairs, walking into the first room I came upon. It was lit with red lights and filled with women. Only women. A projector bounced images of girl-on-girl action off the walls as the women in the room, strewn about on mattresses, blankets, pressed into corners and up against the wall, mimicked the movements on screen. I tiptoed across the room, toward the back, careful not to interrupt the heated action. I spotted a sofa against the wall, designated for those strictly interested in watching. I took a seat alongside two other women, each in her own masturbatory world.

I opened my trench coat, my legs slightly parted. My eyes traveled from the women in the porn on the wall to the ones entangled, grinding, and scissoring in the room. I imagined myself as one of them. I closed my eyes and listened to their sounds as they writhed with carnal fervor. I touched myself below and felt a slow stream of wetness oozing out, dripping down. I rubbed my fingers into the juices, then rubbed them into my clit, stroking myself to the sounds of women cumming against each other and in one another's mouths. I rubbed and rubbed, faster and faster, eyes still closed, until I was surprised by a hot, wet mouth sucking my clit. A finger gently rimmed my pussy, then poked all the way in, stroking against the roof of my steamy canal.

I opened my eyes. A masked, blond Amazonian woman was on her knees between my thighs, parting them wider as she moved deeper into my wetness. The sight of the top of her head as it bobbed up and down on my cunt sent an electrifying thrill throughout my body. I came instantly in her mouth. She lapped desperately at my juices, wave after wave of ecstasy rippling through me as I kept cumming and cumming, the muscles of my thighs tight with pleasure.

I felt ashamed and exhilarated, all at once. Without even looking up at me, the woman slunk away, back onto the floor, blending seamlessly into the writhing lesbian landscape. I cinched my trench coat tight and ran out into the hall, breathless and dizzy.

A black light beckoned from the next room. I stepped inside, spotting another sofa against the back wall. The room seemed subdued, if not completely empty, so I headed for the sofa to take a seat, catch my breath, and process what I'd experienced. Even though I had been to these events on several occasions, I had always remained a voyeur, getting my kicks from watching others. Now the fourth wall had finally been broken. I wasn't just a bystander. I was complicit. I'd been ravaged and was thirsty for more.

As I sat back, replaying what had just happened in the other room, I noticed through the dimness a man on the other side of the room who appeared to be stroking himself. I squinted, able to see the movement of his hand up and down his shaft, but not able to clearly make out his face. I watched, transfixed, until my eyes were drawn to more porn footage being projected on the wall. It was of a three-way—a man, a woman, and a she-male. The man was furiously fucking the woman as he simultaneously sucked off the transsexual, who was massaging the woman's breasts, flicking and squeezing the nipples. Mouth agape, I looked on in horror, then awe, then inexplicable desire. I wondered what it would be like to be the woman, sandwiched between two men, one of them endowed with a magnificent penis but the face and breasts of a woman.

My fingers found their way between my legs again.

Just as I was getting into it, the scene on the wall suddenly went black. I sat in the dark waiting for it to resume, my hand softly caressing my sticky wetness. A few seconds passed and, as the wall lit up with another trio of naked bodies, I found my mouth being stuffed with cock. As cliché as it sounds, it came out of nowhere. A large strong hand palmed the back of my head, ramming my face into what felt like endless dick, over and over again. I grasped at his fingers, trying to pry his hands loose, to no avail.

He rammed. I gagged, barely able to breathe, spittle bubbling up and around my mouth. I hated each thrust, feeling as though he would rip out the back of my throat. He rammed even harder and what I had initially hated, I began to love. Somehow we magically fell into sync as my throat relaxed and my tongue suckled against his shaft. I grabbed onto his rod with both hands, my hips moving below, keeping rhythm with my mouth.

He grew in my mouth, forcing me to open even wider, taking all of him in. I slathered up and down the length of his cock, then gently suckled his balls. His breath was hot on the crown of my head as he bent over above me, caught up in my exquisite tongue ballet. A moan escaped from deep within his body. I fastened onto him, sucking, stroking, coddling, taking all of him in. His moan turned into a scream as his throbbing dick, pressed against the back of my throat, released itself. His body jerked and shook as he squirted inside my mouth, his warm, thick load sliding down my esophagus. I tried to breathe as I swallowed, my eyes wet with tears inside my mask. Was I crying? What for? Was this shame? Euphoria? A crazy mix of both? It was as though my mind, faced with an overload of pleasure, had reacted with the only logical emotional response it could think of. Tears.

I touched myself below. My eyes weren't the only things that were flowing. I needed fucking. I needed it now.

The projector shut off and the room went black again. I couldn't see a thing around me. Just as quickly, the dim light from the projector returned, more images flickering against the wall. I reached out for him, the stranger who had just busted an enormous wad in my mouth, desperate for him to service me. I blinked in rapid succession, adjusting to the light.

He was gone.

I pulled my coat together and ran from the room. I wandered crazily through the hall, spinning as I searched for the bathroom. I'd had my pussy licked and my mouth fucked by two different strangers. I felt violated, but I'd walked into this of my own free will. Had been excited by it. Had cum and over-cum. Still, I felt dirty. I needed to clean up.

I searched the manse, stumbling past two other rooms, one lit in green, one in blue. A third room beyond them was completely devoid of light. It was the bathroom. I quickly rushed in, closing and bolting the door behind me, locking out the deviance.

I turned on the light and found myself facing a large mirror. I studied my reflection, alarmed at how disheveled I looked. My lipstick was smeared; driblets of cum lingered on my chin. I looked down. A long blond hair was entwined in my garter belt. I blushed with shame as I plucked it away. I lifted my mask, determined to wash my face, but was interrupted by sighs and moans coming from the water closet. Unable to resist, I inched closer and pressed my ear against its door. The sighs and moans grew more heated. Curious, compelled, I turned the knob and peeked inside.

A couple was inside in the dark having sex. He stood behind her, pounding her pussy as she stuck her head in the toilet. In the toilet! Without missing a beat, he turned and saw me, reached back, and pulled me in. The woman didn't make a sound as he continued drilling her. Was she okay? Was she drowning? She didn't object or protest in any way. He resumed fucking her. The whole freaky thing turned me on.

I slid down to the floor and watched them go at it as I recalled the woman who had sucked my pussy and the strange man who had ravaged my mouth in the previous rooms. I felt like such a whore...so dirty and worthless. I touched myself at the thought of it all, surprised that feeling so low could make me feel so ready to fuck. I closed my eyes and flung my head back as I rubbed my clit and fingered my hole, quickly bringing myself to full pleasure.

"I'm cumming! I'm cumming!" I cried out and just as I reached orgasm, my body felt warm and wet all over. It was as if my entire body was cumming all over itself. It was as if...

The man was pissing on me! He towered over me and was dousing me in his sun-yellow piss. I was disgusted, appalled even. Still I rubbed my clit furiously and continued to cum even harder, surprising myself. And as I thrashed around in orgasmic bliss, he continued standing above me and began to jack off, excited at the sight of me covered in his urine. I just sat there and let him, feeling outside of myself as this whole bizarre situation took place.

Moments from orgasm, he grabbed me by my hair as he continued to stroke his cock. He pulled me to my feet then bent me over, right next to the woman with her head still in the toilet. He rammed his cock inside me and pushed himself deep, thrusting wildly, thrashing against me and pummeling my pussy like he'd never fucked a pussy in his entire life.

Then he switched up the game.

He fucked her and then me, back to her, then me again. He played musical pussies, going back and forth between us. I cried out while she remained quiet. He moaned. She was quiet. I grew quiet. I was caught up in the role.

He came inside of me, then threw me to the ground.

I lay in a puddle of his cold piss as he stepped over me and then unceremoniously exited the water closet. I heard the bathroom cabinets open and close. He returned with a towel.

"Here, honey," he said as he offered it to me. "Let's grab a shower, clean up this mess, and go to bed." He flicked on the light and revealed a life-like sex doll bent over the toilet.

"How was I tonight?" he asked.

"Perfect," I said. "I especially loved you as the blond lesbian."

"Yeah. Me, too!"

Reality

Ahhh, swinging! A subject that has secretly fascinated many of us because of its call for what seems like the complete abandonment of inhibitions and convention. Being fascinated about swinging, however, doesn't necessarily mean that you want to engage in it. Curiosity is one thing, but actually trying it out is another.

Swinging, obviously, isn't for everybody. And even though some of you might think it would be fun for you and your husband to try, go in knowing this: **Swinging is not for the faint of heart.** Leaving your inhibitions behind is not the same thing as abandoning the rules, and having rules is the only way you and your mate will be able to enter such a liberal and potentially liberating phase of your sexual relationship and remain strong (or become stronger) as a couple. Swinging, for two people who claim to truly love each other, is about more than just getting to sample an expanded menu, with your partner's permission. At its core, **swinging tests the very mettle of your relationship and whether you and your spouse are truly and completely in unconditional love with each other.**

First off, let's try to understand exactly what swinging is, so that we can make sure we are all operating from the same point of reference. What I'm referring to is a situation where a married couple mutually agrees to have sex with others outside their marriage, usually as a couple, with one spouse watching as the other spouse engages in sex with others, or in locations separate from each other. This mutual agreement is based upon their expressed interests in specific sexual activities and a desire to fulfill such sexual activities with their spouse's approval, participation, and support.

WTF, Vixen! you scream. *Who the hell wants that? That's just a glorified excuse for having your cake and eating it, too!*

Well, first off, the phrase is actually "eating your cake and having it, too," but that's neither here nor there. Second, apparently lots of folks want exactly *that*, because "the lifestyle"—a more subdued and respectable euphemism that refers to the world of swinging—has grown exponentially in recent years. **Swinging has been around for centuries, but because of how mainstream pornography has**

become, it is no longer greeted with the shock and awe it might have inspired in the past.

That's not to say that everyone is cool with swinging. I wouldn't dare make such a statement, because it would be far from the truth. There are many people who bristle at the thought of something that sounds so daring, unconventional, and ungodly (if they're religiously-centered), especially if they don't understand how it works. The human mind in relationships is often wired for ownership and possession ("You're mine, all mine!") and the ego is not always able to process the idea of physically sharing one's mate. We're told by the greater society that such behavior is dirty and that only amoral, hell-bound (yes, hell-bound—*you're going to hell!*) people engage in such things. As a result, swingers have historically kept their swinging to themselves for fear of being judged, being shunned by neighbors, getting fired from jobs, having their children taken from them, or being seen as aberrant freaks on the fringe of society. It is hard to do things outside the norm of societal expectation and not be met with scandal, scorn, or some dreaded scarlet letter that threatens to follow you wherever you go. And even though, in the last three decades, swingers' clubs have cropped up all over the world—from posh parties in mansions and elite members-only clubs with attractiveness requirements, to hush-hush cells of sexual activity within quiet suburban neighborhoods—people in the lifestyle are still cautious about just whom they share this information about themselves with. Interestingly, though, despite the fact that swinging is not the societal norm, there are reports and studies that indicate **marriages where swinging plays an active part are often stronger and more stable than conventional marriages, with solid foundations of honesty and trust.**

What does that mean, Vixen? you ask. Are you saying I need to let my man be with other women and be cool with it, encourage him even, just so we can have a happy marriage? And I have to let strange men have sex with me and maybe do threesomes and orgies and all kinds of nasty whatnot, just so my husband can get off? Am I supposed to let my freak flag fly? What if I don't have a freak flag? What if I don't want one!

Now, now, ladies. Cool your jets. That's not what I'm saying at all. I would never suggest nor recommend that you engage in any act that makes you feel as though you aren't being authentic to yourself. You should never be so compromised that you lose your dignity, damage your sense of self-worth, or feel demeaned in any way (unless, of course, that's what you were going for).

What I *am* saying is that you should be honest about who you are sexually, and try to get your man to be just as honest in turn. It may take some coaxing, prodding, and some really deep and candid conversations over several bottles of wine, brandy, Grey Goose, Cîroc—whatever your drink of choice is. Most of us spend much of our married lives trying to get to the heart of who our partner really is, hoping that our mate isn't hiding something—some sexual kink or quirk—and that the proverbial other shoe doesn't one day drop, exposing that kink or quirk, thereby catching us unaware. *The Oprah Winfrey Show* and *O* magazine are full of such stories. Confessions of women who never knew what manner of kink their husbands were into. "All these years I just thought he held on to his late mother's dresses because he couldn't let go of the memory of her." No, honey. It was because he was wearing them. And he's wearing *your* clothes, too, when you're gone. One more sexual kink undetected because you weren't bold enough to ask the tough questions and deal with the answers, if he was open enough to tell you.

The advantage that many couples in the lifestyle have over those in conventional marriages is that they already know exactly who their mates are, through and through, and are happily and orgasmically celebrating each other along the way.

No shoes are dropping. The shoes are off!

Think about it. Aside from issues dealing with money, what is the one thing that constantly rears its head as a source of marital problems and, ultimately, divorce? Sex. Lack of it, more than you'd like, not enough of the kind that satisfies, too much of the kind that you don't want, extramarital affairs, wandering eyes, those who stop caring about being attractive for their spouses, not telling your partner what turns you on, not being able to handle learning exactly what turns your partner on (especially if, to you, it sounds aberrant)—all these things revolve around the issue of sex. Heck, just the thought that you will never do it with another person other than the one you're married to *for as long as you live* is enough to send some people into a panic-driven, extramarital fuck frenzy.

Whatever the reason for straying outside your relationship without your spouse's knowledge, it is still infidelity, which is a major breach of trust and intimacy in your marriage. And once infidelity comes into play, everything else tends to unravel around it. You find out that perhaps you never really knew each other. Every lie, even the little ones ("I'll take the trash out in a second"), becomes an issue that results in epic emotional battles. You suddenly can't trust anything. The foundation of your bond is broken, possibly irrevocably. Perhaps your man feared telling you what he was really into, thinking you might judge him or think him some kind of perv. He wants to see you get stuffed with two penises, maybe three, while he watches? It's been a fantasy of his? What the hell! When did he start having thoughts like this?

Maybe he's always had fantasies like this, but now he has them about you because you're the woman he loves. Did the two of you ever discuss such things at the start of your relationship? Were you afraid to do so because you thought it might put each other off? Maybe you like watching others having sex, but wouldn't dare tell him because he might think you're a whore (heaven forbid!). This kind of holding back of one's true self happens every day. People enter into relationships and marriages without ever being honest about who they are and what excites them sexually. Then they sneak and do it, and are shocked when things fall apart once they're discovered. But if you talk to your average swingers in long-term marriages, they'll insist these problems were eliminated early because they were forthright about who they are very early—first with themselves, and then with their mates.

Baby, I like having trains run on me. Do you have a problem with that? It has nothing to do with my love for you. It's just for fun. Just for excitement. I'd love it if you watched. Are you cool with that?

It takes a confident woman to be able to say something like that to a man, and it takes an extremely self-assured man to be down with such a request. That's not to say you're not confident or self-assured if you're not down with that kind of thing. But you can't be down with that kind of thing and not have the spine to back it up.

Consider it, ladies. Seriously. Just how honest have you been with your husband, and he with you? Do you secretly watch porn online, but read him the self-righteous riot act if you catch him doing the same? If so, shame on you! What a hypocrite you are! Perhaps if you had shared with him that you get turned on watching porn just like he does, the two of you could watch some together and turn up the heat in your relationship. Have you ever been in a threesome or an orgy...and liked it? If so, now that you've "settled down" into straitlaced monogamy, do you ever fantasize about that past adventure? Do you ever think about it while you're having sex with your husband? And does your husband know you ever even had the experience? Why not share it with him? Are you afraid he'll be disturbed to learn his precious little wife ever did such a thing?

Ladies, so many of the sexual problems in our relationships are brought on by our refusal to simply tell the truth, sometimes even to ourselves. What do you think would happen if you told your husband that, while you're not a lesbian and have never had nor wanted a lesbian experience, you are very much turned on by watching girl-on-girl porn? Do you think he'd leave you or be disgusted by your admission? What if he then made a confession of his own that catches you unaware, admitting the same thing in reverse, saying that while he's not gay and has never wanted to have a gay experience, he gets turned on watching gay sex because it seems so taboo. Would you freak out on the inside, fearing you'd married a ticking time bomb that would eventually explode and go full-on gay? Would your whole universe suddenly be turned on its ear? Or are you (or any of us, for that matter) brave enough to listen to your man without judgment or fear?

Don't be afraid to ask your man questions about his innermost sexual thoughts and desires, even if what he tells you makes you somewhat uncomfortable. Assure him that you will not use this information against him, then keep your word and hold his confessions close. The same applies to your opening up to him with the knowledge that he won't treat you any differently for what you have shared. This is intimacy building at its purest. The objectives are to learn about each other and to trust on the highest levels possible, when you feel most vulnerable. Perhaps you'll find out something about each other that pleasantly surprises you. If that pleasant surprise involves learning that you both would be open to trying out a swingers' club to test the

Vixen Tip

Reasons to Swing and Who Should Do It

For those of you who are seriously thinking of exploring swinging in your marriage, your best bet is to first educate yourself. There are a vast number of sites on the Internet where you can examine the pros and cons of the lifestyle.

One of the most famous swingers' clubs in the world, Fever Parties* (www.feverparties.com), is known for its exclusive parties for the wealthy elite. While these parties are far more lavish and upscale than most, with strict requirements for attractiveness, age, weight, and

Vixen Tip

personality (unlike many swingers' clubs, which welcome all or most comers), the website offers excellent reasons to consider swinging that might prove helpful as you make your decision. Other swinging sites—such as Swingular* (www.swingular.com) and USASwinging* (www.usaswinging.com), which offers an extensive listing of various swinging clubs and parties across the country—all outline typical reasons why couples choose to explore sexual satisfaction with other couples, groups, or random individuals in this kind of open environment.

Most of these reasons span a range of possibilities, including:

• The desire to mix things up sexually in your relationship. Some of you may refer to this as "getting some strange." The problem with "getting strange" is that this is often done behind your partner's back. Swinging not only allows you to get all the strange you can eat, er, handle, but also lets you do it without getting in trouble!

• Maybe you've been together for so long, you feel like your partner takes you for granted. Perhaps he doesn't even notice that fly new haircut you just got, or the fact that you just lost ten pounds. Maybe you don't notice much about him anymore, not in any great detail. You did notice, however, that he forgot to take out the trash and that he's always hogging the remote. Swinging allows you to rediscover each other through the eyes of someone else. Nothing stokes the flame of passion like seeing a hot stranger lust after and/or step to your mate. Hey! Maybe your man's not such a lump of coal after all!

*Internet sites can be fleeting. This information was available online as of this writing. If it's no longer there by the publication of this book, there are countless other sites with more information. If you Google, they will come.

Vixen Tip

• Perhaps your man has always wanted to try anal. You have no plans to let him anywhere near your back door, but feel bad about depriving him of the opportunity to fulfill this fixation. If you're confident and secure enough in yourself and your relationship, then swinging may be the ideal option. Your man gets to go back-door crazy and you get to watch him enjoy himself. And if you don't want to watch, you can always wander off and enjoy whatever it is that you're into but haven't indulged in your marriage. You both get what you want and can come back together to discuss what happened. In many instances, the excitement of your encounters with others outside your relationship can serve to heighten the intensity of your own couplings.

If any of the above motivations makes swinging sound appealing to both you and your partner (and it must be mutual, not just one of you pushing this on the other), then perhaps this is something worth exploring further. Remember, however, that it can be a very bold step, especially for the insecure and faint of heart. The thought of watching your partner bang or be banged by a stranger might sound thrilling in theory, but could evoke an entirely different response once you see it in action. Before you proceed with swinging as a couple, make sure you are each:

• **Not the jealous type.** The last thing you want is to end up in jail or thrown out of a swingers' club because one of you came unhinged when you saw the other getting (or giving) it really good to someone else.

• **Not a germaphobe.** For obvious reasons.

• **Very open with each other.** Entering the lifestyle should make you more expressive in your relationship and bring you closer. If

Vixen Tip

you suddenly find yourself keeping secrets from your mate about the things you experience in a swinging environment, this defeats the purpose. You may as well be cheating if you're going to keep secrets. Swinging is all about permission and openness. The two of you should be aware of everything you both experience.

• **Into pleasing each other,** even if that means letting the other explore sexual frontiers you have no desire to venture into.

• **A good cheerleader!** Your partner should be willing to root for you to get off, and you should be willing to root in return.

waters, so be it. If that's not the case, you've still taken a bold step in strengthening your relationship by being honest with each other, which is always a good thing.

Those are some pretty good arguments for swinging, aren't they? But hold your horses there, Randy Mandy. Don't start searching for the

Vixen Tip

Reasons Not to Swing and Who Shouldn't Do It

Obviously, there are plenty of reasons *not* to enter the swinging lifestyle, many of which have to do with society's general response to something that inherently seems to be the opposite of a healthy marriage. Society, however, would oppose most of the things in this book, so let's toss that reason aside for a moment. Let's get deeper

Vixen Tip

into personal motivations and self-esteem. If any of the following apply to you, please, don't even think about swinging as an option for your marriage.

- **You're the jealous type.** Fights, hospitals, jail, even potentially the grave, may ensue, not to mention the inevitable divorce. Of course, there's nothing like a murder charge to shake up your sex life, especially when you meet the three-hundred-pound cellmate who's your new, albeit unsolicited, sex partner.

- **One of you wants to cheat with permission.** That's right, you really just want your mate's blessings to sexually pillage, even though your partner's not that gung-ho about it. So you pull an okey-doke, a Jedi mind scramble that makes him or her feel that this will bring you closer together, make you impervious to outside attack, blah-blah-blaggedy-blah, even as you know the entire time you're trying to sell this thing, it's really because you're tired of the monotony of sex with your mate. Or you're just tired of your mate, period, but don't want to jump through the hoops of a divorce. If your relationship isn't strong enough for you to honestly say these things to your partner outright, then swinging is definitely not for you. This lifestyle is a step that should be taken together with mutual awareness of all motivations, or not taken at all.

- **The two of you have a gift that you'd like to share with the world.** No, not that big baseball bat your husband's packing. Not your sorely underutilized contortionist skills. I'm speaking of a much more insidious gift, the sexually transmitted kind. If either of you, or both of you, knowingly has an STD and, for some ungodly reason, wants to inflict it upon an unsuspecting audience,

Vixen Tip

don't. First of all, it's a crime. You will go to jail for it. Second, it's despicable. Third, you should both be tested anyway before even considering getting into the lifestyle. Many clubs demand proof (as in, recent documentation) that you are free of STDs.

• **You think it's going to save your marriage.** If this is your reason for swinging, then honey, you're already doomed.

---

nearest swingers' club yet. Just as there are couples that are prime candidates for the lifestyle, there are those who shouldn't touch it with a twenty-foot stick. Could this be you and your man? You really need to think this thing through.

Did any of those points describe you and your man? If so, then please, quickly skip to the next chapter. You need swinging in your marriage like you need a third tit. If, however, all systems are go for you and your hubby, before you take the next step—and, ladies, I cannot emphasize this enough—it is imperative that you establish some rules. Rules that you both agree to abide by, no matter how turned on or adventurous you feel once you're there and in the moment. As I said earlier, swinging is *not* for the faint of heart. Many a woman who believed herself capable of seeing her man bang another woman in a way he has never banged her before has found her spirit, self-esteem, and, ultimately, her marriage broken by the night's end. Many a husband who thought he would be turned on watching his beloved wife—the mother of his children—stuffed balls-deep by another man has folded under the pressure of witnessing her become extra-eager and, um, let's just say "multiply excited" while being mounted by an over-endowed human satyr far more skilled than he is in the art of giving pleasure. It gets even worse if he sees said wife whip out some exotic moves (moves long put away after her wild college years) that have never been used on him. Insecurity can rear its ugly head when least expected, bringing along its fraternal twin, that green-eyed beast, Jealousy. Soon the

Vixen Tip

Rules to Swing By

• Be honest about why you're doing this. If it is to explore mutual fantasies together, with the goal of strengthening your relationship, then sally forth! If you're hoping to fix a long-standing problem, this will be like putting a Band-Aid on your face after major plastic surgery. Things are only going to get uglier.

• Find a swingers' club together, researching until you locate one that feels acceptable to you both.

• When you visit the club for the first time to investigate, ask to speak to others in the lifestyle, preferably couples who have been married a long time and have been swinging for many years. See if they will meet with you for drinks or dinner so that you can learn more about how their world operates. Ask forthright questions about how swinging has affected their marriages, for better and/or worse. Ask how long it took them to adjust.

• Be very aware of each other the first time you decide to participate sexually with other swingers. If either you or your husband is uncomfortable, for whatever reason, call it a night and readdress whether this is something you really want to do.

• If either of you, at any time, begins to feel a deeper attraction for someone other than your mate, disconnect at once and find another sexual partner. While you and your husband may eventually build lasting friendships with couples you come to

Vixen Tip

trust and enjoy being with socially and sexually, anything that threatens to interfere with the stability of your marriage is a no-no. Put on the brakes.

• Honor your mate's feelings of jealousy. They are very real and mean your spouse is threatened or insecure in some way. Swinging should enhance your marriage, not put it in danger. If either of you feels uncomfortable, insecure, or jealous about seeing your spouse with others who may be attractive or very sexually experienced, this lifestyle is not for you.

• Introduce each other to your sexual partners. Neither of you should feel as though you're hiding something from the other. There should be no secrets between you regarding sex with other people, or it becomes infidelity and the ability to trust each other is breached.

• Agree beforehand on how far you're willing to go. Are you there just to watch and be turned on? Is oral sex the limit the two of you will go with others, and if so, is it giving, receiving, or both? If penetration is involved, what's the limit? Vaginal? Anal? DP (double penetration, vaginal and anal simultaneously)? DV (double vaginal, where two penises are in one vagina)? Multiple penetrations (vaginal, anal, and oral)? How do you feel about seeing your husband performing cunnilingus on another woman after another man has given her a creampie? How will your husband feel about seeing another man, or several, cum in your face? Exactly how many men are you allowed to be with at once, and per night, and how many women for him? Can you be with other women? If it is a swingers' club that allows it, can he be with other men?

remaining members of the Displeasure family—Anger, Resentment, and Scorn—make their appearance, and what started out as a well-intentioned evening of sexual exploration can go *poof!* in a matter of minutes. **Do yourselves a favor and set some boundaries before you begin!**

With couples in the lifestyle, it is often a case of two like-minded people finding each other and daring to bare their souls honestly. They elect to accept each other's sexual proclivities and quirks unconditionally, understanding and defining that, first off, their marriage, family, and love for each other come above all else. Once that absolute has been established, everything can proceed from there. **Deciding to become a part of the lifestyle could make your marriage stronger than ever, absent of judgment, secrets, and sneaking around.** Swing for the fences and, if you and your husband get it right, this could be just the home run you were looking for to spice up your lives!

Recap

- Swinging is not for the faint of heart.

- Swinging tests the very mettle of your relationship and whether you and your spouse are truly and completely in unconditional love with each other.

- Swinging has been around for centuries, but because of how mainstream pornography has become, it is no longer greeted with the shock and awe it might have inspired in the past.

- Marriages where swinging plays an active part are often stronger and more stable than conventional marriages, with solid foundations of honesty and trust.

- Do yourselves a favor and set some boundaries before you begin!

- Deciding to become a part of the lifestyle could make your marriage stronger than ever, absent of judgment, secrets, and sneaking around.

V-Log #7
The Curious Case of Dick & Dick's Dick

So the two of you have been swinging—hardcore swinging, the real deal—for several months now after reading about it in this book. You mutually agree that getting into "the lifestyle" is the single greatest decision you've ever made as a couple, besides deciding to marry, of course. You're happy. You're beyond happy; you're downright euphoric! You're sexually excited with each other and in love on a level that's soul-deep, a love that transcends mind, body, spirit, and time. You never want to leave this man and he never, ever wants to leave you. You've even joined a swingers' club and made friends, some of whom you regularly pair up with. Some you actually look forward to seeing more than others. Emphasis on *you* looking forward. Namely, one Dick Stein, a tall, tan gregarious attorney with a handsome face and a gorgeous, lean athletic build. Of all the men in your swing club, Dick is your favorite. He is just a naturally likable and sexy guy. Easy to be with. Fun, fun, fun!

Your husband knows this and is cool with him, too (not like *that*, you sillies!). He doesn't mind when you hang out with Dick, because he enjoys connecting and sexing with Dick's wife, Peg, whom you also happen to like (yes, sometimes *that* way). Peg is fun, funny, pretty, smart, and, as the owner of a successful bistro downtown, has shared with you some delicious recipes and cooking tips. As couples, you often come together for foursomes at the club. Your man has his way with Peg. Dick has his way with you. You and Peg go at it. Then Dick and your man ride the rodeo on you both, alternating, sometimes lining you up and switching from hole to hole. After a night of exhausting fun, everyone usually goes their separate ways until the next time. It's all fun and games, isn't it? Such a refreshing addition to what you already consider a wonderful marriage.

Still... lately something keeps nagging at you as you snuggle next to your husband and drift off to sleep at night. What could it be? It seems you keep having this single recurring dream. Night after night, the same dream rears its big, throbbing head. The whole thing started out sporadically at first, once every few days, but now it's as reliable as the daily soaps, and it always starts out exactly the same way. Within moments of your dropping off to sleep, here come the Dicks. That's right, Dick Stein and his big ol' purple-headed pretty peen. Both are eager and ready for action. Neither will be denied. How can they? You are absolutely helpless to their wiles.

You see, Dick's dick *is* beautiful, and that's not an oversell. At a full nine inches flaccid and hanging at pure center—curving neither to the left, nor to the right—it is the Holy Grail of your swingers' club. All the women want it, but Dick and Peg are particular about who gets dibs. Right away, they took to you and your husband. They found your conversation scintillating and considered you both attractive; the four of you fit together easily and well, and in short order you became the fastest of fucking friends. You and your husband are indeed the envy of many a couple for having accomplished such a thing.

But now you're suffering for it. Each night, you can't wait to get to bed, just so you can dream about Dick's dick. You desperately hope that you don't talk in your sleep, but your husband hasn't indicated that you've said anything untoward, so all seems to be fine. Your man has no complaints anyway. Because of all your dreams about Dick's dick, you wake every morning—and sometimes in the middle of the night—completely turned on and down for some action. You stay wet on a regular basis, a phenomenon your husband finds most fascinating and which he very much appreciates. It means less work for him to get you to the boiling point, not that he minds. He mistakenly thinks all this is happening because the passion between the two of you has been reawakened since adding swinging to your lives, and, yes, he is partially correct. You wouldn't be feeling this way if you'd never entered the lifestyle and joined a swingers' club and met Dick. And had you never met him, you would have never experienced the nirvana that is the way Dick's dick feels when it's in you, on you, near you, above you.

Dick's beautiful dick. Dick's dick is now the center of your universe. He is the sun upon which you want to set. Er, sit.

Holy shit, lady! This is a problem! What on earth are you going to do? The chapter on swinging was perhaps the most difficult for me to write and the one with which I took the most care. Choosing to enter the lifestyle can be an extremely complicated and precarious thing for a couple. I'm not saying it's that way for every couple. Some are so mutually in tune about their needs, desires, and how they will handle things that they are able to dive right in and get acclimated without drama. Others have to really pore over taking such a serious step, making sure that there is an absolute synchronicity of intent when it comes to why they're doing it.

As I noted elsewhere, jealousies, infidelities, secrets, and the like all have the potential to be perceived as slights that can destroy the trust in your marriage. Your marriage has to have a solid foundation or it cannot, will not, weather the storm you are rushing into, and it *will* feel like a storm, with winds of change coming at you at speeds you aren't equipped to withstand. You thought your marriage was solid, that you and your man stood on terra firma, but suddenly finding yourself lusting after and regularly dreaming of Dick's dick could be a strong indication of the burgeoning of a breach of trust. It is a sign you're growing attached to Dick in a way that could pose a threat to your own relationship. Sure, you may love the way Dick's dick feels. Who doesn't love the feel of good dick? Okay, great dick. Okay, *spectacular* dick. *Beautiful* dick. Perfectly centered dick. All right, all right, I get it already. Get ahold of yourself. Sheesh!

Seriously, though, you do realize that this isn't a good sign, right? You are going to either have to talk about this to your husband, or find a way to put some distance between you and Dick. Yes, I said it. Distance. Step away from Dick's dick. Right now you're teetering on the brink of falling for Dick in a way that supersedes the supposed harmlessness of friends coming together at a club to swap and share partners for sex. Dick has officially become an object of your affection, and when you start to dream of something repeatedly, that means it's becoming an obsession. Unless you and your husband have agreed that this kind of thing is okay, obsessing over someone outside of your marriage is an invitation to disaster. It's a wedge between you that will ultimately grow into a chasm. People fall into chasms and disappear. That's not a good thing, especially if you're the one falling in.

I can see it all unfolding now. First, you'll start throwing shade at Peg. Perhaps you'll grow short with her and begin inappropriately critiquing her body in Dick's presence. That's what obsession makes you do. You will see Peg as your enemy, the person who keeps you from having Dick and his dick all to yourself, so the barbs will fly. You may not even be aware you are doing it.

Maybe you'll ask if she's gaining weight from all that tasting she does at the restaurant, ha ha ha. And Peg will be like, "Ha ha huh? Bitch, what?" Your husband will wonder what the heck you're doing, saying such a thing to someone who has been so gracious to the two of you. He likes Peg. Peg gives great head and has a fat, juicy, welcoming ass. But unlike you, he could take her or leave her. He's not having late-night dreams and morning wood about Peg and her juicy, fat ass. When he wakes up in the morning with wood, it's all for you, inspired by you.

When that tack fails, maybe you'll redirect the attack and start in on him. First you'll accuse him of the very thing you're guilty of, because that's what we do, isn't it? That's the ultimate giveaway. You Jedi mind trick 'em. Whip out the okey-doke. You accuse him of wanting to be with Peg and insist he enjoys her sexually more than he does you, thus putting him in the unfortunate position of having to defend himself. Of course, he'll put an end to that immediately by saying he can prove that he doesn't and will do so by quitting the lifestyle altogether. Oh noes! We don't want that, now do we? So you say your mea culpas and abandon that failed approach in search of something more subversive, more cunning, more likely to get you access to more of Dick's dick.

You play it cool for a while, but the dissension bubbles and brews inside you, eventually making appearances in other ways. You begin doing the inevitable: comparing your husband's dick to Dick's. It starts off quietly at first, as just a mental observation. Then, tragically, you begin musing aloud. How could you not? Dick's dick is the be-all and end-all of dicks. It is Dick of Dicks, Lord of Meat Swords. Should your husband fail to hit a spot the way Dick's dick hits it or, heaven forbid, not match up to his stamina, you begin to nitpick. It's subtle at first, but it is definitely there.

Don't think your husband won't realize what's happening. He will feel a pang of something that he might not recognize at first, but soon he'll understand that it's brought on by the threat of something encroaching on his marriage, the threat of his wife longing for greener, longer, better-hung grass. Once the full realization of what's going on washes over him, he will understand that this is where all the attacks are coming from—the barbs at Peg about her weight, the accusations about his lusting for her, and your dissatisfaction with the size and performance of his formerly more-than-acceptable manhood—all of it stems from your addiction to Dick's dick.

The worst will be when you insist on frequenting the swing club more. You and your husband started out attending once a week, which seemed more than sufficient to satisfy your urge for some fun-filled strange. That is, up until now. Dick and Peg are on the scene at least five times a week. Now *you* want to go five times a week as well. You insist. It'll be fun! Meanwhile, your husband is growing more than a bit concerned. He is ready to take action in the form of an ultimatum. It is him or the club, your man or Dick's dick.

Do I really need to tell you that it's time to pump the brakes? Seriously? In fact, it might be time to make a clean break altogether—but not from your husband. He's the good guy in all this. In this little cautionary tale, *you* are the villain, although you may not have started out that way. You just stepped into a situation that was—*ahem*—much bigger than what you were capable of handling emotionally. It might be hard, especially now that an addiction seems to have taken hold, but you need to find a way to disengage from your attachment to this outsider. It has even begun causing a bit of tension between Dick and Peg. She is none too appreciative of the jokes you've been making at her expense. Peg is shrewd, however. She has seen this routine before. She knows the prize that is Dick's dick and has had women throw shade at her before. You're not the first, honey, and you won't be the last. Women have even tried to fight her about it, but those silly fools just ended up kicked out of the club. Peg shakes off such drama especially well because she knows that gilded, hysteria-inspiring magic meat wand goes home with her every night. She's got her shit together. She's been in the lifestyle for more than a decade and she knows exactly how to navigate the emotional landscape.

You, however, need to gracefully exit this complicated, dead-end scenario. You're not equipped for this kind of hardball, not just yet, even though you and your husband probably thought you were when you both decided to do it.

Take a break for a while. Be with each other and just each other. Don't even think about allowing any third, fourth, or fifth parties in. Put the kibosh on it all, for the sake of all that's important to you. You can do it. It might be hard, but you can definitely do it. Just think, you and your husband were married for years before you introduced the idea of sexing outsiders. You've only been in the lifestyle for a very short while, so while it may hurt a little, it's not going to kill you to give it up. Amiright?

Chill. Enjoy each other. Try this fantasy with just you two and a bit of costuming and dolls, if you must. Revel in the fact that your love is strong enough and trusting enough that you were willing to try out the lifestyle to see if it was something that could work for your marriage. Well, um, obviously it can't, at least not without one of you freaking out a little . . . okay, a lot, but take heart knowing that no matter what, being together is all that matters. I'm not saying that you should leave the lifestyle completely, especially if you both really enjoy it, but maybe taking baby steps wouldn't hurt. I mean, you got sprung on a specific dick after a mere two months of experimenting with swinging, which means you haven't mastered the ability to separate the act of having sex from the person you are having it with and can't leave those momentary feelings at the club once you and your hubby head back home.

Take your time. Reacquaint yourselves with each other. Re-meet his meat. Your husband's, that is. He's got a dick, too, you know, and his dick has feelings. His dick isn't stupid. It knew you were transferring your affections to another. It's not blind. Well, maybe it is, but still. You get my point.

His dick knows you, literally, inside out. It's there for you when you're wet, and even when you're dry. Good dick isn't always about how a man puts it down, but where he wants to put it, day after day, night after night.

Show his dick some love. Give it some praise. Give it a fist bump with your mouth. It may not be Dick's dick, but, by golly, it's yours!

Chapter Eight

Glory Hole

Fantasy

Most of my days were exactly like the ones that came before: the same old routine at work and at home. My husband and I, though still very much in love, were more mechanical than passionate, much of our focus placed on raising our family rather than on giving each other the personal attention we deserved. Sex was stimulating at the most basic level, but for a long time I'd been feeling that it wasn't enough. I hungered for more, and was beginning to look for it in the unlikeliest of places.

There was a seedy sex shop in an unincorporated area on the other side of town. I saw it every day on my way to and from work, and it always piqued my curiosity—the pink neon lights that never seemed to shut off, day or night, the large, cheesy lettering on the billboard above. NOVELTIES! LINGERIE! MOVIES! PEEP SHOWS! it shouted as I passed, beckoning me. I often wondered what was in there, and if it was more interesting than my one-trick-pony sex life at home. Cars in the parking lot were always sparse; just a few, never a crowd.

Each day as I approached, I'd gaze for a long moment, then look away, staying inside the boring lines of my life. Then one day after work, I found myself steering into that lot, the pull of curiosity too strong. There was only one other car besides my own. I parked in the space next to it, near the door, and approached the building. The glowing neon invited me in by way of a giant arrow above the door, pointing to the entrance. I glanced back at passing cars, wondering if anyone saw me. What if I ran into someone I knew? How would I explain? I could always pretend I came to buy lingerie—a reach, yes, but a credible one.

My worry was needless. Except for a man leaning against the building with a ball cap pulled over his head as he drank a beer, no one was around. I entered with my head down, anxious to duck into one of the tiny rooms to maybe watch some porn. I desperately needed some excitement. Perhaps I could even learn something new.

A row of doors lined a wall at the end of a long, dark hall. A bulb just above each indicated whether or not the room was occupied. Only one of the bulbs was lit. I went to one at the far end. A mini-machine mounted next to the door accepted cash, credit, or debit. TEN DOLLARS, TEN MINUTES, a sign on it read. I opened my purse, pulled out a ten, and pushed it into the slot. It disappeared with a whir and, for a moment, nothing happened. Did that damn machine just steal my money? Suddenly the lock clicked free and the bulb above the door came on. I looked around nervously, almost changing my mind. Then I took a breath and went inside, determined to get my ten dollars' worth.

The lock clicked behind me, which was a bit scary. I figured they locked you in so no one else could enter. I squinted at my watch, my eyes adjusting to the light or, rather, the lack of it. It was 5:32 p.m. My ten minutes had started. How would I use them?

The room was darkened, but not dark, just enough light for me to make out my surroundings. There was nothing, not even a place to sit. Just four walls, three of them covered with graffiti, and one of them padded with a hole cut into it. The hole was about waist-high, maybe lower, and slightly bigger than a softball, with duct tape around the edges. I stared at it, confused. As I stared, I heard a noise behind the wall. Someone was coming. I froze.

Flesh stepped in front of the hole. I saw hair and a cock—a hard, throbbing cock and balls, pushing themselves through the hole in the wall. I suddenly realized what this was. A glory hole. I'd heard of them, but they seemed almost mythical, so far removed were they from anything I'd ever experienced. Finally, here was my chance for some adventure. An anonymous dick to be used as I chose!

Wasting no further time, I walked over to it and fell to my knees, forming a fist around the base of the dick. I made circles around the tip with my tongue, and then enclosed it with my lips, sucking just the head. He moaned with pleasure. I smiled, eager to service, his cock still in my mouth. I fastened my lips tighter around the tip and sucked and sucked and sucked, savoring the gamy taste of his delicious meat. He kept moaning. And then I stopped.

"More," he says.

"Say please," I whisper.

A long pause, and then . . .

"Please."

I obliged, covering his rigid member with my ready mouth as I reached my free hand beneath my skirt and pleasured myself.

I flattened my tongue, cradling his cock at first, followed by a waving motion. He groaned deeply, excited by the undulation of my hot, hungry muscle. He pressed his pelvis closer against his side of the wall, trying to give me every inch. I wanted every inch. I wanted both of us to experience more.

I parted my lips wider, pressing them flush against the padded wall so he could shove his dagger deep into my mouth. As I gagged from the pressure, he began to thrust in and out, each more furious than the last, finding pleasure in the back of my throat.

I wrapped my hand tighter around his member, the fingers of my other hand plunging in and out of my wetness. I tightened my lips around him and sucked with a long, slow motion, all the way down the length of his shaft to the tip. He tried to thrust again, but I gripped him tighter, controlling the moment. I opened my mouth wide, taking his entire cock inside, and repeated the motion, sucking long and slow from the base of his shaft all the way down to the tip. I did it again. He was in agony, begging for more.

"Keep doing that," he pleaded from the other side of the partition.

I did, syrup-slow, my tongue sucking furiously on its way down, spit coating his dick and oozing from my mouth. I continued to deep-throat him, stroking his cock with one hand—up and down, back and forth, side to side—increasing in speed.

My whole body was hot. I had to have more. Still sucking him off, I pulled down my panties with my free hand. I could feel him building toward ecstasy and I didn't want to miss a drop. I released his cock and pulled away my mouth, then raised my skirt and backed against the partition, my ass aimed high in the air so he couldn't miss my pink, wet flesh. I reached between my legs and grabbed his raging dick, guiding it into my steaming pussy. Once he was inside, I let him take over, as I tipped forward on my toes and wrapped my hands around the backs of my ankles. I bounced my ass back and forth as he plunged in and out.

I tightened my walls around his dick and squeezed.

"Oh shit," he cried. "Damn, you feel good!"

He sank deeper and deeper as I opened wider with each stroke. I could feel every inch of his dick as he swelled to capacity. His thrusts grew faster, the wall shaking as his knees banged against it. The vibration, coupled with his pounding, sent shocks through my body. I placed my palms on the dirty floor and pushed back, bucking against him, meeting his fervor with a zeal of my own. I could hear his balls slamming against the other side of the wall.

"Fuck it! Fuck my pussy!"

I could feel the pressure growing inside me, ready to burst.

As I was bent over, I noticed my watch: 5:40 p.m. We were running out of time.

"Hurry!" I said. "Fuck me! Fuck me!"

I pushed my hot wetness against the wall as he pierced me again. Two more thrusts and I was cumming, hard and heavy, my pussy gushing.

"Oh, oh, oh…"

My legs shook I was cumming so hard.

My spasms pushed him over the edge.

"Quick," he ordered, "give me your mouth!"

I pulled away and turned around on my knees, ready to receive him, wanting to feel him explode on my taste buds. I stroked and sucked for a few short seconds, and then he was cumming, his cock like a geyser, shooting a load so big, my mouth couldn't contain it all. His goo coated my throat and my tongue, dripping past my lips and onto my chin. He grunted and shook, releasing every drop. I licked and swallowed all of it, quite pleased with myself for this adventure. A buzzer went off in the room. The lock clicked free. Our time was up. He withdrew his spent, glistening cock from the hole. I pulled my panties up over my still-dripping cunt.

I straightened my clothes and left the room, my head down, my body glowing, as I made my way back down the long, dark hall toward the exit. I could hardly keep my mouth still. My lips wanted to burst into a grin. I felt wicked, naughty, daring. In just ten minutes, I'd become brand new.

I pushed the door open and stepped out into the daylight. He was waiting for me, leaning against the wall, his ball cap tipped back. His dick, safely zipped away in his jeans, still tingled from our romp. He reached for my hand as we walked to our cars. He opened my door and I got in. He closed it. I let the window down. He leaned inside.

"See you at home," he said.

"I can't wait."

Reality

I'm pretty sure none of you happens to have a wall in your home where you've decided to cut a hole big enough for your husband's penis and plums, nor do I expect you to run around your house looking for a wall in which to do this. On the other hand, **if you're lucky enough to have an unpatched hole about groin level just lying around, then I say use it!**

Equally as lucky are those of you who have craftsman husbands who love building and tearing apart things. Men like that, if asked to make a glory hole, will usually leap at the chance, just for the thrill of cutting into drywall and getting out the sander to smooth the rough edges. He probably won't even ask why or give a what-for. Once you reveal that the hole is for acting out a sexual fantasy, he'll be extra thrilled. Why, it's a downright twofer—getting to cut through drywall *and* get some freaky sex out of the deal!

Just for fun, we've come up with instructions for creating your very own glory hole. If you're crafty enough, do it as a surprise for your husband. If you're not-so-crafty, the two of you can build it together. Or you can watch as he does all the work. No matter what, just making the hole can be fun, fun, fun!

For those of you who don't have the attention span for a visit to Home Depot or a husband who's inclined to build anything more than a sandwich or a plate of nachos, you can always **use the Internet to find**

Vixen Tip

Let's Make a Glory Hole!

1. Measure the thickness (circumference) of your man's erect penis.* If you're building the glory hole as a surprise for your husband, this is very tricky for obvious reasons. The hole is going to need to be able to accommodate his erect penis and possibly his balls. If the hole is too small, well, you can always make it bigger. If the hole is too big, you can't make it smaller, not without retrofitting a piece of wood inside it, which is way too complicated. If this glory hole is supposed to be a gift for your hubby, the last thing you want is to mess with his ego by having him flop around in a hole that is entirely too big for his package (lowered expectations, et cetera). A gift should make him feel good, not remind him of his shortcomings. Or skinny-comings, if you will.

2. Cut a hole in the wall where you plan for your glorious glory-holing to take place. For discretionary purposes, it shouldn't be in an obvious place, like your living room or somewhere that will prompt questioning from visitors (unless, of course, that's what you want or you happen to run a glory-hole establishment). The wall should be one you can easily press your backside against. Your man should easily be able to access the wall, via the hole, from the other side.

3. Make the hole approximately two and a half inches wider than the circumference of your man's erect penis. You can even go three inches wider, just to be safe. His balls, unless they're boulders, should be able to cram through that. Note: If you're a renter, it is highly advisable to get your landlord's permission first. In all likelihood, the landlord will say no. If the landlord says yes,** but wants to know what the hole is for . . . good luck with that!

Vixen Tip

4. Sand the hole. Please. Unless you want to give your man snaggledick and spend what was supposed to be a night of fun picking out splinters and salving his wounds. Sandpaper and/or sanding equipment can be found very cheap at your nearest Home Depot or Lowe's. A smooth hole guarantees an evening of smooth love.

*If you're doing this as a gift for your husband and he wants to know why you want to measure his erect penis, go ahead and tell him it's for a surprise. Odds are, in all the surprises he tries to think of, he'll never come up with a glory hole. He'll think you're knitting him a dick sock before he thinks of a glory hole. If he's not satisfied with "it's a surprise" as an answer, distract him with your talents (which may vary, depending on what you're good at; no point in wasting an erect penis).

**If your landlord says no, you can always build a freestanding wall that's mounted on a wood platform that you can take out whenever you want to use it and tuck away discreetly (in a basement? in the closet?) when you're done. I can't help you with that, however, because I'm not that crafty. Ask someone at Home Depot. If they want to know what the wall is for…good luck with that!

the location of a glory hole near you. Search for "glory hole" plus your city and state and see what you come up with. **Depending on the state or country where you live, glory holes may be considered illegal.** You could be arrested for having sex in a public place, sodomy, and who knows what else. Some of these places can be dangerous, at the very least seedy and not exactly sanitary. Proceed with caution. **Do your research** before you have your man stick his dick in some random hole in the wall. And for goodness' sake, whatever you do, don't just walk into someone's establishment and start drilling holes in their bathroom walls and blame it on me! I will not bail you out!

Recap

- ∂ If you're lucky enough to have an unpatched hole about groin level just lying around, then I say use it!

- ∂ Use the Internet to find the location of a glory hole near you.

- ∂ Depending on the state or country where you live, glory holes may be considered illegal.

- ∂ Do your research!

V-Log #8
Aye, There's the Rub!

Look how industrious you are! You were so enthusiastic about the idea of having your own glory hole at home for you and your man to reenact the whole anonymous-sex thing as a fantasy that you built it yourself, without your husband's help. Without him knowing about it at all. What a busy little beaver you've turned out to be. First you read the previous chapter about a glory-hole fantasy, decided it was the one for you, then made a trip down to the nearest Home Depot to get yourself some plywood, a drill, drill bits, sandpaper, et cetera, unaware that your husband already had those very items outside in the toolshed. No matter. One can never have enough drills lying around, right? So yeah, off you go to Home Depot for all the appropriate goodies, get back home, head down to the basement, erect the plywood, then drill and sand your very own hole of glory. Congratulations! You win the Industrious Wife of the Year Award for that one. There's no way I would attempt to do such a thing.

What's even more impressive is how meticulously you went about it. The hole is smooth, inside and out. No ragged edges, no stray splinters. You followed directions down to the minutest detail. Your husband's going to love this. You know him and what he likes, so you're already sure of it. Once you share with him all the exciting details of the glory-hole fantasy as I laid them out, he is going to be just as excited as you.

So now here you both are, about to take the plunge. He has read the Glory Hole chapter and, as you expected, he is super-turned-on at the idea of sticking it to you from behind a wall as though you are a stranger. You're already a bit of a hot mama, so the two of you have decided to take it that extra mile. You're going to pretend to be a cheerleader in a locker room changing out of her attire. Your husband will play the part of a Peeping Tom on the other side of the wall bold enough to stick his piece through the opening and offer it to you for service. You already have a cheerleading outfit from your previous role-playing fantasies. This time, instead of the panties you would normally wear under the skirt, you go for a tiny, frilly pink thong that can easily be pulled aside to allow him access. He gets into position on his side of the wall. You get into position on yours. Let the games begin!

Your man is on his knees, peeking through the glory hole as you primp and dance about in the "locker room," changing out of your clothes. You pretend to catch him and gasp with surprise. He disappears from view. You draw closer. Suddenly, his crotch appears in front of the hole. He unzips his fly and places his flaccid penis through the opening, inviting you to partake of his flavor. He loves for you to suck him off until he is hard. You, in turn, always love doing it. You drop to your knees on your basement, oops, I mean locker room floor, clasp his limp peen in your hand, and encircle it with your lips. He instantly begins to moan as he leans against his side of the wall. You lick and stroke him as you fondle yourself with your free hand, majorly aroused by the moment, especially the fact that you made it all possible. *I the woman*, you think to yourself. You can build a glory hole, be a cheerleader, and suck your husband off like it's nothing. You're so awesome, you're making yourself hot just thinking about you. Your husband swells with excitement as you lap at his shaft and suck on the head. You're wet from fingering yourself, sucking him, and thinking about how awesome you are, so you stand and back up against his hardness, rubbing your thong-clad ass back and forth over his flesh as he moans with pleasure. You pull the thong to the side and slide your wetness onto his shaft. The two of you groan simultaneously at the incredible sensation. The smooth wood between you heightens the moment as you press your backside against him. You pull away, making sure not to pull all the way out, and then push back against it, plunging him deeper inside. He is groaning in agony, it feels so good, as you push-pull, push-pull, and push-pull against him. He is damn near screaming at this point, which excites you even more.

You're the bitch, that's what you are. You're *that* bitch, the maker of glory holes, the bitch that makes her husband holler, which is exactly what he is doing right now as you push-pull and push-pull against him. Damn you're turned on right now, mostly at the thought of you. You're about to pop as you squeeze your breasts, your eyes shut tight, your ass pushing and pulling up and down your husband's sweet meat. There's a ringing in your ears that's surely the sound of a killer cum on the way. The ringing grows louder, louder, super-loud, until you realize that it's not ringing, it's screaming. It is your husband screaming, but it's not a scream of pleasure. It's definitely a scream of pain.

You immediately disengage from him, asking what's wrong.

"It hurts!" he cries.

"What hurts?" you ask, confused. Were you humping him too hard?

"I'm stuck," he replies, his voice thick like bleating sheep.

"Stuck where?" you ask, still confused. Until you look closer and notice he is stuck in the hole.

His penis is beyond erect. It is engorged with blood, blood that was able to flow into his penis and make it erect, but can't flow back the other way because he is too swollen for any kind of movement, let alone a flow, to take place.

You husband keeps bleating like a poor, beaten sheep. You can't even begin to guess how bad his dick hurts right now. The bleating should be a clue. What grown man bleats? Bleating is grounds for having his man card snatched.

"What should I do?" you ask, now seriously freaked out.

"Bust it open," he bleats.

"What? I can't hear you."

"Bust it open with a hammer!" he cry-bleats. It's a strange sound. A sound you realize you never want to hear again as you race off in search of a hammer. You don't see one in the basement. Perhaps you need to make a trip to Home Depot.

"It's in the toolshed!" he bleat-screams. The worst sound human ears have ever heard.

You rush to the toolshed, juices of excitement dripping down your leg. It is still daylight out and the neighbor next door, a man who's always ogling you, is in the backyard. Your husband's bleat-cries fill the yard. You fly by in your cheerleading outfit, your thong and juice-stained legs clearly on display. You never even look his way as you burst into the toolshed, expecting to have to hunt for the hammer. You don't. There it is, hanging on a hook in plain view alongside rows of other neatly hanging tools. You suddenly realize that this shed is actually a pretty impressive place. You decide to visit it more often as you race back to the house and down into the basement.

"I didn't know we had a drill in the tool shed."

"Hurry up!" your husband pleads, way past losing it. "I feel like I'm about to faint."

Oh no! First bleating, now fainting? You've successfully turned your husband into a punk. Be careful with that hammer when you go for that hole. All you need is to break your husband's dick and your emasculation of him will be complete.

"Don't hit my dick," he bleats, already anticipating that breaking it might be in the plans.

You drop to your knees and desperately go at the hole, taking care to knock into areas of the plywood inches away at from his pathetically swollen member.

"Do you have a saw?" you ask, realizing the hammer is not going to work.

There's a thud on the other side of the wall. You rush around to see if he is okay.

He isn't. He fainted. Whoever saw a man faint standing up?

You grab hold of him, propping him up. His dick, now flaccid enough to get through the hole, pulls out with little damage, although it does get skinned up a bit coming through.

Congratulations, girlfriend. He bleated, he fainted, and he has a skinned dick to boot. He couldn't be any more of a girl than he is right now; you put that cheerleading outfit on him.

If I were you, I'd lay him on the basement floor and while he is still out, I'd dismantle that wall with its failed glory hole and hide it in the toolshed. Then I'd come back and mount him, pretending the whole incident never even happened and act like we were just having sex on the basement floor and I skinned his dick in the process. Better to have him be momentarily confused about the situation than to bring up that bleating-fainting thing again.

On a separate, but strongly related, note—ladies, if you plan to build a glory hole, you are best off if your man is present when you do it. Prepping this fantasy on your own as a surprise for your husband carries some huge risks. News flash: Penises expand. They go from soft to hard and back again. The hole should be able to accommodate the free movement of a rock-hard dick, not just a flaccid one. It should be larger than your husband's penis, but too small for his balls to get through.

So be careful out there. These fantasies are meant to open your relationships to brave new worlds, not open your husband's penis to the pink meat.

Chapter Nine

Virginity

Fantasy

The knock at my bedroom door startled me. I hadn't expected him to arrive so fast. We'd been texting each other for the last two hours, our messages finally jumping the sexual shark into bold statements of outright lust after months of increasing flirtation. His last text read, "Cmng ovr." "K" had been my abbreviated reply. That was more than thirty minutes ago. Since then, I had freshened up, fluffed my hair, and reapplied my lip gloss too many times to count. I was still in my school attire—plaid skirt, white cotton blouse, knee-high socks, and saddle oxfords—a bundle of nerves as I reflected on how we'd gotten to this point so quickly. I was ready. Scared to death, but ready.

"Come in," I said, trying to hide the shakiness in my voice.

The knob turned a slow revolution. The door opened with a creak.

There he was, all handsome and tall, walking into my room. My heart did a quick-step as I realized this moment I'd dreamed about for so long was finally about to happen.

"Your mom said it was okay to come to your room."

He was setting his backpack on the floor near my bed as he spoke.

"She said she'll be back at six thirty with some pizza for dinner."

He was grinning now, unable to contain himself at how conveniently things had worked out. It was five after four, which meant we had more than two hours alone. We were supposed to be doing homework, which was why he'd shown up with his books. It wasn't a lie. Not really. We would be doing homework. Maybe not the kind my mom would have expected, but it would be homework, that was for sure.

The plan was for me to study. He would be my teacher. He walked over to the bed. I was lying on my stomach, surrounded by scattered papers and my economics and history books, clearly looking the studious part. He sat on the edge of the bed, leaned down, and kissed me softly.

"Mmm," he said. "You taste like frosting."

It wasn't our first kiss, but when his lips touched mine, a jolt of expectation raced through me. Now was the time of reckoning. I'd talked so much smack in my text, making promises of what I'd do when I got him alone, how I would take him in my hands, hold him in my mouth, suck him like there was no tomorrow. I knew nothing about fellating, other than what I'd glimpsed furtively on naughty Internet sites and from things my more experienced girlfriends had bragged of doing with their boyfriends. I never knew if they were exaggerating or not. This was all new to me. Seeing him before me now, however, I was eager to try. I reached out for him, my hand in his lap, tugging at his zipper.

"So you weren't playing," he said.

"No," I replied. "I'm ready to do this."

He moved closer to me, his hands on my breasts, as he covered my lips again with his own. He groped my full and fleshy 32Cs as his tongue hungrily probed my mouth. His fingers lingered on my nipples, then circled them slowly, the sensation it ignited below making me squirm. I arched my back as I groaned against him. My tongue danced hotly with his, eager to taste his desire. He pulled me closer and stood, lifting me from the bed. Drunk from his kisses, I wrapped my legs around his waist as I continued to feast upon his delicious lips.

I could feel his hardness just below my bottom as he carried me over toward the wall and pressed me back against it. I released my thigh-grip from around his waist, planting my feet firmly on the floor. His hands scoured my body, running up and down my sides and over my breasts as he dry-humped me against the wall, our loins desperately grinding together. I shyly placed my hand on his crotch, feeling the massive hardness beneath his jeans. I glanced up at him as I felt for the button and opened it, and then unzipped his fly. I wanted to see what I'd been imagining for so long, wanted to explore this brave new world. He opened three buttons on my blouse, raising my bra and lowering his head onto my left nipple. His tongue made circles around the areola, and then flicked quickly, back and forth, over the nipple. The feeling was so heady, my knees buckled slightly. He fastened his mouth onto my nipple, gentle at first, his tongue still flicking over my sensitive bud. I could feel myself growing wet below as his tongue flicks grew rougher, then turned into full-on sucking. I leaned my head back, my eyes closed, hotter than I'd ever been. I reached inside his unzipped fly, into his briefs, for his treasure. It was rock-hard, solid—a staff of steel that pulsated in my hand. I opened my eyes and looked down. It was golden, glorious, the magic wand that was going to turn me into a woman. I sank down the wall, my breast pulling away from his mouth, until I was eye-level with his throbbing beast. I held it in my hand, observing its simultaneous strangeness and perfection. I kissed it, sweetly at first, and then pulled the head into my mouth. He moaned as he watched, pushing his hardness in deeper. I sucked the way I'd seen them do in the movies online, running my tongue up and down the shaft, then fastening upon the tip and sucking, sucking, sucking more. He widened his stance, giving me more room, as I held him with both hands and relished the taste of his hard flesh.

"Suck my balls," he said, confusing me with his words. I pulled away from his dick.

"But won't that hurt?" I asked. I had learned early after a game of kickball that suddenly went bad about how sensitive the scrotum could be.

"Not if you do it the right way," he instructed. "Be gentle. Take them into your mouth. Massage them. Treat them like they're delicate eggs."

I opened my mouth wide beneath his sack, taking one of his testicles into my mouth, rolling it carefully with my tongue as I gazed up at him for his approval. He closed his eyes and moaned again, clearly pleased with what I was doing. I palmed his balls softly as I sucked, hoping to increase his pleasure. He moaned again as he placed his hands in my hair and held on.

I continued to palm his balls as I cradled his cock with my lips and tongue and sucked the tip. My head bobbed furiously as I fucked him with my mouth. He thrust against me, shoving his hardness toward the back of my throat. I tried to take it, then coughed and gagged, pulling away.

"Sorry," he said, stepping back.

"I want to learn," I insisted, still coughing. "Let me try." I reached out for his rod. He placed his hands under my arms and lifted me up.

"There'll be time for more of that later," he said. "This might be the first time, but it definitely won't be the last."

He picked me up and carried me to the bed. He softly laid me on my back, unzipped my skirt, and pulled it off. My panties followed. I leaned up so he could undo the rest of my blouse. He removed it, and then took off my bra. He patiently undid the laces of my shoes, pulled them off, and then removed my knee socks. I lay back, naked and vulnerable on the bed. He stood over me, his eyes glistening as he drank in my body.

"You're so beautiful," he whispered.

"So are you," I said.

He parted my legs slightly, lowering himself between them. He licked his lips, and then kissed the insides of my thighs. They tingled at his tongue, the feeling radiating throughout my whole body. I could feel the wetness growing between my legs as he moved higher and higher until he was face-to-clit with my lustful longing. He touched my love bud with a soft flurry of licks, then ran his tongue up and down my oozing slit. He sucked on my labia and my button as I squirmed with delight at the newfound pleasure. His tongue darted hungrily in and out of my pussy, licking, sucking, flicking, and awakening a fire deep inside my inexperienced loins. As he drank from my well, he reached up with both hands and tweaked my nipples and massaged my breasts. I came hard, right there on the spot, my body quaking violently. He watched me closely as he drank from my fountain. I opened my legs wider, dazed by an overload of feelings, my nervousness completely replaced by wanton passion and heady lust.

"Turn over," he commanded, snapping me out of my delirious state.

I did.

"Raise up on all fours."

I got up on my knees and elbows.

He slid beneath me on his back, bringing his mouth just under my pussy.

"Now sit on my face," he said.

I wasn't sure whether I should sit down all the way. Would I smother him, I worried. I wasn't sure what the proper face-sitting etiquette should be.

When I didn't respond quickly enough, he took charge, placing his hands upon my thighs and moving me into a sitting position over his mouth. I rose slightly, out of instinct. He picked up where he'd left off, sucking and feasting upon my lips and swollen bud, then plunging his tongue deep inside me.

I felt myself growing limp. The feeling was too incredible to describe. My hands made their way up to my breasts, my fingers squeezing my nipples, increasing the pleasure I was already experiencing. I gyrated against his mouth, his tongue darting in and out of my wetness.

I closed my eyes, still fondling my breasts, hovering above him. He pulled away and slid from beneath me, pushing me forward, back onto all fours. I glanced over my shoulder at him, unsure of what was happening. He lowered his jeans and stepped out of them, completely unleashing his gorgeous manhood. He pulled his shirt over his head and approached me. I suddenly realized what he was about to do. He was going to take me from the rear, doggy-style.

He slapped my bottom a few times, making it jiggle.

"I love the way your ass bounces."

I giggled, raising it higher in the air. His jacked himself with his right hand as he took in the view of my fleshy cheeks, then placed his left hand in the middle of my back and ran it slowly down until he reached my wetness. He fingered the opening, feeling around inside. I pushed back against his hand, wanting more. After a few quick finger-thrusts, he moved his pelvis closer, his golden hardness poised for entry.

This was the point of no return. This was the moment that would forever make my virginal state a thing of memory. He pushed the head inside my portal, as if that was as far as he planned to go. An instant later he plunged in deep, all the way to the balls, his girth and force almost taking my breath away. I was beyond well lubricated, so it didn't hurt. It felt glorious, in fact. But the feeling was so unexpectedly intense, all I could do was gasp in pleasure.

"You okay?" he asked.

I responded by grinding my ass farther back onto his dick.

He pulled out, then thrust again deep, taking care not to apply too much pressure. I welcomed him in, my body freed of all semblance of restraint.

"Your pussy's so tight," he moaned between strokes.

"How tight?" I asked, knowing his range of experience far eclipsed mine. He'd been with four others before me, he'd confessed once during a phone conversation, but had never been in love. I was the first to break the cherry of his heart. The thought of him being more experienced sexually both excited and comforted me. The last experience I wanted during my first time was two inept people fumbling in the dark.

"You're the tightest of them all," he said.

I laughed, thinking of the evil queen in Snow White. *Mirror, mirror on the wall. He says I have the tightest pussy of them all.*

He plumbed my depths, simultaneously reaching beneath me to massage my clit. The rhythmic motion of his hips and my backside bouncing off his waist heightened my excitement as I looked behind me and watched our bodies moving together.

"You're so tight and wet," he whispered, not missing a stroke. "I can't get enough of this sweet, sweet pussy."

I could feel his cock growing inside me, swelling to capacity. He pumped faster, groaning as if he was in some sort of pain.

"I...I don't think I can hold it," he said. "I won't cum inside you. I promise."

He tried pulling out, but I wouldn't let him, my tight, newly explored crevice clamping down hard. When he felt my walls grip onto him, he immediately let go, filling me up with his cream. He collapsed against my back, the pressure of his body pressing me flat onto the bed. He rested above me until he could catch his breath, and then rolled onto his back, still panting.

"How did you do that?" he asked.

I cut my eyes at him slyly. "I read in *Cosmo* about these exercises I could do down there. I do them all the time, just for practice."

"I think you've got it down."

I glanced over at him. He was smiling. I laughed, suddenly not feeling like a novice anymore.

I rolled over onto my back and stared at the ceiling. His hand slid across the sheet and clasped mine. We both lay there for a long moment staring up, savoring the power of what had just transpired.

"I love you," he said finally, breaking the silence between us.

"I love you, too."

We spent the next hour just like that, enjoying the freedom we'd been afforded. Our children would be home soon, so I'd have to get up and put away the fake schoolbooks, backpack, papers, and costume. This was why I loved my husband so much. After two kids and four years of marriage, he could still manage to discover a way to take a schoolgirl's virginity all over again.

Reality

There are certain fantasies floating around in a man's mind that many women may consider appalling. If your mate is turned on by the idea of being with a virgin and you obviously aren't one, don't feel dismayed. Also, assuming you really know your man and are confident in who he is, rid yourself of the thought that his desire to experience a virgin teeters on the brink of pedophilia. Most men love the idea of conquering uncharted territory, so rest assured that a fantasy involving him having his way with an unsullied woman is just that. It is what it is. This is a man thing, a moment where he gets to be the ultimate chest-beating teacher and lover (and, um, revisit the "tightness" that goes along with it!).

There are at least two ways of becoming that virginal flower he desires, over and over again. All you have to do to make this fantasy a reality in your sexual life is choose one.

First off, there's what I like to call the "lady's days" virgin. I'm sure you can figure out what "lady's days" means. No? Are some of you stumped, seriously? Well, you may know "lady's days" by other euphemistic phrases. Like "Aunt Flow," a "visit from your friend," the "red tide," or "riding the cotton pony." Heck, I've even heard it referred to as "Shark Week," which is both hilarious and clever. So do you get it now? Good! Yes, "lady's days" are your menses.

It is not nearly as bad as you think. In fact, I find there's something quite primal about having sex while on your period. It is true that some women and men are uncomfortable with the idea of intimacy during that time of the month. It can, sometimes, prove messy, awkward, and seemingly more trouble than it's worth, but that's only if you have hang-ups about it. If it's not against your religion or personal dictates, and doesn't upset you visually or psychologically, I say go for the gusto!

There are actually lots of women who find themselves extra aroused when their period strikes. If you're down and your man is, too, why not take advantage of the urge and scratch that bloody itch? If your husband is, indeed, seriously harboring a virgin fantasy where you are to be the virgin in question, **you may want to take another look at those lady's days as a way to satisfy the beast before a *real* virgin steps in and does it for you.** By having it off with your man when you're in the red, you can re-create the feeling—and visual—of him literally busting your cherry all over again. Talk about your "ocular proof"! Throw in a little (or a lot of) theatrics, including the occasional *"ow!"* and *"ooh, that hurts,"* and you've got the makings of a bona fide revirginization. Add to the equation the rumor that chemicals released during sex help ease the intensity of the cramps that sometimes come with menstruation, and it's a win-win scenario all around.

Hey, who needs Midol or Aleve when you can bone those pains away and make your man feel like William the Conqueror in the process? Virgin-fantasy sex on your period may not solve the bloating issue, but at least you'll feel good as you waddle around with all that extra water weight. Your husband won't even notice those swollen ankles and mini-muffin-tops Aunt Flow gifts you with because he'll be too busy grinning from getting a virgin a night for a few days in a row. And we all know that nothing beats a happy husband. So let's examine this idea further, shall we?

Vixen Tip

Prepare the Room

Okay, let's be honest: You're about to do something you've probably never done before. At least, not on purpose. So before you invite your hubby into his new virginal reality, let's run through the checklist of preparations you'll need to ensure that this potentially messy exercise will be the mutually exciting adventure you'd like it to be.

- **Cleansing supplies.** For immediate cleansing during and after the act, be sure to keep a container of pop-up **baby wipes** handy. For a more thorough cleansing, keep dark-colored **washcloths** in the bathroom and near the scene of the crime. Soak and rinse them in soothing **warm water** and use **mild soap**, if desired. And

Vixen Tip

although you're free to have your bloody virginal sex wherever you'd like, my recommendation is a smooth, flat surface, like your bed. You don't want to be somewhere less comfortable or controlled and wind up with blood spatters on a kitchen towel or your kid's car seat. Be adventurous, but don't get too crazy!

• **Bed dressing.** Cover your mattress with **dark-colored sheets, blankets, or towels** if you don't want to ruin anything. If, however, you *want* to see blood, I recommend using linens that you don't mind ruining or treating, soaking, and laundering within an inch of their cotton to remove the stains. If the thought of having to "Shout It Out" the next day with a bottle full of spot remover doesn't strike your fancy, I'd stick to Plan A and go with the dark sheets.

Now that your boudoir is prepared, let's get *you* ready. **Virginity comes with the notion of innocence**, so this will not be that fantasy-turned-reality that calls for hooker boots and a whip. Put away your grown-up toys. Now is the time to think like a girl—a sweet, pure, inexperienced girl. Your demeanor and appearance should reflect this. You should seem simple rather than worldly, a naïf embarking upon an exciting—if borderline frightening—adventure. Since this is your husband's fantasy, his job will be to make that sweet, nervous girl feel safe, trusting, secure, yet willing, all while exposing her to the ways of passion and the joys of erotic love.

Okay. So now it's on. You've got your Pollyanna thing going and you're ready for the plucking. This is where the role-playing comes in. You've created the look. Now you have to be believable. In most people's minds, a virgin is shy and unsure, most likely young, although

Vixen Tip

Don't Just Think Like a Virgin, Look Like One!

You can pretend to be a virgin all you want, but if you don't look the part, this whole exercise will be like theater of the absurd. What's the sense of acting coy and skittish when you show up looking like your seasoned, married, maternal self? This is an all-or-nothing fantasy, so take it all the way. Set the stage by creating the look. Here are some suggestions for delivering on the promise of giving your man some "brand-new."

- **Hair.** Try a truly young style for the occasion. **Pigtails**, **braids**, **curls**, or the like will surely do the trick.

- **Makeup.** Nothing conveys innocence like a clean, beautiful face. Wearing a little **foundation and powder** is okay, even a light touch of **blush**, something pink and fresh, like flowers in springtime. Forgo the lipstick and opt instead for a sparkling, glittery **lip gloss** with a cheeky flavor reminiscent of your gum-popping grade-school days. Drugstore favorites like Bonne Bell offer several girlish glosses, including a line called lipLITES, with flavors like Cream Pop, Angel Food Cake, and Cherry Berry Kiss. Go even lighter by wearing a plain **lip balm**, like ChapStick's 100% Naturals line or Kiehl's. A little **mascara** on your top and bottom lashes is just the right touch to emphasize your wide-eyed innocence.

- **Attire.** When it comes to underwear, ditch the granny-panties and the super-lacy thongs. Instead, present yourself in a colorful, even printed, cotton pair of **knickers** (yes, I said *knickers*!). Try the full back, thong, Brazilian-cut, or any variation thereof. Even boy shorts can go a long way toward giving off that oh-so-naive

---

Vixen Tip

air. Your outerwear can run the gamut from a traditional school uniform to whatever's being touted in the pages of the latest *Seventeen* magazine. Go for girlie shoes, like oxfords, loafers, or a simple pair of white canvas Keds sneakers. Oh, and don't forget socks. There's nothing more innocent than knee-highs with oxfords or the classic **ankle socks** worn with white sneakers, especially the ones with the fuzzy little ball on the back!

• **Skin.** The way you smell also plays an influential role in bringing this fantasy to life. Avoid musky scents that suggest seductive allure. Tonight, you are the seduced. Go for something plain and innocent, like a baby lotion rubbed all over your body. Add the hint of a light, fresh fragrance at your pulse points (behind the ears, at the wrists, behind the knees, between the thighs, and lightly sprayed onto the panties).

• **Accessories.** Feel free to throw in some additional accoutrements to flesh out the look. Bows, ribbons, book bags, backpacks, even a giant lollipop can help complete your virginal transformation.

---

not necessarily a schoolgirl. A virgin is definitely not a woman who is married with three kids so, **whatever you do, don't be yourself!**

When the time comes, **don't ruin the fantasy by showing him this isn't your first time at the rodeo.** Act as if you've never seen one of these penis thingies before and you have no idea where it goes and what to do with it. At the most, pretend you've maybe caught glimpses of it in furtive peeks online while hanging with your girlfriends, but be giggly, awkward, and much more skittish about seeing one in the flesh. Once you're in the act, squirm in discomfort or pain, even though having sex with your husband after all this time is as natural, instinctive, and synchronous as a veteran tango team performance. Allow yourself to bleed all over him. This is when the fantasy will begin to feel all too real for your man. Bask in your newly found innocence, asking him if you're doing the right things and if your body pleases him. Seek instruction on how you should touch, kiss, and respond to his every move. Let him know you are eager to learn!

Vixen Tip

Be Convincing from the Inside Out

Before you get into character for this wonderful fantasy, soak in a hot **Epsom salt** bath. You can also add a bit of **vinegar** to the water if you like, but beware of emerging smelling like tartar sauce, which could destroy the entire illusion. The purpose of this bath is to cleanse the more prominent blood from your vagina and temporarily tighten the area for that genuine unpopped-cherry feel.

I trust that you can handle yourself from this point, so let's move on to the second option for creating a virgin fantasy for your husband. I'm sure some of you have your thinking caps on and already have it figured out. For those of you who haven't, well, I'll just cut right to the chase. I'm talking about the ultimate virgin territory: that ass! All right, maybe that was a little harsh. Let me dial it back a little and try to be a bit more PC. I'm talking about anal sex, ladies. Rectal exploration. "That undiscovered country from whose bourne no traveler returns..."

My bad. I waxed a little Shakespeare for a sec. Your husband, however, might want to wax more than just Shakespeare. He might seriously be entertaining waxing that ass. *Your* ass. So here's where you decide whether you're ready to give up that last legitimate bastion of purity.

That being said, are you ready for some back-door loving and the potential pain that might come along with it?

For those of you who've already been having parties in your backyard, this option is moot. Go the sex-on-your-period route to fulfill your husband's desire for a virgin because your ass will be old hat to him. For those of you, however, who are seriously behind the idea of delivering to your husband the authentic feel of breaking in a virgin, doing it in the butt is the way to go. **There is no definitive answer to the question of how you should have anal sex for the very first time.** Aside from brutal, forceful entry (definitely not advisable), there's really no wrong way to do it, as long your husband is mindful of your feelings and does his best to minimize any pain (unless you actually want him to be rough). So while I can't tell you exactly what to do, I hope the following advice illuminates how to approach the experience for minimal pain, maximum pleasure, and a night of deflowering the two of you will never forget.

Vixen Tip

Patience Makes for a Perfect Virginal Experience

For obvious physical and emotional reasons, this is one sexual fantasy where tender loving care is mandatory. Your husband should be mindful of your needs now, more than ever. The following tips should help facilitate the moment:

• **Try not to eat within hours of the experience**, and empty your bowels as much as physically possible. An inexpensive enema from the drugstore can help ensure you've completely evacuated. While anal sex isn't the most sanitary act, that doesn't mean it has to be the most disgusting thing you've ever done,

Vixen Tip

either. Trust me, there's nothing like seeing a man come at you with a penis covered with the dregs of yesterday's lunch to kill the desire to ever to do this again. We won't even talk about how it would smell. Cleansing your bowels in advance of the moment can mean the difference between a totally awesome new experience and a horror show you'll want permanently burned from your memory.

• **Avoid the use of blood-thinning analgesics and anti-inflammatory medications on the big day.** Drugs such as naproxen sodium, like Aleve, and aspirin are anticoagulants, which thin the blood. Having them in your system during a sexual act that may cause tears to your rectum could result in excessive bleeding. Avoid using them at all in the days prior to the event, if you can.

• **Implement toys,** if you can, such as anal beads or butt plugs, to segue into anal sex. Be careful, however, to avoid the insertion of small, loose objects, as things can get lost inside your rectum and travel up into your bowels, which can be very dangerous. Butt plugs are often tapered, designed to expand the sphincter by degrees. Anal beads typically feature smaller beads that increase in size along the length of the strand. Using either of these generously lubricated aids (see the following tip), insertion can be accomplished with as little pain as possible.

• **Don't forget the lubrication.** You'll want your husband to play with the area a bit before he decides to dive in. He should lubricate your anus first with any of the wide range of products available on the market, from Astroglide to K-Y, and myriad others in between, including flavored lubricants, in case he

Vixen Tip

wants to taste your ass before he enters. This is why bathing and emptying your bowels before this fantasy is critical. He can start with one finger, then two, or whatever toys you have on hand to ease the transition, until you feel comfortable with entry in that region. Though it may not seem so initially, the anal cavity is fairly elastic and resilient. With a little practice and patience, it, and you, will begin to relax.

• **Take your time,** ladies, please! I cannot emphasize this enough. This is the least ideal scenario for someone to be in a rush. Just as in the case of your actual vaginal deflowering, not the fake one you reenact for your hubby, this might hurt and/or take a few tries before it feels truly pleasurable. The lubrication will help, so be sure to apply it liberally.

• **Clean, clean, clean!** Please be mindful of cleanliness when venturing to and from your and your partner's anal regions—a caution that extends to any toys and instruments used during your explorations, too. A sexual fantasy is one thing, but the reality of infection is a whole other story. There are special cleaners for your toys that can be found at your neighborhood adult store or online. I recommend, however, choosing toys that aren't so porous, made out of hard plastic, rubber, aluminum, or glass. These toys can withstand high degrees of heat and can be more easily sterilized. Also, be very careful not to go ass-to-mouth or ass-to-vagina. The risk of infection is too great! For a quick cleanse when switching positions and holes, simply clean your pudendum with a clean washcloth, hot water, and antibacterial soap. There are even antibacterial wipes and washes made especially for your perineum. These can also be found at

Vixen Tip

adult stores as well as your local drugstore. Don't be afraid to ask your pharmacist; many people use these sorts of products to help care for the elderly. So if you must, explain that it's for your granny!

Once you've had your butt broken in, you may find that you love it almost as much as vaginal penetration. Many couples include anal sex as an active part of their repertoire, so it could very well go from being the fulfillment of a fantasy for your husband to par for the course in your everyday romps. Be mindful, however, that the overuse of toys and large penises that expand your anus may cause you to lose some of the elasticity of your sphincter muscles, which could open up a whole other can of worms you never even anticipated. Can you say *Depends*, ladies? Too many parties in the butt, and you may find yourself wearing diapers on a full-time basis because you can no longer control the muscles back there. But it would take a whole lot of anal sex to make that happen. I'm talking *a lot*. Still, don't say you haven't been warned.

Govern your asses accordingly.

Whether vaginally or anally, losing your virginity is considered a big deal to most women. Sex is an incredibly invasive and personal act and should always be undertaken with the utmost care and consideration. As a role-playing experience, the virgin fantasy should allow you the opportunity to **remember yourself back at the moment when you crossed the threshold into womanhood.** Many of us, sadly, regret our first sexual experience, later realizing it came too soon and with someone whose name we hardly remember and whose face we'll never see again. This is your chance to recast and replay that moment with the love of your life. There should be no moment more satisfying than this, no matter which of the two versions of this fantasy you decide to employ.

Oh, and remember to take your bows and return for that second curtain call, ladies, because this will be one fine act you're putting on. If, after years of marriage and having children, you can still get your man to feel as though he is taking an untarnished peeper for its first spin around the block, that's grounds for an Oscar. Move over, Meryl.

A star is born!

Recap

- There are at least two ways of becoming that virginal flower he desires, over and over again.

- You may want to take another look at those lady's days as a way to satisfy the beast before a *real* virgin steps in and does it for you.

- Virginity comes with the notion of innocence.

- Whatever you do, don't be yourself!

- Don't ruin the fantasy by showing him this isn't your first time at the rodeo.

- There is no definitive answer to the question of how you should have anal sex for the very first time.

- Remember yourself back at the moment when you crossed the threshold into womanhood.

V-Log #9
Because Abs Aren't the Only Things That Get Ripped

It's 12:09 a.m. You're in one of those little curtained-off areas they put you in when you come through the hospital's emergency room. You're lying on your side on the cold bed with its thin sheets, your face blank as you stare at the wall, your ravaged rectum smeared with soothing ointment and taped up with gauze. Your husband sits bent over in a chair beside you, a riot of nerves, occasionally throwing up into a wastebasket. A nurse comes in and gives him something to quell his lurching stomach. What a pitiful scene. Do I even need to explain how we got here? Of course I do. How else are others ever going to learn?

Welcome to *What Not to Do During a Virginity Fantasy Involving Anal Sex: A Cautionary Tale.* Pull up a chair. This one's a doozy.

Goodness. I almost don't even have the words for this one.

So, as we have noted, you and your hubs chose the virginity fantasy. You have been married for eleven years, having wed in your early twenties. It has been a long, long time since he's had anything fresh, let alone virginal. You were still pure when the two of you met as college freshmen and he had the proud distinction of being your deflowerer. It was a beautiful moment, one you both have reminisced about over the years, but never once did you consider that you could replay that special, magical time. Not until now.

So you read the Virginity chapter together and your husband's eyes nearly swell with tears at the thought of being able to take you all over again. Your heart is full at the promise of what can once again be. You love him so very much and live to make him happy in every way you can. You allow him the choice of which type of deflowering he would like: sex on your period or via that safe house of innocence, your butt. You mentally cross your fingers, hoping against hope, never daring to speak your deepest fears aloud. He quickly blurts out that he wants . . . the butt. Damn you, crossed fingers! Damn you to hell!

Your man explains that he wants to do it anally because he has already experienced what it is like to have sex with you on your period. While it wasn't intentional, there were times when he accidentally struck red gold when he was dipping in for a marital visit. Each time it happened, he was out of there, posthaste. Although he doesn't need to, he reminds you that he is none too fond of blood. In fact, the sight of too much of it makes him quite ill. He explains that sex in the butt will be far less bloody than sex on your period. He'll be able to suffer through it, if it means getting to devirginize you again. He admits that he likes the idea of the tightness that will come with venturing into your booty. He hasn't had tightness in a long, long while—eleven long years, to be exact. He reminds you of that. Not in a passive-aggressive way, of course. Not like he's trying to pressure you. He is sincere, saying it with just a hint of wistfulness, as if reflecting on some paradise lost. You melt inside. You love him, so you let go of your fears and give in. Of course he can do it in the butt. It's just a butt, after all! *Mi culo es tu culo*, you tell him. And with those words, your husband claps his hands together happily, a schoolboy once again, and covers you with a shower of honeyed kisses. "We're doin' it the butt!" he sings, dancing around the room with his rump in the air.

"Doin' it in the butt," you chime, rooting your patootie right along with him. The two of you grab hands and dance like giddy children as you sing your silly song, oblivious to the world of ugly waiting just around the corner.

The Big Day arrives and you do your due diligence, right in keeping with the recommendations in the prior chapter. You eat a light breakfast, just one piece of toast and a smoothie to get you through the day. By afternoon, you empty your bowels using the Fleet enema you purchased. You empty them again a few hours later, just to be sure. You purchased three enemas, after all, since you were unsure just how much poop might be in there and you couldn't remember if you'd evacuated your bowels the day before. You've picked up several of the suggested items from a local sex shop, even though you were mortified to even go in. You bought a butt plug, Astroglide, and anal beads, your head down, eyes averted as you paid for it all. As the cashier bagged up your goodies, she gave you a friendly smile and said,

"Have a good day!"

That one simple phrase sent you scurrying out of the store, flush with embarrassment, certain she was making fun of what you're about to do.

At home, after your enema, you spend some alone time getting your mind right. You soak in a hot bubble bath while drinking a glass of Chardonnay. Two glasses of Chardonnay. A few glasses of Chardonnay. You pop an Aleve in advance of any potential pain. Like the commercial said, "All day strong. All day long." You hope they mean it.

Your husband arrives early with an enormous bouquet of multicolored tulips, your favorite flower in the whole wide world, the same size bouquet he gave you the night you made love for the very first time. How apropos: flowers in exchange for your butt flower. Nice. He kisses you. You're dressed almost exactly the way you were that very first time—in a simple sundress, sandals, with a band in your hair. Suddenly you are an eighteen-year-old college freshman all over again. The beads, butt plug, and Astroglide are on the nightstand next to the bed. You coyly glance at them, but do not speak their names. You are innocent, you see, and innocence knows nothing of anal beads and butt plugs. Innocence and Astroglide have never been friends.

Your husband's eyes light up when he notices the items. He's eager, so eager, and rushes off to shower while you turn down the bed and wait for him to take you.

He emerges moments later, freshly shaven, sleek and clean, wearing a buttondown shirt, jeans, and the same inexpensive cologne from that very first time. You're sitting on the edge of the bed as he walks up to you. Each step he takes, each move, is exactly the way you both did it before. He takes your hand as you stand before him. You glance into each other's eyes, deeply in love. He kisses your neck, your shoulders, down the length of your arms, carefully unzipping your sundress as his lips have their way. The dress slips to the floor, exposing your virginal white cotton bra and panties. Your husband breathes in deeply, something close to a gasp. Your body looks just as young as it did back then. He reaches around you, unfastening your bra. He kisses the delicate buds of your nipples. You giggle like a bashful teen. He picks you up in his arms and lays you on the bed facedown.

This part of the narrative of your love story differs from the first deflowering. Back then, in your dorm room, he laid you on your back. But he's ready for the gusto now, so your honey wastes no time. He gently pulls down your white cotton panties, leaning his face into the crack of your backside. He parts the cheeks and breathes in. You're fresh after your double enema, a living tulip of wonder. He reaches for the Astroglide and squirts a good measure of it into his hands to warm it up. He spreads your cheeks apart and smears it on your rectum. You're trembling, slightly, and not for show—you're shaking for real! This is brand new for you, but it is being done under the cloak of love. You are partly nervous, partly excited. You wonder if the feeling of him sliding in and out of your bum will be comparable to the sensation of him sliding in and out of your vagina. What if you like it more than vaginal sex, you wonder. What if you hate it, but your husband loves it and wants it on a regular basis? Your heart pounds, the sound disappearing into the mattress. Your husband smears more unspeakable on your butthole. He pushes in a finger. Then he pushes in two.

You squeal in the beginning, but it is nothing major. It's the squeal of surprise. He didn't warn you when his finger first went in, but it doesn't hurt at all. It feels different, but it definitely doesn't hurt. Your husband sticks in a third finger, twirls all three around, checking to see if it's causing you pain.

"I'm fine," you whisper, sensing his concern.

"Are you sure?" he asks.

"I'm sure. Everything's okay."

You hear him unzipping his jeans. He steps out of them and kicks them away. You glance back to see his rigid penis angled up and ready for action. You glance at the beads and the butt plug, but your husband has no time for them. In his mind, three fingers going in means you're open for business.

"Honey?" you mutter, but he doesn't hear you. He is busy squirting the lube onto his shaft. He slathers it up and down with his hand as he crouches above you, aiming for entry.

And now he's at the back door, cramming the head in. You squeal for real this time. Not in surprise. This time, it does *actually* hurt a little. He pauses, waiting for you to collect yourself before he begins anew. You breathe in, breathe out. It's okay now. He pushes in again.

This time his shaft goes deeper and you feel it intensely, but what you are feeling isn't unbearable. He pushes harder and this time, he goes all the way. You gasp. It hurts, but not too badly. He begins to move in and out slowly, gradually. It doesn't feel bad.

And now your husband is in asshole heaven. Your pucker pouch is tighter than tight. Vaginas wish they gripped him the way your backside has him right now. He caresses you as he pumps in your booty, kissing along your spine, losing himself in the wonder of butt-bliss.

And now you're getting into it, grinding against him, raising your derriere to meet him halfway. He's burning hot with passion and lust, furiously pumping in and out of your bum. He notices a trace of blood along his shaft, but he closes his eyes to avoid the sight, letting himself get lost in this magnificent sensation that trumps your first deflowering a thousand times over. He pulls you up toward him, doggy-style, and goes at you with rabbit-fast desperation.

You can't really feel anything in your butt anymore, just him moving in and out. He's too caught up in the moment to notice anything, either. You feel nice and wet back there, super-wet, but his eyes are closed as he jackhammers you like it's the end of days. He doesn't see all the blood dripping on the bed until he pops, and boy, does he pop. Hard. He empties his big fat I-just-busted-my-wife's-cherry-for-the-second-time-oh-yeah load into your posterior and you take it, raise your butt up to receive it, and as he collapses onto your back on the bed, he wonders at all the wetness beneath him. Was he sweating that much? He checks. Nope. Were you sweating that much? There's a nope to that, too. He rises and sees the blood. You glance back and see the blood. And as he slowly pulls out of your booty, you feel the pain—the shredded pain—of the ripping your rectum has taken without either of you really being aware.

Cut to: The hospital, 11:28 p.m. You and your husband arrive at the emergency room and stand at the desk, shamefacedly explaining to the intake nurse exactly why you're there. You've got a maxipad stuffed inside your cotton panties, but it's not under your vagina, it is under your bleeding ass. Your beloved is wearing the face of a thousand shames. The nurse asks if you were on any medications and you say no, not at all, until you remember...*dun-dun-dunnnnnnnnnnnnnnn*: the Aleve.

The Aleve. The Aleve. The fucking Aleve! The very Aleve that I warned of in a Vixen Tip earlier. The same Aleve that I mentioned you shouldn't take on the day of The Big Deflowering. The aforementioned Aleve I noted was an anticoagulant that could very well make any rips in your rectum that occur during anal sex bleed way worse than normal.

So now at 12:09 a.m. you've got a shredded booty as you lie on your side in the hospital bed and your husband's still throwing up at the thought of all that blood. His penis still has blood on it, too, because he didn't have time to wash it before you left the house. There was no time. He had to race to get you to here, lest your bottom bleed out.

Let that be a lesson to you, ladies, and you, too, butt fuckers. Read these fantasy chapters carefully. Pay attention to the fine print. If the fine print says avoid a certain kind of medication, well, dammit, then avoid that medication. The worst part of all this is that it isn't even fine print. It's written out plain as day, in a font large enough for you to clearly make out. Also, your hubby could have been a little less rabid to get at your ass. Just because he was able to get three fingers in without much difficulty, it didn't mean you were ready to have your ass plunged into. That's what the beads and the butt plug were for. They would have helped ease you into the situation, and maybe you wouldn't have had the tears that you did. Not that the rips were critical or life threatening. They just bled a lot because of the Aleve, but that's already been taken care of.

Look at that poor soul vomiting into that can and you there with the smear of ointment on your pucker. Next time, try the *sex on your period* version of the virginity fantasy. Sure, it may be bloody, but at least it won't put you in the hospital. And there's definitely a way that your husband can enjoy it. Blindfold him if you have to and then wreak bloody havoc with his cock and balls. He won't see the blood, but he'll feel its gushy wetness. Of course, the whole purpose of the sex-on-your-period fantasy is for him to actually see blood so that it replicates the experience of busting your cherry all over again. But your husband is a bit dramatic, now, isn't he? The last thing you want is for him to hurl on you during sex.

Now that I think about it, why don't you guys just skip this fantasy and try something else? Maybe the next chapter will work better for you. At least it won't involve blood, hospitals, and asses smeared with ointment. And vomiting.

At least, I hope not.

It better not. If it does, then I'm going to have a talk with you two!

Chapter Ten

Video Voyeur

Fantasy

My morning at work had been so hectic and draining that when noon rolled around, I didn't have the time or the energy to go to lunch. I was deep into a financial report, double-checking the numbers by calculator, when my supervisor knocked on the open door of my office and walked in.

"Why are you still at your desk?" he asked.

"I've got too much to do," I said, surprised by his visit.

"That's no excuse for not taking the time to eat. What do you want people to think, that I'm some sort of slave driver?"

"No," I stammered. "I just wanted to make sure..."

He chuckled softly at my nervousness, clearly making sport of me. My eyes were immediately drawn to his dimples, which were so deep, I could have fallen in. He was gorgeous, well built, and tall, easily six-foot-five. It was the perfect recipe for the Boss From Hell, a label not referring to how he treated his employees but rather what it meant to be anywhere near someone so attractive. Everyone in the office, men and women alike, secretly lusted after him. I'd always played it smart, maintaining a professional distance, but he was undeniably sexy and charismatic. As he stood before me now, I couldn't look away.

"Come on, let's go," he said, with a wave of his hand.

"Go where?" I asked, startled.

"I'm taking you to lunch."

"No," I began, "I can't. I'd love to, but I really do have to finish this report. Otherwise I won't be able to make any headway with the rest of this paperwork and I'll end up spending another late night here at the office. It'll be my fourth one in a row."

"Well," he said somberly, rubbing his cleft chin. "That's not good. We wouldn't want your life to be all work and no play."

I couldn't tell if he was mocking or serious. Maybe I was reading too much into his words. My energy was running way low. I took a sip of the room-temperature Red Bull I'd been nursing for the last two hours.

"I'll be fine," I said. "I had breakfast, so I'm good."

"What, Red Bull? That constitutes breakfast?"

"It gets the job done."

"Are you sure?" he said, laughing. "Because right now, you clearly look like you're running out of gas."

I laughed along with him, charmed by his dancing dimples.

"All right," he said finally. "I'll leave you alone. I wouldn't want to be the cause of you spending another late night here at the office."

"Thanks for the offer, though," I said.

"Of course. Maybe we can do it another time. I like to make a point of getting to know everyone in the office individually, and I haven't had the chance to do that with you."

"Sure," I said. "I think that'd be great."

I watched him walk out of my office. He glanced back, catching my eyes on his ass. I shuffled the papers on my desk awkwardly, pretending as if I hadn't just been ogling him, but I'd been caught. Embarrassed, I returned my attention to the report. The numbers and line items were a blur, all washed together. I took another drink of Red Bull, yawned, stretched, rubbed my eyes, and resumed crunching numbers.

It wasn't even ten minutes later when I was distracted by another knock at the door. I looked up. It was my supervisor once again, standing in my doorway. This time, he was holding a large brown paper bag.

"I got sandwiches and chips. Do you like corned beef?"

I could barely think of anything to say.

"Of course you do," he said, coming in. "Who doesn't like a good corned beef sandwich?"

He walked over to my desk, opened the bag, and pulled out a large sandwich wrapped in waxed paper, along with chips.

"It's nice and hot, straight from the deli across the street." He lifted a bottle from the bag. "Some refreshing Snapple." Then he held up something fat and long, wrapped in waxed paper.

"I even got you a pickle."

His eyes twinkled with mischief. I laughed.

"Wow. I can't believe you did this for me."

The delicious scent of corned beef filled the room, awakening my hungry stomach. I was so appreciative of what he'd done that, without thinking, I stood from my desk, went over to him, and thanked him with a hug.

"You're the nicest boss I've ever had," I said.

Our bodies pressed close as I felt him pull me in a little tighter. His hand ran softly, discreetly, down the small of my back, and I tingled with satisfaction at knowing I wasn't alone in my repressed lust. He apparently wanted me just as much as I wanted him. I stood there in a sensuous daze, savoring his touch, when reason suddenly kicked in. This was my boss. What was I thinking?

Blushing furiously, I pulled away from his embrace and rushed out of my office. My door had been wide open the whole time. I wondered who might've seen us. The last thing I wanted to risk was being labeled the office tramp. I'd worked hard for my position. I didn't need anyone thinking I'd gotten there on my back.

Fortunately, everyone had already left for lunch and the phones had been forwarded to our messaging service. I'd been so caught up in work, I hadn't even noticed. He and I were all alone. My hands shook slightly as I got myself a drink of cool water, then crumpled the paper cone and threw it away.

I lingered near the watercooler, expecting him to walk out of my office and head back to his own. He didn't. I leaned back slightly, trying to get a better view. He was sitting at my desk with his pants down at his ankles, his boxers around his calves. He was holding his dick in his right hand, jerking it slightly. I stepped closer, shocked at his brazenness. He licked his lips as he watched me approach, his dimples beckoning me in.

"You know you want me," he said. "So get over here. That's an order."

Hypnotized with lust, I obediently walked back into my office, stopping just inside the door.

"Closer," he directed.

I moved toward him, stopping barely a foot away, my eyes glued to his hand yanking his beautiful instrument. Suddenly I remembered something and glanced up toward the back right corner of the ceiling. "There's a camera trained on this room, recording everything."

"I know," he said. "I shut it off on my way back from the deli."

"Oh," I replied, shocked. "So you…"

"Had this planned all along?" He smiled devilishly. "Something like that."

He reached out for me with his free hand, pulling me in. He placed my hand on his dick. I instinctively dropped to my knees, wrapping both my hands around it in a full-on squeeze. It was hard, firm, solid, pulsating. He let go of his grip, leaving his penis all to me.

He pressed gently on the back of my head in a not-so-subtle hint. I licked my lips and lowered them onto his hardness, breathing him in as I tasted his manhood.

I moved my hot, wet mouth up and down his shaft, his hand pressing my head farther, coaxing me to take in more. Holding the base of his dick with my left hand, I teased the tip of his dick, glazing it, then gliding it in and out, taking him in deeper each time, until all of him finally disappeared inside. He groaned with pleasure.

"You're good," he said, his breath coming fast.

I bobbed faster, increasing my pace.

"I take that back. You're great."

I cupped his balls and squeezed them gently, massaging them as my mouth and tongue worked over his throbbing rod. He reached inside my blouse and wrestled with the front of my bra, freeing my breasts from their cups. He massaged their fullness, then ran his fingers delicately around the nipples, setting me on fire. I kept sucking his dick, harder this time, forcing it toward the back of my throat. As I lathered his piece with my warm saliva, he abruptly grabbed the back of my head and pulled me away. I was confused, embarrassed. Was it over, just like that? Had I fallen for the okey-doke, the oldest trick in the book...giving my boss great head, only to be dismissed like a common whore?

"What's wrong?" I asked, mortified. "What just happened?"

He was silent as he pulled up his boxers and pants, straightening his clothes.

"Get up," he said, not even looking at me. "I can't do this. We can't do this."

I was beyond ashamed as I got up from my knees, my heart thumping inside my chest. I should never have let this happen, I thought. He has lost all respect for me.

He hurriedly stepped past me without a word, exiting my office. My pussy was hot and my heart was heavy. I was both turned on and humiliated. It was an overload of emotion that I couldn't even begin to know how to process. I'd been hit by a train. As I stood there catatonic, he suddenly walked back in, grabbed my hand, and led me away.

We rushed down the hall, stopping at his office. He pushed me inside, took a quick glance down the hall in both directions, stepped in after me, and closed the door. He locked the bolt.

"I thought you changed your..."

He put his finger over my lips, shaking his head.

"Never," he said. "I've wanted this from the moment I met you."

He guided me over to a large mahogany armoire. Was he going to fuck me against it? I couldn't wait, my pussy hot and wanting.

He opened the cabinet's double doors, revealed a large television.

"Let me show you something," he said, his expression sheepish and cryptic.

He picked up the remote and turned on the television. My office immediately appeared on his screen, complete with the image of me on my knees, going down on him. He was staring directly at the camera as he pushed down on my head.

I was furious. "I thought you said you'd turned the camera off."

"I know." He glanced at the floor, then up at me, holding my gaze in his own. "I wanted to see us together. I think about you so much, I just wanted something of my own to watch in private. You and me."

My eyes were flames.

"I know it was wrong," he explained, feeling the heat of my ire. "That's why I stopped things. As much as I want to hold you, taste you, feel you, fuck you..." His breath was hot against my neck. "I don't want it under false pretenses. Me telling you I had turned off the tape was a false pretense. It was a lie that I couldn't go through with."

"Is this the first time you've ever taped me?" I asked, my blood rising to a slow boil.

"Honestly?" he replied.

"Yes."

"No. It's not."

He opened a drawer in the armoire, revealing a stack of DVDs with handwritten scrawl in black, permanent ink. He handed them to me. I rifled through them, half horrified and half aroused. *Melinda, 2/14,* one read. *Melinda, 3/21* was the label on another. *Melinda, 6/4* had four stars. I glanced up at him.

"You were wearing a tight red skirt that day that hugged your ass and exposed it in perfect form. Your breasts were so full and ripe; I could taste them through the screen. You were bent over your desk a lot that afternoon. I've jacked off to *6/4* more than any of the others."

"You say 6/4 so casually, like it's the name of a close friend."

"It is. You are. At least, that's how you feel now that I've watched you so much."

"Surprisingly, I feel dirty. Violated. Raped. I wonder why that is?"

I put the DVDs back in the drawer and headed for the door.

I was halfway there when he came up behind me, both hands covering my breasts. He massaged them, squeezing the nipples between his fingers. I felt heady, drunk with passion and rage. He spun me around, pushed me toward his desk, and bent me over the hard wood. He unzipped his pants, pushed them and his boxers down, and hiked up my skirt. His finger slid along my wetness. He brought it up to his mouth, sucking on my juices.

He rammed his cock inside me, all the way up to the balls.

I moaned in exquisite agony.

He pulled all the way out, and then thrust in again. He dropped to his knees behind me and fastened his mouth on my pussy and clit, licking and sucking at my nectar like a man in the desert stumbling upon a luscious oasis.

I held on to the desk, my knees weak and quivering. He ate and ate, his tongue plunging in and out of my aching slit. I rubbed my breasts, lifting my ass higher into his face. He squeezed my cheeks tight with both hands as he devoured my nether region. I began to gyrate. He flicked his tongue against my clit with rapid-fire strokes.

"Is there a camera in here?" I asked, my words short and clipped.

"Yes," he answered between licks.

"Is it on?"

"Yes."

"Good," I replied. "Now fuck me."

He stood, gripping my ass firmly. He parted my legs with his own. I could feel the tip of his hardness at the door of my heat. He moved it up and down, burrowing his way in, then pumped, slow and rhythmic at first, shifting quickly to hurried strokes. He hunched over me, thrusting with desperation, his rushed movements electrifying the walls of my pussy.

He pulled out, flipped me over, and leaned me all the way back against the desktop, entering me from the front. I was so hot, so aroused, my head felt light. He squeezed my breasts and his eyes held mine as he downshifted into a long stroke, stirring my flowing juices with his stick.

"I'm going to faint," I whispered

"I'm going to fuck you till you faint," he said.

He bent over me, still pounding my pussy, fastening his mouth on my right nipple, first flicking his tongue over it, and then fastening down. I was so turned on I could barely breathe. His thrusts sped up. I wrapped my legs around his waist. He moved to the other nipple, flicking and sucking. His hand made its way down below, between my legs clamped around his body, and he began to rub my clit—first slowly, then in time with his thrusts. I couldn't take it. Too much pleasure had begun to build. As he pumped and rubbed and sucked me, the room began to spin. The combination of being overworked, hungry, and on the downside of a Red Bull energy high collided with the splendid thrashing he was giving me. The sensation ballooned in my loins until I couldn't hold back anymore. I burst, cumming hard against him, my juices gushing around his cock as he continued to pump and rub and suck. I squeezed my legs tighter and clung to him desperately. I couldn't stop cumming, as wave after wave after wave of pleasure roller-coastered through me. The room spun like I was on a carousel, a ride I never wanted to get off. I stared at the ceiling as he kept on fucking and I kept on cumming. The fluorescent lights above me flickered teasingly.

My heart felt like it would burst from my chest. The light grew brighter and brighter and brighter, and suddenly...the ceiling went black.

He was wiping between my legs with a moist cloth when I came to. I smelled the delicious scent of corned beef. He'd brought the sandwiches back to his office.

"What happened?" I asked, sitting up.

"Um, you fainted, my dear," he replied with a grin.

"I did?"

"I told you I was going to make it happen. You really shouldn't go without eating breakfast, you know. A Red Bull will never replace a well-balanced meal."

"Yeah, yeah," I said. "Whatever. I noticed you didn't have breakfast before we left the house this morning, either."

"That's because I was planning on making you faint today."

"I see. Did you shut off the camera already?" I asked.

"Right after I got mine. I waited a few minutes, of course. You know, so I could get my bearings."

"Of course."

We both chuckled.

I got up from my husband's desk and smoothed down my skirt, patting him on the butt as I passed. We loved this game, especially since we owned our own business. We played Fuck The Boss at least once a week. Sometimes I was in charge; sometimes he was the one who took charge over me. Sometimes the game was Fuck The Employee. It didn't matter what we called it; the result was the same. We always took the tapes home and watched them together. We burned a spare set onto

DVDs that we kept in his office, just so we could see ourselves in the act and get turned on for each other all over again.

Reality

And now we get to one of the most popular ways that couples choose to spice up their sex lives: video voyeurism—or, in layman's terms, making a sex tape. These days, we're living in what could be called The Golden Age of the Sex Tape. Make a movie with your man, find a way to leak it, or claim that it is stolen, and watch your fame shoot through the roof. It might be a brief, meteoric rise, but a rise nonetheless. That's if you're trying to be famous, and trying to garner that fame without putting in legitimate work. But that's not what we're here to talk about. What we're discussing now is making home movies for the sole purpose of enhancing your relationship. **Starring in your own porno is the ultimate way to become the object of your man's visual and physical desire.**

Why send him off to the basement to get aroused watching flicks starring Jenna Jameson or Mary Carey—only to return hot and ready to make love to you with a boner brought on by their images in his head—when he could be jacking off to the sight of you and him getting it on or a video of you pleasuring yourself for him? Why have him fixate on some porn producer's take on what's considered sexy when he's got his own version right at home? He did marry *you*, after all. You are his ideal. If you're not, then you should be. This is the perfect way to make that a reality.

First things first, and this is big: the trust factor.

Hopefully, both you and the person you are married to have a real level of trust rooted in a genuine desire to never do each other any harm, no matter the situation. That means that even if, heaven forbid, your marriage fails, neither of you would ever use the tapes you made together as a means to threaten, hurt, or embarrass the other. If you and he honestly believe, deep down in your hearts, that this kind of do-no-harm policy exists between you, then by all means crack out the camera!

If, however, you or your mate harbors even an iota of vindictiveness, the potential for sour grapes, or a plain old mean streak, stop now. Skip this chapter. Go, on . . . scat! Many lives, too many to count, have been damaged by exes trying to humiliate or control others by threatening to release highly personal and potentially embarrassing material such as this via social network sites and on the Internet. The first and most obvious example of this phenomenon was the infamous Jayne Kennedy sex tape that was viciously leaked by her ex-husband as they were going through a divorce. This kind of malicious act is different from some starlet or up-and-coming entertainer leaking a tape in order to gain fame. We live in an age of camera phones that can capture embarrassing moments on the sneak, YouTube, YouPorn, and videos going viral. Someone intent on ruining the reputation of an ex can destroy lives in an instant. Exposing, or threatening to expose, explicit photographic material created consensually by two people in love with the intent to degrade either party is both criminally and morally wrong. It is emotional extortion, and if you're planning on releasing the tapes unless your ex pays you not to, well, that's actual extortion, prosecutable by law. **I would never recommend voyeuristic videotaping for any person who would use a moment of open and shared intimacy as a tool to hurt someone else.** If this is you, you should move on. Seriously. I'll give you a few moments to gather yourself and go.

Jeopardy! theme song*

Still here? So does that mean you plan on playing fair? Hold up your hand. Scout's honor? All right, then. Put your hand down. Moving on.

Now that we've addressed *that*, there's one other thing we need to get out of the way: the body consciousness issue. While it is a good idea to always be vigilant about your weight and to exercise and eat right as a part of a healthy lifestyle, **filming yourself in the act of making love doesn't require that you be Hollywood-thin and perfect or that your husband be built like Will Smith or Brad Pitt.** This tape will be for your private viewing pleasure, not the masses, so a little (or a lot of) extra poundage here and there shouldn't matter in the end. If you and your husband are both comfortable with your bodies and able to watch each other on screen without feeling embarrassed, judgmental, and insecure, this is a more-than-viable way to keep your marriage sizzling hot!

Vixen Tip

I'm Ready for My Close-Up, Mr. DeMille!

Just like with a real movie, if you're going to make one at home, you're going to need to do some pre-production. That's Hollywood talk for getting your materials together, identifying your location, casting your stars (you and your hubby), adjusting the lighting, even assembling "crew" to help, if necessary. It is all about getting everything just right before the actual shoot. The important things you'll need include:

• **Video camera.** These days, you can find video cameras at all ends of the pricing spectrum, from inexpensive handhelds to high-end HD equipment. If you have a computer with a built-in camera, you're already in business. If not, there are also all kinds of clever gadgets that arrived on the market with a splash, like the Flip (www.theflip.com), which is no bigger than a digital camera but packs a mean punch. It will only do up to an hour of recording at a time, though, and, like many camcorders, doesn't have actual tape

Vixen Tip

in it—you load it onto your computer—but that doesn't mean it can't do the job. Fun, snazzy, available in a wide array of colors and designs, and—at $150 to $230—reasonably affordable, it's like the iPod of camcorders. If you don't already own a video camera, you should have in mind how you want your sex tape to look before you make a purchase. If it's quality of picture you're looking for, high-definition (HD) is the way to go. HD cameras can run anywhere from less than two hundred dollars (like the Flip UltraHD) to several thousand dollars. I'm not going to pretend to be an expert on video equipment. Do your research on websites like CNET (http://reviews.cnet.com/camcorders) and ZDNet (http://review .zdnet.com). Go into stores that carry a large selection of video equipment. Touch the merchandise. Ask questions. While you don't have to tell the salesclerk you're planning on making a porno, let him or her know that you're planning to make some home movies of your family and want the maximum bang for your buck. Once you've identified the model that best meets your needs and budget, shop around. Don't forget to check eBay. You might end up finding a really good one for a steal!

• **Accessories.** Depending on how you plan to shoot your video (from a closet, a corner of the room, the foot of the bed, what have you), and how long you want your movie to be, you may need items such as a tripod, additional flash cards, additional videotape, and more. If you plan to do some outdoor shooting, such as in your backyard or on a private beach, you may need a bag to carry your camcorder and accessories, as well as a charger or extra batteries. Some of these items come standard when you purchase your video camera, but that's not guaranteed. Accessorize accordingly.

Vixen Tip

• **Location and lighting.** Where are you shooting your movie? Indoors? Outdoors? Are you planning to make it like a real porno, with a pseudo-plot that starts in one room, then wends its way to the bedroom or somewhere else in the house? Then make sure the rooms are lit in a way that flatters and conveys the mood. Sex in an outdoor setting isn't too problematic, if you're filming on a bright, sunny day. Just set up your scene, or commence fucking, and record. But too much indoor light can be distracting and reveal flaws you might not exactly want to highlight on film, especially in HD. Too little indoor lighting can find you both squinting as you watch the playback, wondering which body part is which. Having a light meter on hand, while not mandatory, doesn't hurt. That's if you're trying to get things exactly right. If you're going for balls-out, gonzo sex, technicality be damned, then don't sweat the small stuff. Just assume the position and press RECORD!

• **Crew.** Ever see those movies that show amateur couples having sex? Ever wonder who the heck is doing the shooting, getting close enough to zoom in on genitals slapping, penises penetrating, and tongues a-twirling? It's probably a trusted friend of the couple, someone they can depend on to be discreet, nonjudgmental, and willing to lend a helping hand for a "labor of love." By enlisting a friend's assistance, you can frame just the kind of shots you want—close, guerrilla-style and gonzo, even—rather than relying on a constant, unchanging wide shot from a video camera set up on a tripod across the room or at the foot of the bed.

• **Wardrobe.** Dress to be undressed. If you're filming a porno with a plot, dress for the role of your character. Are you a lonely neighbor, stopping by for a cup of sugar? Is your husband a mail carrier delivering a (ahem) "package"? You and your husband should play the parts with zeal and aplomb. If you're just filming yourselves having sex, no plot, be provocative. Do a striptease for the camera. Help your husband disrobe. Tease. Please. Perform to the hilt. Make it a movie, the first of many, you'll both want to watch over and over again.

If you've never seen yourself, or liked seeing yourself, on tape, it is going to take some getting used to at first. Trust me, though, you'll quickly adjust and will find this to be a very fun addition to your marital sex life. Once you've agreed as a couple to make a sex tape, test the waters by filming yourselves individually, just to become at ease with being on camera. If neither of you is camera-shy or modest about being filmed while making love, make it a true voyeuristic adventure. **Make masturbation tapes for each other.** That might mean a video where your husband films you cleaning the house in nothing but an apron and heels, so he can watch it at another time, either with or without you, and jack off to the image of the woman he loves. Film your husband lathered up in the shower, closing in on his hands soaping up his balls and penis, massaging his chest, foam running down his butt and legs, and finally rinsing himself clean. Or make one of him, hot and sweaty, working in the backyard, removing items of clothing one by one as the heat becomes more unbearable, until he ultimately ends up naked. Finish with him holding his own penis, looking directly into the camera at you. Pull that tape out and watch it when you're missing him, getting yourself in the mood for his imminent arrival home, or just because. No reason necessary.

I'm sure I don't need to strongly recommend that you make these erotic tapes when your children are out of the house and you're shielded from prying eyes of the neighbors. I'm sure I don't have to tell you that. But I'm telling you anyway. Just in case.

The more the two of you build your sex life and fantasies around images of each other, the stronger you can become against outside forces, even common marital distractions such as the seemingly limitless amounts of online porn. When you become each other's favorite porn stars, your passion can potentially go into overdrive, and that's exactly what we want, ladies. Am I right?

Lights! Camera! Action!

Party like a porn star!

Recap

- Starring in your own porno is the ultimate way to become the object of your man's visual and physical desire.

- Hopefully, both you and the person you are married to have a level of trust rooted in a genuine desire to never do each other any harm, no matter the situation.

- I would never recommend voyeuristic videotaping for any person who would use a moment of open and shared intimacy as a tool to hurt someone else.

- Filming yourself in the act of making love doesn't require that you be Hollywood-thin and perfect or that your husband be built like Will Smith or Brad Pitt.

- Make masturbation tapes for each other.

V-Log #10
Rhymes with "Lardashian"

Who doesn't love a good sex tape? Certainly not you. Certainly not your husband. We know this because you guys made a sex tape. You did a bona fide video voyeur fantasy according to the guidelines I detailed in the prior chapter. There was role-playing, dramatic acting, and the works. None of that boss-employee business like in my example, though. Nuh-uh. My example was pedestrian compared with what you laid out. You guys got all Cecil B. DeMille with it, shooting an epic outdoor scene where you pretended to be Cleopatra and he was your Marc Antony. You geared up for it and everything, with full-on makeup and attire from the era. Not that the outfits were on for very long. The sex was hot. The sex was steamy. Your husband did some pretty freaky things. We don't even want to talk about the stuff that you did. It made for excellent viewing again and again and again, so much so that, in addition to having DVDs of the event, you both kept digital copies loaded on your computers so you could watch it whenever you needed a quick thrill.

And then your husband let one of his friends borrow his laptop and, in less than twenty-four hours, all hell and evidence of Egyptian kinkiness coincidentally broke loose.

Of course your husband's friend denies being the one who stole the video from the laptop, and there's no way you can prove that he did it. Now things are really jacked up. The video has anonymously been uploaded to YouPorn and, as of the last time you checked, had over a million viewings. It shows up all across the blogosphere, and people are beginning to acknowledge that they recognize you. The video makes its way to the inboxes of your family and friends, and is inevitably discovered by people at your job. Your boss has even seen it. You know this because he keeps showing up at your office door, asking for information about things for which you're not even responsible. Your boss never comes to you in person for information. Ever. He sends emails. He's notorious for it. These days, however, he's at your door. That's surely the sign of a man who has gotten a glimpse of your naked body and seen you in explicit action.

And now you're beefing with your husband. You want him to do something about this. File a lawsuit for defamation of character or something. Your guy insists that his friend—a buddy he has known since college—would never do something as vile as leak such a sensitive video. He thinks maybe someone hacked through the firewall at your house and stole it off his computer. You don't believe it. The problem didn't rear its head until after his friend used the laptop. Things grow strained between you and your man. He is not nearly as freaked out about the video leaking as you are. He runs a web design company from home and has no fear of his clients getting wind of it. Besides, he comes across as a stallion in the video, something that he is actually quite proud of. You, however, have so much more at stake. Your colleagues have seen it and now they know that you and your hubby like to get freaky. They also now know that you've got skills not listed on your résumé.

Ladies, this is why it's critical that you take the necessary precautions with this kind of fantasy. Even though we live in a time when sex tapes seem to leak every other week, it can still be very damaging and humiliating to have your personal sexual capers seen by the world, especially if you're in a profession that demands a certain level of gravity and decorum to do business. Also, in case you're still not getting it, there's one thing you should remember: The Internet is forever. A video of you that leaks onto the World Wide Web will always be out there hiding, long past when the hoopla dies down. The second someone goes to Google you, up you will pop in all your spread-eagled, lined-eyes, asp-holding glory. Thus your primary goal should be making sure that never happens. A video in digital format, residing on a computer, can easily get away from you. Before you even turn on the camera, make sure all the necessary precautions have been addressed.

As I noted elsewhere, if you and your man decide to record yourselves, there must be enough trust between you to ensure that this video is for your eyes and your eyes only, unless you mutually agree to share it with others. That's not to say that it's your man's fault that your video just leaked. You both are responsible for not making it secure enough. Keep the DVD version locked away in a cabinet for which only you and he have the key. Never leave that cabinet unlocked, not even casually. How many times have we heard of sex tapes being stolen by visiting friends? As for digital files kept on computers, require a password to be entered before any action—from viewing to copying—can be done. You can even make it so that only those with administrator rights on your computer can access the file. This keeps just anyone from getting a gander at it.

For optimum safety, do not keep the file in a digital format at all. The DVD should be enough. Digital files resident on computers can always be hacked. For every safeguard you set to protect digital data, there's a techie out there who can take it down in record time. Odds are, your husband's friend was just such a guy. He probably went exploring around your man's laptop and found it sitting right there in plain sight. Who could resist double-clicking something named *Cleopatra Bones*? It was sitting right there on his desktop, no password required. Once his friend got an eyeful of the two of you going at it, all he had to do was drag it onto a flash drive or, even easier, email it to himself.

Don't make it easy to show your ass to the world. The collateral damage simply isn't worth it. And don't think that by having the video leaked to the world, it will turn you into an instant celebrity. Even though it may seem like that happens all the time, it really is much more rare than you think. Don't believe me? Visit YouPorn.com, if you dare. There are thousands, nay, hundreds of thousands of videos uploaded to the site every day, every hour, of people doing some really freaky things. Most of those people will seem foreign to you . . . they are just regular people who like showing off what they do. Yes, they have their fans, the people who visit the site and click on their videos again and again, so, in that regard, you will be famous. But you won't be reality show/celebrity boyfriend/*People* magazine famous. You won't be invited to go on Letterman to giggle, act silly, and talk about your plans for a clothing line. You won't be on the *Today* show flipping your hair as you promote your new perfume. You won't walk the red carpet at the Emmys and the VMAs. Designers won't fight to dress you. Free clothes and shoes won't arrive at your door. You won't have a stylist, a PR person, and a makeup artist. Your phone won't be ringing with an offer of a fifty-thousand-dollar appearance fee just for showing up at Tao in Las Vegas and pretending to party for a couple of hours. No, honey. You won't be having any of that. You'll just be really, really popular with the hand-job-and-lotion-loving folks who prowl for porn. You and your husband will have the go-to video for getting off. That is, until the next video leaks, which will be any minute. It's being uploaded right now.

So please, take precautions. And if your husband insists on having files in the wide open on his computer desktop, make him give it a name as repulsive and uninteresting as possible. Something like *Grandma's Wart Removal* or *Our Baby's Birth*. No grown man wants to see either of those things. Grandmas, warts, and babies covered in afterbirth are about as safe from prying eyes as you can get.

Chapter Eleven

MILFs

Fantasy

I was in the middle of doing laundry. It was hot outside, over a hundred degrees, which wasn't unusual for this part of the Valley. Even though it was cool inside the house, my body was just as hot as it was outdoors. I'd been running nonstop since six that morning, first a blow job for my husband, then rousing my teenage sons from sleep, getting breakfast together, sending my boys off to school and my husband off to work. Once they were gone, I threw on a baby tee, some jean shorts and sandals, and made my morning rounds: dropping off dry cleaning, stopping at the grocery store, then on to Costco for some household supplies. I returned, cleaned the house, and then started on the laundry. Next up was a quick dip in the pool, and after that I was going to meet one of my girlfriends at the Burke Williams Spa in the Sherman Oaks Galleria. We were treating ourselves to an afternoon of pampering before our kids and husbands came home. I desperately needed it after such a busy morning.

I placed the last load of clothes into the washer, and then searched through a large basket of freshly laundered delicates for my favorite bikini. I changed into it, tossed my old clothes into a nearby hamper, stopped by the kitchen for bottled water, slapped on some sunscreen, and headed outside.

I immediately dove in, my body knifing through the water as I kicked like a frog, my legs propelling me to the other side. I emerged, my head tilted back, my drenched skin drinking in the blazing sun above.

I swam over to the floating lounge chair and climbed onto it carefully, lest it overturn. I stretched out and closed my eyes. I floated like that for a long, much-needed moment, my body deliciously heated by the rays overhead, my left foot dangling in the cool, soothing water. I fell into a light sleep for who knows how long, until I was awakened by a sound at the back gate. I opened my eyes but couldn't make out what it was. I raised my hand to my forehead to minimize the glare. A tall, handsome young man in a T-shirt, cargo shorts, and sandals was coming inside, carrying a long-handled leaf skimmer, a vacuum, and supplies. It was our pool guy. Our very sexy pool guy. I hadn't realized it was his scheduled day to clean the pool.

He came over and stared down at me, his surprise undisguised.

"I didn't think you'd be out here," he said. "You're usually in the house."

"It's hot today," I said, my hand still arced over my face to block out the sun. I scanned his body from top to toe. My eyes lingered over the front of his pants. Was that the beginning of a growing bulge?

"I forgot you were coming," I said, my eyes still on his crotch. The sun was beaming too brightly for him to notice exactly where I was staring.

"Today's not my regular day," he explained. "My ten o'clock class at Pierce College was canceled, so I wanted to use the time productively."

"Oh," I replied, wondering if the moisture growing between my legs was from the sight of his hard, lean, muscular body, was sweat, or was maybe from the water lapping up onto the sides of my chair.

"I figured I'd come over here. You were the client I wanted to service first." He caught himself, embarrassed. "I mean, you know..." His words trailed off.

"Oh really?" I asked. "You want to service me?"

"Yeah," he said with a half-shy, half-bold grin. "You're my favorite client. I'm always excited when it's time to do you. Um, your pool. You know."

The bulge in the front of his pants was definitely growing. It had clearly formed a tent. He casually placed his hands in his pockets and ballooned the material outward in an attempt to hide the erection. I chuckled to myself.

"Why am I your favorite? Like you said, I'm usually inside. You hardly ever see me."

"Oh, I see you," he said. "I catch glimpses of you through the sliding glass door as you run around in your cutoff shorts and clingy T-shirts. Sometimes I stop what I'm doing and stare. I can't help it."

Now it was my turn to be embarrassed. "I didn't know you could see inside that well."

"You can."

I glanced at the sliding glass door. I could see quite clearly, from the kitchen and family room all the way past the foyer to the front door. How had I never noticed this before?

He pulled his hands out of his pockets, no longer attempting to camouflage the tent. I lowered my hand, playing with the water. I was definitely moist from excitement. I wondered how far I should let this conversation go.

"So what are you going to school for?" I asked, deciding it was best to change the topic.

"Did you know that I won your house in a bet?" he replied, ignoring my attempt at diversion.

My face flushed red.

"Excuse me? *Won my house*? What does that mean?"

"That came out the wrong way," he stammered. "What I meant was, all the guys at my job wanted to do this house. We put our names into a betting pool to see who would get it. I won." He said this last statement with beaming pride, like he had hit the lottery.

"Why would you guys bet on something so silly?" I asked, startled by his confession.

"Because," he said, "you're the hottest mom...um, I mean, the sexiest housewife...I mean..."

I waited to hear how he was going to get himself out of this.

"You're the hottest chick in the neighborhood," he finally blurted.

I laughed out loud. "Okay, now you're bullshitting me," I said. "And I wouldn't exactly call myself a 'chick.' I'm thirty-seven, which makes me more like a hen. Maybe even an old one. Besides, there are plenty of gorgeous girls running around here that put me to shame."

He stepped out of his shoes and sat on the side of the pool, his strong, taut calves dangling in the water.

"None of them can touch you," he said. "Your body is out of control."

"Really?" I asked, now very turned on.

"Really. If I didn't know you were married with teenagers, I wouldn't even believe you were over twenty-five."

I made slight paddling motions with my hand, the motion gently inching the lounge chair his way. The sun blazed down across my breasts, my loins, and the tops of my thighs, stirring my desire even more.

"I don't want to be twenty-five," I said. "I knew so little at that age. I've got experience now, lots of it. I wouldn't trade that experience for anything in the world."

"I wish you'd share some of that experience with me," he said, his voice thick. His right hand moved boldly to the tent in his pants as he ran his palm across the hardness. I could see the outline of the head of his cock. He clearly wasn't wearing any underwear.

"What are you doing?" I asked.

This situation was careening out of control.

"Nothing I haven't done whenever I think about you running around on the other side of that sliding glass door."

His eyes were on mine now. Even the sun couldn't come between our gaze.

"So would you?" he asked.

"Would I what?"

"Show me some of your experience. I'm an apt pupil. At least, that's what my professors at Pierce always say."

My lounge chair floated closer.

"What do you want to know?" I asked. My voice was so soft, it was nearly a whisper.

"Everything."

I was hot for this guy. Me. Married me. Me with two teenage sons who probably thought their mom was busy making the beds, not preparing to roll into one with someone not much older than them. After all, he couldn't have been more than twenty-one or twenty-two, just seven years older than my fifteen-year-old. What was I thinking? He was way too young for me to even consider.

But he was so hot. So sexy. Right in front of me for the taking. How could I not take advantage of the moment?

I floated closer, now within arm's reach. He massaged his crotch blatantly, running his hands up and down his shaft, still trapped inside his cargo pants.

I slid off the lounge chair and into the water, walking slowly toward him. His eyes were on my body as he dry-jacked his dick.

I stood between his legs, removing his hand from its preoccupation.

"Let me show you a better way to do that," I said.

I unzipped his cargo pants and reached inside. His cock was thick, solid, and long. I groaned with pleasure just touching it.

"Omigod," I muttered.

"Does that mean you approve?"

"Most definitely," I said as I pulled out his thickness, lowered my head, and encircled it with my mouth.

He threw his head back.

"Oh geez..."

I took him in deeper, all the way down to the balls.

"What the fuck," he breathed. "I've been dreaming about this. I can't believe it's actually happening. I've been wanting to..."

"Sssshhh," I said, momentarily removing his dick from my mouth. "Don't talk. Just feel."

I feasted on his young hard meat, relishing the taste of his skin. I slurped and sucked up and down the shaft, taking it in all the way to the back of my throat.

He grabbed my head with both hands, pushing it down farther. I kept taking him in. I gently massaged his balls as my tongue kneaded his cock. The pressure from my jaws sucking in produced a pussy-like tightness that made him scream.

"Sssshhh," I repeated, this time with his hot rod still in my mouth. "The neighbors might hear."

I sucked and massaged, massaged and sucked, my own pussy welling with excitement as I dined on his dick.

His hands moved from my head to the string of my bikini top. He untied it. The wet top fell down, unleashing my heaving breasts.

"Unbelievable," he whispered.

He reached out for their fullness, rubbing the nipples between his fingers. The feeling made me dizzy, almost drunk. I let go of his rigid shaft and pulled his cargo pants completely off. He took off his T-shirt, revealing a perfect, rippling six-pack. Holy mancocks. He was a god.

He stepped down into the water with me and lifted me onto the side of the pool where he'd been sitting. I parted my legs.

"Eat my pussy," I commanded.

He thrust his face into my wetness, pulling my bikini bottom down with his teeth. He reached around my back and undid the rest of my bikini top with a singular motion. It fell into the water. Perhaps he wasn't as inexperienced as I believed.

He pressed his mouth against my clit, his hot breath steaming my skin. He flicked his tongue across it first, then fastened on and began to suck, his arms wrapped around my thighs, opening them wider.

I closed my eyes as he worked me with his mouth, my body tingling all over from the pleasure it gave.

"Put your tongue in my pussy."

Eager to oblige, he thrust his hot red tongue inside me, darting in and out, lapping at my building juices.

"You are so fucking hot," he said around my pussy lips. "The guys at work would never believe this."

"And they're never going to know," I said.

"Never," he insisted as he nibbled at my labia.

I lay back against the concrete as he continued to flick and suck at my nether region. I rubbed my hands across my breasts, squeezing them together. I leaned up, flicking my tongue across my nipples.

He opened my thighs wider, his face completely pressed against my flesh, drinking, sucking, and breathing me in.

My hand found its way to my clit and I began to rub—first softly, then hard and fast—while his tongue did swan dives into my cunt.

The phone began to ring inside the house. It was probably my friend Lisa calling about meeting up at the spa. I ignored it. A ringing phone couldn't compare to the way his tongue was ringing my body right now.

"I want you to fuck me," I said.

"I want to fuck you," he replied, raising his head from between my legs. "I've been wanting to fuck you since Day One."

"Then you've got a lot of fucking to make up for," I said.

I stepped down into the water, facing him.

"I'm going to plant my arms on the side of the pool to steady myself," I explained. "Then I want you to grab hold of my legs and raise my hips so they're perpendicular to yours. You do know what *perpendicular* means, right?"

He grinned broadly. "I told you, I'm an apt pupil. And I've always been an A-student in math, especially when it comes to angles."

"That's a good boy," I said with a smile.

I backed against the wall of the pool, and then placed my arms on top of the edge. I braced myself.

"Okay, now do it."

He stepped closer, lifting my legs until my entire lower half intersected with his. His dick jutted hard and rigid between us.

"Now," I began, "I want you to slowly—"

He cut me off. "Um, I think I can take it from here."

Still holding me steady, he grabbed his dick with his right hand and guided it until he was perfectly centered over my extra-wet love hole. He rubbed the head up and down against the entrance, taunting me, sending shocks through my body, and then plunged in deep, all the way to the bottom.

"Oh my God!" I screamed.

"Sssshhh," he whispered with a wicked smile, grinding his dick into me. "The neighbors might hear."

He gyrated his hips into mine, his cock digging deeper and deeper, excavating my insides. He pulled nearly all the way out, then thrust in again, pumping slowly at first, then faster and faster, the waves and splashing water compounding the sensation of his shaft moving fluidly into and out of my body.

The phone in the house began to ring again. The spa was so far off my radar right now. Lisa was going to have to wait. I couldn't imagine getting anything at Burke Williams that could top what I was getting right now.

I bucked wildly against him, unable to hold back my squeals of delight. The threat of release grew into a hot, glowing ball of intensity deep inside me as he pounded my pussy again and again. Pool water splashed around us as we thrashed against the wall.

"I want to cum," I moaned, my breath coming quick. "I can't take it. I'm going to cum."

"Cum for me, sexy mama," he coaxed. "I want to drown in your juices."

He banged me rapid-fire, jackhammer-style, his youthful body a bottomless well of vigor. I wrapped my thighs tightly around him as my love walls began to quiver. The quivering quickly turned to powerful spasms as I gasped and shook against him, wrapping my legs around him tightly.

"Oh! Oh! Oh," I cried.

He unleashed another flurry of rabbit-quick pumps, banging against me as my orgasm swelled upward through my pelvis, then outward, from my pussy through my thighs, all the way down to my toes, which clenched and curled with absolute delight.

"You like that?" he urged, still pounding me, causing a fresh wave of spasms to course throughout my body. He moved as close to me as he could get, grinding and stirring inside my pussy with his hardness. I let go of the edge of the pool and threw my arms around him, hanging on. He squeezed me tight and moved farther away from the edge, thrusting harder, fucking me with a desperate, gluttonous passion, as if he was trying to fuck me to oblivion, as though he had something he needed to prove.

I came again, unexpectedly, a tidal wave of ecstasy rushing through my entire body. I held on for dear life, my chin on his shoulder, my breathing short and erratic. He was murdering my pussy, beating it senseless with the barely legal monster between his legs. I gasped and sputtered, pool water sloshing into my mouth.

"Keep fucking me," I panted.

"Don't worry," he said, still thrusting. "I've just gotten started."

He carried me toward the shallow end of the pool, his dick still rock-hard, planted inside me. He walked up the steps, out of the water, and carried me over to a nearby chaise, his throbbing cock inside me the whole time. He laid me down and resumed his business, this time pumping with hard, slow, deliberateness as he sucked my nipples and tasted my tongue. I wrapped my legs around him, my hands on his ass. I was trying to pull his whole young body inside of me. I wanted to feel every inch of his exuberance, wanted to drain him like he was the fountain of youth. I bucked against him, hungry for more, as our tongues twirled and our wet bodies slapped together. I came again. Hard. He thrust one last time, then threw his head back and let out an enormous moan.

"*Unnnnnnnhhhhhhhhhhhhhhhhhhhhhhhh!*"

"Give it to me," I urged, my nails digging into his ass. "I want all of it. Give me your cum!"

He writhed and bucked, his thick, gooey richness filling my entire tunnel. He pulled out, glancing down between my legs at the creampie oozing from the entrance of my swollen, beaten slit. I reached for his dick, pulling him toward me. I sucked the creamy fusion of my juices and his spunk from the entire length of his meat.

The phone began to ring again.

"She should be super-pissed by now," my husband said, laughing.

"She'll get over it," I replied, lapping him clean. "If it were her, she would have done the same thing."

Lisa knew all about the MILF-and-the-Pool-Boy game we liked to play, even though my husband's "arrival" today had not been planned. She and her husband often played games as well. What woman didn't want to be reminded that she was still hot, even after kids and years of marriage?

Luckily, we both had husbands who loved making us feel that way.

Reality

MILF: Mother **I**'d **L**ike **T**o **F**uck. If that's not one of the funniest, most clever postmillennial acronyms to hit the scene, I don't know what is. The term, obviously, refers to a woman who is someone's mother, often but not necessarily married and of a certain age—usually in her thirties, forties, or fifties—but is still considered very attractive and sexy. Yet another term with a similar context has emerged on the scene in recent years—*cougar*. Let's be clear: **MILFs and cougars are not the same thing.** The term *cougar* suggests someone predatory and desperate, hungrily seeking the young and vulnerable. A cougar may or may not be a mother. She is typically single. She may or may not be sexy. She is just a well-seasoned older woman looking for young meat. But a MILF? She is one hot mama!

MILF fantasies are popular because MILFs are usually just going about the business of being themselves, but exude a knockout quality that catches the attention of everyone around them, from their children's friends to their husband's buddies and their own colleagues and friends. The bottom line of the message they give off? **Sexy is sexy, age be damned.**

Among the most high-profile examples of an attractive woman paired with a younger man on the pop-culture landscape are Demi Moore and Ashton Kutcher. Demi is usually referred to as a "cougar" who managed to snag one of Hollywood's most eligible young bachelors. Ashton has sometimes been painted as a naive and unsuspecting fly who got ensnared in her cunning web. I personally think this assessment is about as wrong as it gets. I'm guessing that when

Ashton and Demi met, she saw a handsome man with his head on his shoulders, who was mature beyond his years and very shrewdly building his empire. And perhaps he saw a gorgeous woman who was the complete package: sexy, accomplished, intelligent, fun, and devoted to her children. Maybe he wanted to know more, maybe she did, too, and once they got the chance, maybe they realized here was everything they had been looking for in a mate, age be damned.

Ladies, even if you've never heard the term *MILF* before—or if you have and you never liked it—consider its inherent complimentary nature. It really is a compliment. Oh brother, I can hear you already. You don't believe me, do you?

But Vixen, there's nothing complimentary about some stranger saying I'm someone they'd like to fuck!

Oh really? There isn't? Because I'd happily take being considered fuckable any day of the week over the alternative—a **MIWTWATFP** (**M**other **I** **W**ouldn't **T**ouch **W**ith **A** **T**en-**F**oot **P**ole). Not only is that second option undesirable, it's practically unpronounceable! But being called a MILF? Heck yeah! It means I'm doing something right. I don't just work out for my health, you know. Wait. I mean, I do, but that's not the sole reason. I also work out because I like looking good. I revel in the fact that taking care of my body and appearance makes my husband both more attracted to me and proud to be the man who was able to win my love. After all, what woman doesn't want to feel as if she was The Big Get? Men love having bragging rights. **Your husband** *wants* **other men to consider you fuckable, which is why the idea of a sexual romp with a MILF is so alluring.** If your husband's got a MILF on his hands, it increases his stock, the implication being that he must be some kind of fierce to have pulled a woman like you, a woman who spat out a passel of babies, runs the household, has a fulfilling career, and still looks like she just stepped off a runway. There's nothing wrong with being just as proud of your outer sexy as you are of your inner vixen.

Mind you, I'm not suggesting that you suddenly start donning cutoff shorts and baby tees on the regular. Preserving your sexy is one thing. Suddenly turning into a homespun Pamela Anderson is another. Yes, your man wants others to see you as fuckable, but most men don't want you flaunting said fuckability in front of their friends and the public at large. Save the skimpy outfits for the actual MILF fantasy we're about to discuss, not for everyday wear around the house...unless, of course, that is your and your husband's thing!

Think about it: Here is a woman who has given birth to one or more children, children who are possibly now adults, but she has managed to take care of herself and maintain a level of attractiveness that inspires lust and envy all around. That's what being a MILF is. The term gives a whole new meaning to the phrase *motherfucker,* which, when you boil it down to its most rudimentary truth, is exactly what your husband is, if you have children.

Since you're married with children, why not go all the way and introduce the MILF fantasy into your relationship? Why not go ahead and officially join a club of which you're already sort of a member?

Come on, you hot mamas! Let me show you the way!

Vixen Tip

MILFs vs. Cougars

First of all, you need to be clear about the difference. This is a MILF fantasy, not a cougar one. The focus should be on playing the role of a hot and sexy mature woman who catches the eye of everyone when she walks into the room. Any older woman—and by *older,* I mean "above thirty-five"—can be a cougar. Being a cougar doesn't

Vixen Tip

guarantee that you'll be noticed, it just means you're on the prowl. But a MILF? Ha! All eyes will be on you, baby, especially the eyes of the young guns, one of whom your husband will play in this most delicious fantasy.

So what's MILF-like, you ask? Here are some clues:

• **Oblivious-sexy.** A true MILF seems to be blind to the fact that she is stopping every man in his tracks. She doesn't appear to be trying too hard to be this way, either. She's hot and that's just the way it is. In order to best experience this fantasy, this is a trait you must adopt when you play the role. That *Who me? Sexy?* thing works for MILFs every time. Of course, you're going to know you're sexy. Just don't act like you do.

• **Positive accentuation.** A true MILF knows what to showcase without looking like a flat-out slut. Her breasts are seductively displayed without being all *Boom! Pow!* in your face. Her ass is showcased in a provocative, figure-hugging skirt that's not so short that it makes her seem skanky, and not so long that it screams she's boring. Or maybe she's in low-slung jeans and a hoodie, but still manages to ooze an organic irresistibility. Even if she dons cutoffs and a baby tee, the look feels natural and doesn't come across as though she's trying to look younger than she actually is or compete with twenty-year-old girls. (For great examples of women who truly represent for the MILFs of the world, see Halle Berry, Heidi Klum, and Angelina Jolie.) Know how to *work what ya mama gave ya* while still keeping it classy and aboveboard.

• **Sexperience.** MILFs know from sex. Seriously. They really know their way around the sexual landscape, and they navigate

Vixen Tip

it with confidence and ease. They know what turns on a man and how to introduce him to sensations and pleasures he wasn't even aware of, which is why younger men are so hungrily drawn to them. A MILF can put you on, show you the ropes, and then set you free, ready to take on the world. She is not going to throw herself at you, but she is not shy or inhibited, either. She is both gregarious and independent, as easy traveling solo as she is in the company of others. That's because she knows herself and is comfortable in her own skin. What better woman to teach you the ways of the sexual world?

By adopting the above characteristics, you're almost ready to step into your role. Just make sure not to incorporate the following traits, which are the telltale signs of a cougar, which is *not* the role you should be playing in this particular fantasy:

• **I want your sex!** That's because she does . . . want your sex, that is, fellas. When a cougar walks into the room, the men may or may not all pause, but they definitely know this lady is on the prowl and ready for action. There are certain signs that a woman open to a sexual encounter gives off, and the cougar is slinging all of them at once. She makes eye contact with you, she sends the waiter over to you with a drink and maybe her business card that has a provocative note scrawled on the back. She's got the *Boom! Pow!* tits and ass going on, displayed for maximum exposure in a too-tight top and too-short skirt. She has on a pair of five-inch-high Louboutins that she is semi-struggling to walk in, because, yeah, Louboutins, that's what the hot young chicks are wearing these days, right? She wants to *f-f-f-fuuuuuuck*, and she's got her eyes on the hottest, freshest, tastiest meat in the room, the one guaranteed to give her a night of prolonged pleasure fueled by

Vixen Tip

the natural stamina of youth, not some pharmaceutical boost (read, Viagra, Cialis, ExtenZe, et cetera) that any old fart can pop to produce wood. Ladies, this is *not* the kind of sexy you want to be giving off as a MILF. A MILF doesn't need to do anything along these lines to garner attention. A MILF just shows up, and everyone else will take it from there.

• **Freeze frame.** Why is this lady's face so stiff? Even when she laughs, it's only from the mouth down. Her brows don't move. Her eyes blink robotically. Her forehead is frozen still. This is a major giveaway that separates cougars from MILFs. While MILFs rely on natural beauty, cougars are terrified that time will ultimately betray them, so they jump the gun and try to head aging off at the pass. That frozen forehead? It's shot full of Botox. That weird puffiness around her eyes and mouth? Reservoirs of Restylane are resting within. All a plastic surgeon has to do is hint at a new miracle anti-aging drug or remedy and the cougar will be first in line to get it. After all, you can't lure a younger man with a face full of wrinkles. Better to have your face a little stiff (but smooth!) than look like the Crypt Keeper, right? Trust me, for every facial-peeled, lip-plumped, collagen-injected, Botox-browed cougar, there's a Dorian-Gray-esque "before" photo in a file in a plastic surgeon's office that depicts what she really looks like. And it ain't a good look, son. It ain't a good look.

• **The not-so-sweet smell of desperation.** Something's ticking on a cougar, and it is not that thirty-thousand-dollar, diamond-encrusted Chopard wristwatch, either. (*Sidebar:* Cougars are, in many cases, financially independent and well heeled. The better to eat you, er, I mean, *take care of you*, young man. That's

Vixen Tip

the trade-off you'll get for all that sweaty, on-demand sex and round-the-clock doting she'll expect.) Now, back to that ticking. Do you hear it? Listen closely. *Aaah*, there it is! It's the sound of her biological clock. That thing's about to blow some gaskets, and if you're standing too close, you just might lose an eye. A true cougar is newly divorced, perennially single, or has been divorced so long, she's afraid she'll never: (a) marry again; (b) have sex with a real man (as opposed to the rabbit-eared vibrator in her nightstand); (c) have children; (d) all of the above. She is in a bit of a panic, you see, and her pheromones are leading the charge as a sort of advance guard, if you will, alerting all those in the vicinity that it is time to put up or shut up. There will be no doubling down with this one, fellas. Either make your move or get out of the way. A younger man will do best, because he is more likely to have staying power, he's great for her ego, and—because she's older—he'll be enthralled at how worldly she is (at least for a while). Also, if she is in the market for a sperm donor to give her that elusive child, his swimmers stand a better chance of reaching and awakening her eggs, which have been cooling on the shelf a little—okay, a lot—longer than expected. She is going to need some potent stuff to rouse those puppies. I'm talking missile sperm, the long-range kind that can navigate her withering fallopian tubes and hang around for a few days without dying off. *Ladies, don't show up in your fantasy as this woman!* This woman needs to take a chill pill. Several of them. *Stat!*

• **Welcome to cougar country.** Cougars often travel in packs. It provides moral support and helps take some of the edge off getting back into the game. If a cougar is shot down when she tries to make a move on some unsuspecting tenderfoot, it helps to have other cougars nearby to run to for reassurance. Those other cougars serve as the female equivalent of a wingman—"cling girls," if you will, who help process the rejection and offer encouragement. Then there are the ones who tend to travel solo. They are what I like to call "professional cougars," women who've always liked their men younger and don't want any other women around providing competition. Professional cougars can sometimes be mistaken for MILFs, mostly because of their sexual confidence, but Pro-Cous (pronounced *PRO-cooz*, and it's my word! I just coined it!) tend to be strident, almost abrasive, in how strong they sometimes come on to men. Don't be a Pro-Cou, ladies.

The goal of this night is to initiate your "young man" into a wide world of sensuous adult pleasure—the kind that can only be had in the arms of a truly grown-ass woman.

Of course, none of that was meant to be offensive to cougars. Sometimes the unplanned circumstances of life have a way of bringing out the cougar in all of us. But that's not our thrust here. By pointing out cougar characteristics, we are distinguishing them from those of a MILF, which is what this fantasy is about. What we want to focus on now is turning you into the kind of woman men salivate over. Not some young sex kitten or a desperate housewife. We're talking a real sexpot. Who needs Halle, Heidi, or Angelina when you're about to step out as the ultimate MILF?

By incorporating this kind of fantasy into your marriage—especially if you are, in fact, a woman of a certain age and not just pretending—in addition to stoking the fire of your relationship, you might also find

Vixen Tip

Come to Mama!

Let's be clear here, ladies: Just because you and your man are about to indulge in what's considered an older woman/younger man fantasy, there is nothing that suggests the incestuous and Oedipal here. This isn't a fantasy involving your man wanting to be with *his* mommy. This is a moment of role-play with you in the part of a mature woman whose attractiveness transcends age, which makes you a *hot* mama. Men of all ages are drawn to hotness. In this particular case, your husband will be playing the part of someone much younger than you who gets a crack (ha!) at an older woman who incites his lust in a very big way. This is his chance to act out the kind of fantasy his teenage wet dreams were probably made of. It is important to set the right mood and tone.

- **What's the scenario?** MILF fantasies work best when you create a setup as the lead-in to sex. Pick a theme, any theme, as long as it fits with the MILF concept and profile. Classic examples include the male college student who is turned on by his sexy married professor and finally sees an opportunity after class to close the deal, or a junior lawyer alone in the office after hours with a seasoned partner at the firm. Also, the pool boy bit never fails, and neither does the one where you end up getting it on with your son's best friend. With the right scene and the right tone, this adventure is sure to deliver!

- **To seduce or be seduced?** This one is up to you. You can play it either way: as the object of a young man's lust, or the one who initiates the act. All that matters is that the attraction is depicted as mutually irresistible, not inherently predatory, à la the cougar.

Vixen Tip

The "young man" in this scenario should want you just as much as you want him. He has been waiting for the right moment and is trying to figure out an opening, or he has been fantasizing about you for months and can't believe that you're the one who finally makes the move. Whether you are the seduced or the seducer, the feeling should be that, once the ice is broken, things are going to be on and popping!

• **Teach me tonight.** The beauty of playing a MILF is that you get to demonstrate how much you know about the art of love. Your husband's role should be as a willing student, letting you take charge and show him what you want him to do. If he is the aggressor, then he should portray himself to be a formidable match for you: a young stud who wants to impress knowledgeable you with skills equal to or surpassing someone your age. Sit back and let him have at it!

your self-esteem getting a much-needed boost. Once you and your husband realize that being a wife and a mother don't have to preclude being the object of sexual desire, then you're free to roam territory that may have long been abandoned after children, marital responsibility, day-to-day chores, and time constraints entered the picture.

No territory ever has to be lost. Marriage and aging should be the beginning of exciting and adventurous sex, not the end. **This fantasy reaffirms the idea that a woman growing older should be seen as ripening into full, fragrant fruit, not as withering on the vine, beyond desirability and usefulness.**

As Confucius once alliteratively said: "Man who make MILF make more merry than most." Okay, so maybe he didn't say that, but it makes a whole lot of sense to me!

Recap

- MILFs and cougars are not the same thing.

- MILF fantasies are popular because MILFs are usually just going about the business of being themselves, but exude a knockout quality that catches the attention of everyone around them.

- Sexy is sexy, age be damned.

- Your husband *wants* other men to consider you fuckable, which is why the idea of a sexual romp with a MILF is so alluring.

- This fantasy reaffirms the idea that a woman growing older should be seen as ripening into full, fragrant fruit, not as withering on the vine, beyond desirability and usefulness.

V-Log #11
When 69 Is Not Just a Position

In what has proved to be an interesting turn of events, your man—your normally very reserved and conservative beloved—somehow stumbles across this book in a bookstore (or on his iPad, Kindle, Sony Reader, et cetera), buys it, quietly reads it all on his own, then brings it to you one evening to discuss some of the fantasies. How impressive and forward thinking is that? Men usually have to be coaxed and encouraged to do certain things, but in this case he's the one with the initiative. Girl, if you didn't know it before now, your man rocks! Let's give him a rousing hand!

Not too heartily, though. Hold on a sec. This *is* a book of erotic fantasies for advanced and adventurous couples. Most women won't have to press too hard to get their men to indulge in sexual role-playing they'd probably be game to do anyway. This book is a great way for a whole lot of husbands who want to put some of the fire back into their relationships bring it to the attention of their wives, so while we applaud those who pick it up on their own for being proactive, it's not exactly like leading an unwilling horse to water and forcing him to drink. This book of suggested fantasies is exactly the kind of water most hot-blooded men with half a sex drive—if given the "go" sign—would be eager to chug.

So yeah, your man brought you this book. Notice I didn't say *bought* you this book. He bought it for himself, then brought it to you to excitedly share what he discovered inside. Together the two of you look through it for the fantasy you think will best suit what mutually excites you. For the record, you don't have to settle on just one. This book is filled with lots of adventurous possibilities—possibilities that are limited only by the boundaries of your willingness and creativity. You flip through the pages. Hmmm...the One-Man Gangbang fantasy looks like fun. So does the Paid Escort chapter, or maybe you could try swinging? No, not swinging. You're not sure if you're ready to go that far just yet, if ever. You look up at your husband. He quickly shakes his head. He doesn't want swinging, either. He knows how slippery that slope can get. That is definitely not an option the two of you will be trying.

But wait…what is this? You notice a group of pages toward the back that are already earmarked, as if to single them out. You flip through to investigate. Ah! It is the chapter on MILFs. You glance up at your husband. He gives a sheepish look, a half smile on his face. *Is this the one you like,* your expression silently queries. His half smile goes to full grin as he nods eagerly, takes the book from your hands, and points out how fun and easy the MILF fantasy would be to implement. He quotes the chapter's content from memory, as though he wrote the words himself. He reminds you that he has always had a thing for older women—you're six years his senior, so you already know this—and he prattles on giddily about how he'd love to see you get into the part of the perfect older woman, someone perhaps even a tad older than you are now, and he'll pretend to be a teenage neighbor whose parents force him to come over to see if you need anything, um, you know, serviced around the house.

Okay, you think. *That sounds doable.* You read the fantasy part of the chapter and realize that, yes, this could be quite fun. You could use an escape from the everyday. Some explosive, role-playing sex would be just the thing. You scan through the rest of the chapter, taking note of the Vixen Tips. Your eyebrows rise with alarm. Your husband quickly emphasizes that you are definitely a MILF, not a cougar. You sigh with relief. You've never been a woman who aggressively pursued men, so you wouldn't be comfortable pretending to be that kind of woman. But a MILF? Yeah. You're a MILF, for sure. You take pride in your sexiness, and men other than your husband constantly find you attractive. Playing that kind of role would be an easy transition, a great way to ease yourself into trying out a fantasy for the very first time.

Oh, and look. Your man already has the details of your adventure worked out. He informs you that, in your MILF fantasy, he is going to be the one going after you. Your character won't be making the first move. You like the sound of this. Yes, you tell him. You're definitely in!

Your husband hugs you and gives you a high-five. You didn't know people still gave high-fives, but apparently your husband is among the diminishing few that do. He wants to do the MILF fantasy tomorrow, during the day, when the kids are in school and the two of you have the house all to yourselves. Is that okay? Tomorrow?

Um, okay, you think. Wait, tomorrow? Isn't that kind of soon? Don't the two of you need time to figure out the details and work out the, er, kinks? No, he stresses. You don't need time! There is no time like the present, blah, blah, blah, he says. The best way to do it is to just jump in. He is even going to take the day off from work, he is that excited about making it happen.

Now you're finally getting excited, almost as excited as he is. You jump up, about to head to the bedroom to go through your closet to find a sexy, mature outfit for the big event. You need attire an older housewife would wear, but something provocative, not frumpy and unappealing. Not too *Penthouse* Forum, I'm-sitting-around-waiting-for-you-to-show-up-and-fuck-me, but not classic June Cleaver, either. That would be way too off-putting. It should be somewhere in the middle of those two things, maybe more like Teri Hatcher's character on *Desperate Housewives*. Yes, yes, that would work.

Wait a minute...what's that? Your husband next informs you that he's got a surprise for you. Another one? Girl, you have the best husband in the world! Turns out he already stopped and picked up some things on the way home tonight, just for this very occasion. He purchased some mature and sexy clothing for you to wear, exactly the kind of attire that, once you put it on, is certain to get him off. He picked up a youthful outfit for himself as well. A khaki T-shirt and some cargo pants, since that's what the teenage boys are wearing these days.

Look at that. He just saved you some work. You don't even have to go through your closet now to put together something to wear for the fantasy. All you have to do tomorrow, your husband points out, is put on the getup he picked out for you and wait for him to show up. It is going to be *fun, fun, fun*, he promises. He is going to love you, literally, like he's never loved you before. Er, rather, like you've never been loved before. Or something. Whatever. It's going to be a whole lot of never-had-before loving, that's for sure. That he can promise.

You fling your arms around your husband's neck and give him a long, sensuous kiss. He has never been this proactive about anything. Ever. This book of fantasies just might be the best thing that has ever happened to your marriage. It is exactly that, by the way, particularly when implemented properly. But we'll discuss that in a minute. Back to you. Back to this. This is about to get *really* interesting. Let's take a look.

You wake up the next morning and get the kids fed and off to school. Your husband is already gone, having exited the house before anyone else in the house was awake. That's cool, though. You discussed this very thing the night before. It is all part of the plan, his already-mapped-out itinerary for how this fantasy would go down. Once the kids are gone, you head upstairs for a long, hot shower. Your stomach has butterflies, like the very first time you went on a date with your husband. In a way, that's what all of this is. You and your husband are rediscovering each other. You are trying something new, something fresh, and something hot, after years of being stuck in the routine of day-to-day life. Your somewhat uptight husband is finally letting down his guard. The wildest part of it all is that he is the one who prompted the whole thing. You giggle to yourself as you stand under the stream of water and let the bubbles from the fragrant body wash rinse away. *He* is the one who wanted a fantasy. A MILF fantasy, of all things. He didn't want to fantasize about being with some impossibly young twenty-year-old. He wants to engage in a fantasy with someone older, someone mature. Someone like you! You giggle again and touch yourself down there, thinking about what lies ahead. You quickly pull your hand away. Best to leave that to your husband. Let him do all the work today. You put your hand back, noticing something. You glance down. Your bush is out of control. Oh no! That will not do for today. Just because you're playing an older woman doesn't mean you can get away with having a yeti camped out between your legs.

You step out of the shower, drip your way over to the medicine cabinet, pull out your tiny trimming scissors, and step back under the water. You begin snip, snip, snipping, trimming your trim into a nice little triangle. You place a light amount of Nair around your bikini line to take care of the excess. Then you get an even brighter idea. Why not give your husband a treat? Since he was proactive enough to encourage you to introduce a role-playing fantasy to reinvigorate your marriage, why not be proactive and do something for him? You've heard your friends talk about their Brazilians, landing strips, and clean-shaven mounds, but you've never dared to do anything like that. Who has the time to maintain such a thing? The upkeep, to you, has always seemed like it would be too much for any woman with half a life to handle. But hey, today is a new day! Why not go with the new? And just like that, you decide to do it. You contemplate whether to smear some Nair on your mound to remove the remaining hair, then decide against it and reach for a razor. A few strokes of your mound and careful maneuvering in the areas around your labia and near your butt later and . . . *voilà!* Your hoohah is as clean as a baby's. You step out of the shower again, wipe away the steam from the bathroom mirror, and check yourself out. It is so fresh and so clean-clean. It's gorgeous. You're gorgeous. Oh yes, your newly hairless peeper is going to blow your hubby's mind!

You dry yourself and slather soothing oil over your body, taking special care with your newly clean-shaven lady parts. You spray a light fragrance into the air and step into the mist, letting it fall lightly onto your body.

You head into your bedroom in search of the outfit your husband selected. There is a handwritten note on your lingerie chest. Your husband must have put it there before he left this morning. You never even noticed. You pick it up. *Look in the back of the closet*, the note says. You rush over, excited to see what he got for you. You burrow past the dresses, suits, slacks, and blouses hanging in the way. There it is: a shopping bag way in the back, shoved into a corner. You reach your arm all the way in, pull it out, and take it over to the bed, dumping out the contents. There is a white Playtex 18 Hour bra, oversize white panties, a full slip, a boxy floral dress, support hose, a pair of clunky black shoes...and a wig. A gray wig. Gray. WTF?

You plop down on the bed, examining the items. Is this all a joke? Surely, surely, your husband is kidding. You look at the items again, picking through them one by one. You hold up the matronly bra. It is the correct size. So are the panties, the slip, the shoes, and the dress. Your husband knows your measurements, that is for sure. You have to give him credit for that. Maybe he has something funny planned. Yes! That has to be what it is. Your man has always been a prankster. Of course that's what this is. All right, you're game. Why not go along with it? It is a fantasy, after all.

You don the giant panties, put on the bra, slip on the slip and the support hose, and pull on the dress. You step into the clunky black shoes and cram your hair under the wig, fitting it onto your head. You walk over to the dresser, glancing at yourself in the mirror. This is freaking hilarious. What is your husband up to? Wait, there is yet another note taped to the mirror. *Put this on.* An arrow points to a brand-new tube of fire-red lipstick.

You put on the lipstick, pursing your lips together. You check yourself out again in the mirror. Even though you don't know where this is going, you definitely make a damn cute granny.

You go back into the living room and begin the day's chores. That is what your husband wants, for you to act as though you're just a MILF (albeit this getup certainly stretches the definition) going about the regular course of her day.

The doorbell rings. Your heart races. It's him. The games are about to begin!

You smooth down the front of the dress as you calmly walk to the door. You look through the peephole. Yes! It's him!

You open the door and are instantly taken aback. He has a fresh haircut, one that almost makes him look like a little boy. It's a rather silly haircut, and he's going to have to live with it for a few days, long after this fantasy is over. He really is going all-out for this. You can't help but giggle as you study him from top to bottom. He's dressed in the T-shirt and cargo shorts and a pair of sneakers with white socks that almost come up to his knees. The transformation is downright hilarious. In contrast, he gasps with wonder at the sight of you, his eyes lighting up in a way you've never seen.

"Wow," he mumbles. "You look great."

Great? Is he kidding? You're dressed up like a granny.

"Can I help you, son?" you say according to the plan he previously laid out.

"Uh, yes, ma'am," he stammers. You notice that his stammering is genuine. He seems honestly taken with you right now. "I was wondering if there were some things you needed done around the house."

"Well, now let me see...oh yes! I do have some dusting that I can't reach. It's pretty high up." You point inside the living room. "On that ceiling fan there and the ledges at the tops of those windows. And I can't reach up very well on that armoire."

"I can help you with that."

"Why, thank you, young man. Why don't you come on inside."

You wave him in, doing everything in your power to keep from laughing. Your husband had been adamant the night before about the two of you not breaking character. He wants this to feel as real as it gets; otherwise, he insisted, what's the point of trying out a fantasy?

Your husband is dressed like an overgrown child. You're dressed like a granny. How are you going to keep from breaking character? It'll be nearly impossible for you to keep from laughing your way through the whole thing.

"Where should I get started?" he asks.

You walk across the room to the tall armoire.

"Up there," you say, standing on your tiptoes. "I can never reach all the way to the top."

Your husband, your man-boy, is already unable to contain himself. He falls to his knees, grabbing hold of your ankles. He kisses your calves desperately, and then begins to rip the support hose.

"Oh my!" you cry, trying to stay in character. "What are you doing? Shouldn't you be doing the armoire?"

"I'm doing what I've been wanting to do all year," he says.

Your man-boy picks you up in all your granny glory and carries you over to the couch. He places you down softly, gets on his knees, lifts up the dress, and finishes tearing the support hose away.

He holds the torn hose in his hands, breathing in the scent. You are partly amused, partly horrified. Who knew your husband was such an actor! He was acting, after all...right?

He throws the torn hose down and reaches up for you, covering your neck with kisses.

"God, you're beautiful!"

I'm eighty, you respond in your head.

With one Herculean snatch, he rips open the dress and the slip, exposing your missile-shaped cones pointing skyward in the 18 Hour bra. He squeezes the missiles together, sucking each one through industrial fabric that was in no way designed for pleasure. There is an enormous tent in front of his cargo pants. You reach out to touch it. He is harder than physics. You grasp that hardness, wanting to release it, but he pushes your hand back, maintaining control.

Your man-boy kisses your stomach, then lower, making his way toward the oversize panties. This is all very strange, but, admittedly, it has gotten you quite hot. You're already wet just from watching how excited this whole thing has made him.

He tugs at the panties. You can't wait for him to see your surprise. His surprise. You did it for him. He pulls at the panties, tugging them lower, then stops halfway. He freezes at the sight.

"Noooooooo!" he cries frightfully, filling you with instant alarm. *"What did you do!"*

"I shaved it," you say proudly. "I figured since we were having a freaky fantasy, I'd do something freaky that you would really like."

Your man-boy backs away, livid.

"But this was a specific fantasy! This was a MILF fantasy! I needed you to have hair down there!"

And now you're confused. You consider yourself a MILF, but you would never dress in the outfit he picked for you. You have plenty of MILF girlfriends and none of them dresses like this, either. You've seen movies where younger guys refer to older women as MILFs. Stifler's mom was a MILF in *American Pie*, wasn't she? She wasn't dressed like this. She didn't have on an 18 Hour bra!

Maybe you don't know what a MILF is, after all.

"But I thought...," you begin.

"Never mind," he snaps. "It's over. You ruined it. The first time I ever get the nerve to try something different, you have to go off script and fuck everything up."

Go off script? What script? He never gave you a script. He just provided a few suggestions for what you should do when he showed up in character. You tossed around a few things to maybe talk about, but there was no script, per se.

Too late. Your man-boy storms away, leaving you splayed on the couch with your skyward missiles, ripped-open dress and slip, granny panties, clunky shoes, gray wig, and tattered support hose. Your fire-red lips were never even kissed.

You don't know whether to be indignant or embarrassed. Maybe you're feeling a combination of both. Even worse, your freshly shaved peeper itches. What the hell. No fantasy is worth all this.

What is the moral of this story, ladies? Can you figure it out? First, if you and your husband are going to do a MILF fantasy, make sure you are in accord regarding your definitions of a MILF. Unbeknownst to your Norman Bates of a husband, he had a GILF fantasy. **GILF** is an acronym for **G**randmother **I**'d **L**ike **T**o **F**uck. That explains the outfit he so eagerly picked out for you. Now, as for why your man is fantasizing about shtupping a grandma, well, that is a subject for another time and another book, one that deals with the psychology of the sexual mind and the origins of fetishes. I haven't written that book yet. And, well, I'm not sure I ever will. If this kind of thing keeps coming up, though, I just might change my mind.

Just for speculation's sake, however, maybe your man once had warm feelings for an elderly neighbor when he was growing up. Maybe she gave him lots of fresh-baked cookies and other delicious treats and, somehow, in his young mind, the happy feelings he got from those delicious treats transferred into a sort of sexual happy.

Maybe. Maybe not. Hell if I know. I just took a wild stab. Maybe he just has the secret hots for grannies. Sometimes it is what it is.

In the meantime, you're going to need to turn your attention to that freshly shaven cha-cha of yours. Not because your husband is upset about it. He'll get over that soon enough. I'm sure he is going to have enough to deal with now that he's let you "peep his hold card," so to speak, regarding his whole granny fetish. I guarantee you that once he calms down and realizes he played himself, he won't be too keen on giving you grief about your hairless hoohah—he's really into something out on a much farther limb. No, he's not your biggest concern right now. What I'm talking about is the hell that awaits you once those pubic hairs start to grow in.

This is why most women who remove the hair from that area do so by having it waxed. Shaving only gets rid of the hair at and above the surface of the skin. By nightfall, if not sooner, the hairs underneath will be pushing through, causing the area to itch and possibly develop what is known as *pseudofolliculitis barbae*, otherwise known as razor bumps. It is not going to be pretty. A bumpy pussy with a five o'clock shadow is a sad thing to witness. You're going to have to make a decision between two options. You can keep shaving it in order to minimize the bumping and itching. I don't recommend this, as repeated shaving of your pubic mound can result in distressed and damaged skin not unlike gator hide. Talk about your porn pussy. Well, this is its ugly sister: mangle mound.

The ideal thing to do is the second choice: Just let it grow out. This is the more painful option, but it is the one that will be most effective in getting you back to normal. Sure, it will itch like crazy the first few days as those hairs break through. Just ignore it. I know that sounds like an easy thing for me to say, especially since it isn't an easy thing to do. It will be hard. Your hand will make its way down there to scratch without you even realizing it. You must be mindful. Vigilant. You have to suffer through. In the end, when your peeper moves past its crazy Brit-Brit stage and is back to its recognizable self, you'll be grateful you endured.

You can do it. We are women, dammit. Strong women. We have suffered and will inevitably suffer through worse things than growing out a bald pussy.

And if you must scratch (which is highly inadvisable), for goodness' sake don't do it in mixed company. What an awful signal that would send. Just let the damn thing grow wild and free. Don't bother manicuring it at all. Heck, you've apparently got that rare breed of husband who likes a woman with a weed-whacker-worthy bush between her legs. And since he is a GILF-chaser (yes, girl, your husband likes granny ass...own it already), imagine how thrilled he is going to be when your pubes turn gray.

Good times, y'all. Good times, indeed.

Chapter Twelve

Foot Fetish

Fantasy

I'd been on the dance floor for more than an hour, shaking my hot ass to back-to-back hits as the deejay kept the music coming. The club was packed, the heat was thick, and the man I'd been dancing with was relentless. He was tall and super-sexy with killer moves that had all the women waiting for a turn. A few had been bold enough to push up behind him and dance along with us, but he never once acknowledged them. He interest was exclusively focused on me.

"Aren't you hot?" I asked, hoping he wanted a break from all the dancing we had been doing. I didn't want to just walk off from him. One of the skanks hovering nearby would snap him up for sure.

"I'm hot for you," he slyly replied.

I laughed. "No, seriously. I could use a drink or something. If I don't cool down, I'm going to faint."

He grabbed me by the hand and led the way toward the bar, pushing through the throng of people.

"What's your pleasure?" he asked once we arrived.

"Anything with ice in it," I replied. "But I need to hit the bathroom first." I ran my hand across my sweaty neck. "And I need to freshen up a little. This sweat running down my neck is definitely not sexy."

"It's sexier than you think," he said. "What's sexier than a hot, sweaty woman who can dance her ass off?"

"A woman who can dance her ass off who's not flinging sweat all over the place."

"All right," he said, laughing, "you've got a point. Go handle your business. I'll be here when you get back. I'm not going anywhere."

A pack of girls stood a few feet off, eyeing him.

"I don't know," I warned. "Looks like I might need to take a number when I return."

His eyes followed mine, noticing them. He laughed again. "Trust me, that won't be necessary. This ride is only giving out one ticket tonight."

"Well, all right then." I chuckled as I headed off. "I won't be long."

I made my way toward the back of the club. The hall was thick with body heat, lined with people talking, drinking, kissing, popping shit, popping E, texting, sexting, and everything in between. Barely dressed women were pressed up against buff-bodied men. I checked them all out as I navigated through the madness. Damn. There was a line to get into the bathroom. At least six other women were ahead of me. My first instinct was to turn around and head back for the bar, but eventually I'd have to come back and the line would surely be longer than it was right now. I decided to stick it out. Maybe the wait wouldn't be as long as I feared.

I stood behind the last girl, leaning against the wall as I tried to ignore the heat. I closed my eyes, fanning myself with my hand.

"Nice shoes," a deep voice said right next to my ear.

Startled, I opened my eyes, following the sound of the voice. I turned and looked right into the face of a man with fiery dark eyes that dazzled me at once. His full lips curled into an intriguing grin. Or maybe it was a smirk. I couldn't tell in this light. I blinked several times, caught off guard by his presence.

"Giuseppe Zanotti," he said. "The spring-summer line."

"What are you, gay?" I said with a laugh. I quickly recovered. "Not that there's anything wrong with that, if you are."

"Not gay. I just know shoes. And feet."

"I see," I said, unnerved by his closeness. I also found his accuracy unsettling. My shoes were, indeed, Giuseppe Zanottis from the spring-summer line. I had a friend who worked for the company, and she'd gotten me a pair right before they debuted. I turned away from him and faced the line. It had advanced a little. Now there were only four women ahead of me.

"You have supple heels," the man behind me continued. "Soft, pink, delicate skin. Those are the heels of a woman who gets weekly pedicures."

"So you're a podiatrist," I muttered, stepping forward along with the line.

"Not a podiatrist."

"Then you work at a nail shop."

"No nail shop," he said. "I'm just a connoisseur."

He moved up along with me. I turned toward him.

"You know this is the line for the ladies' bathroom, right?" I asked.

"It's a unisex bathroom," he said.

I leaned around, glancing up ahead. A man walked out of the sea-green glass door.

"Oh," I said, surprised. "I had no idea."

"Does that bother you?"

"I don't care," I said. "As long as I can do my business privately, I'm fine."

"Good girl," he replied.

Good girl? What an odd thing for a stranger to say. Like he was my chaperone or something. I glanced over my shoulder at him. He stood behind me, all smoldering eyes and chiseled jaw, not saying a word. He was sexy. I couldn't deny it. And he was right about my feet. I was a weekly pedicure person. Pedicures and beautiful shoes were my biggest indulgences, and I didn't slack on either one. My feet and the way I adorned them were the purest displays of myself as a woman.

"Paraffin dips," he whispered.

"Yes," I replied, my voice just as low as his. This was a game now, a way to kill time, and I was beginning to enjoy it.

The line moved closer to the door. Only two girls were ahead of me now.

"Polish?" I asked, challenging him.

"Hmmm...," he muttered, "let's see..."

I positioned my foot so he could get a clear look.

"OPI. Definitely OPI."

"Very good," I giggled, quite impressed. "What color?"

"Chocolate Moose. Spelled with two o's and one s."

I turned all the way around to face him.

"Oh my God. That's exactly what it is. Who are you?" I pressed. "What do you do?"

He made a nodding gesture. "The line just moved up."

I looked over my shoulder. The two girls were gone. I was now at the front of the line.

"How did they both go in at the same time?"

"The bathroom has two stalls," a woman passing by said.

Now, that would be interesting. It meant that possibly the foot man and I would be in the bathroom at the same time. Unless, of course, one of the women came out and the other took longer to finish what she was doing. Hopefully, that would be the case. This man made me nervous. He was fascinating, alluring, mysterious, but I wasn't quite sure he was someone I'd want to be alone with. Why would a straight man who didn't work at a nail shop know that much about nail polish, shoes, and caring for feet?

"No need to worry," he said, as if reading my thoughts. "I'm the good guy. I'm the one who gives the bad guys something to think about."

"So you're a cop," I said, my eyes on the bathroom door, waiting to dart right in.

"I guess you could say I police things, yes."

My skin was tingling. I glanced down at my forearms. They were covered with tiny bumps. He was giving me chills. Just moments ago I had been hot and sweaty, but now I was cold with the brisk thrill of excitement. My nipples were even hard. Everything about him had me aroused. *Please, oh please, let that bathroom door open. Let one girl walk out so I can go in alone.*

"Relax," he said softly, all inside my head. "Only one will come out."

His breath was warm on the back of my neck.

The bathroom door opened and one of the women exited. I rushed past her, brushing against her shoulder on my way in.

"Hey!" she exclaimed.

"Sorry," I said. "I really have to go."

I'd expected to see a bathroom attendant on my way in, but it was just the two stalls and a long counter with two sinks. It was surprising that more people weren't gathered in the bathroom, waiting their turn to get into the stalls. I grabbed some paper towels from the dispenser against the wall. That's when I noticed the sign that read, NO MORE THAN TWO PEOPLE ALLOWED IN RESTROOM AT A TIME.

How odd, I thought, especially for a unisex bathroom. Anything could happen with just two people in the bathroom, especially with a man and a woman. Then again, I realized, the same could apply irrespective of gender, so I guess it really didn't make a difference.

I ran cool water over the paper towels, squeezed them out, and wiped the sweat from my neck, my nape, and the tops of my shoulders. I looked at my reflection. My skin was still flushed and tingling from the thought of the foot man. A toilet flushed and the woman from the occupied stall emerged and washed her hands. She smiled at me in the reflection of the mirror. I smiled back, tossed the paper towels in the trash, and stepped into an empty stall, locking the door behind me.

As I was adjusting my clothing, I heard her exit. My skin tingled anew at the sound of someone else walking in. The sound was of a man's shoes, not the heels of a woman. I could smell his scent on the air. We were in the bathroom together, alone, as I feared. I stood rooted in place, unsure what to do. I could hear him walk up to my stall. His feet stopped at the door. I could see the tops of his shoes.

"I want to touch them," he said softly. It was more of a demand than a request.

I remained in place, my heart racing, my whole body flushed with heat.

"I'm the good guy, remember?"

I still didn't respond, my hand clasped against my chest, my breath coming quick.

"Out here, in the open," he said. "I want to see them under the light."

Inexplicably powerless, I obeyed. I unlatched the lock on the bathroom stall. He pushed the door open, his hand extended. I reached out and took it and he led me over to the fluorescent lights over the sinks.

He took several paper towels from the dispenser and wiped down the area, then lifted me up and placed me on the counter.

He held my calf in his hands, admiring the shape and the curve of the muscle. He kissed my shin all the way down to the ankle, drinking in the scent of my foot. He held it aloft, gazing at it in wonder.

"So beautiful," he whispered. "Your feet are so beautiful."

I squirmed against the counter, my pussy growing hot.

He slipped off the Zanotti, his tongue running the expanse of my sole, my arch, and my heel. He sucked at the heel for a long moment, and then maneuvered my foot so he could suckle my toes.

Waves of electricity shot through my body. The sensation of his hot mouth on my foot was making me light-headed, almost like I was going to faint. I reached down and touched my wetness, fingering myself as he continued. He unzipped his pants with his free hand, reaching in and pulling out his hardness. He rubbed the arch of my foot against him, rolling it back and forth over his rigid shaft. I moaned with pleasure, pushing my panties to the side and slipping my fingers deep into my wetness. Our eyes held each other as he fucked the arch of my foot, his dick cradling the supple curve, then squeezing itself between my freshly painted Chocolate Moose toes.

He grabbed my other leg and held it high, kissing up and down the length of it as he continued to fornicate my foot. I was high with excitement, one hand tweaking my nipple, the other desperately jabbing in and out of my pussy. I wanted to cum. I needed to cum. Apparently so did he, as he pumped excitedly against my soft heel, clasping my foot tightly in his hand. The pressure built for both of us until it was too much to contain. I came against my own hand, throwing my head back, moaning with pleasure. He came along with me, spewing his hot essence over the top of my foot, his crème brûlée now covering my Chocolate Moose as his oozy goodness dripped onto the floor.

We both smiled, bashfully at first, then the smiles turned to quiet laughter. He removed several paper towels from the dispenser, ran cool water over them, added some soap, and proceeded to clean my foot of his spilled juices. He lifted me down from the counter and handed me some of the fresh paper towels. I moistened them and cleaned myself up. He did the same, tucking his sated cock back into its secret place. He wiped up the floor.

"You first," he said, gesturing at the door.

"No," I insisted. "Let's leave together."

He reached out for my hand and we exited the bathroom as a happy pair, oblivious of the angry stares of the people in line who had been waiting their turn. We floated past them, high on love, headed home to relieve our longtime babysitter of her duties for the night.

This evening out was our weekly ritual, always at a different club, bar, restaurant, whatever. If we went to a club, he allowed me to have my fill of shaking my booty on the dance floor with the man of my choice.

My husband wasn't much of a dancer, but he didn't mind letting me get it in. It helped to get me hyped and ready for what was to come next. No matter what the scenario, our night always ended the same way, with his delicious cum on my feet. Sometimes it was under a restaurant table. Sometimes it was in the corner booth of a darkened bar. Tonight it was in the unisex bathroom of a newly opened club downtown. As we passed the bar, I waved good-bye to the man who had been waiting there, still holding a drink he'd bought for me nearly half an hour before. The ice had long melted. He stared after us with a look of genuine surprise and betrayal. Aw, how sweet. He had been saving himself for me. My husband chuckled, shaking his head as he pulled me closer. The man at the bar would be fine. There were plenty of women eager to get at him.

As for me, I was eager for more of my husband. Our ride home would begin Round Two, as I placed my feet in his lap and expertly used them to massage him to ball-bursting satisfaction all over again.

Reality

Feet. One, rather *two*, of the most telling parts of the human body. Aside from the face and general build of a person, feet are among the first things we notice. Are they well clad or cheaply shod? If exposed, what are the conditions of the skin and nails? Clean, pedicured feet usually indicate a person who meticulously cares about his or her physical appearance. Callused heels and corny toes? Not so much. Are they small and delicate or large and wide? The latter, on a man, can mean the exciting promise of something, um, big. On a woman? Not so much.

Whatever the case, **feet, for some, are considered just as sensuous as more traditional erogenous zones, like the lips, neck, nipples, buttocks, and genitalia**. We've all heard of, known, or perhaps even dated (and/or married!) men who were fixated on feet. Some of you may be foot lovers yourselves. I'm sure there are those of you reading this right now who find the very thought of sucking on some toes both repugnant and off limits. *Why would I want my husband to suck on my feet after I've been walking around on them all day?* you ask. *And I certainly don't plan on putting his nasty toes in my mouth! I hope that's not what you're about to suggest, Vixen!*

Well, that's too bad. While sucking toes isn't for everyone, you may never know if you're not even open-minded enough to give it a try. You just might be missing out on something truly wonderful. Besides, no one is asking you to do anything with unclean feet (unless that is your thing). **Some men with hardcore foot fetishes love the natural aroma of toes fresh out of the shoes they've been tucked in all day.** If that describes your man, why deprive him of that pleasure?

Let me ask you this: Do you enjoy having your feet massaged?

Of course you love having your feet massaged! Done correctly, it can be one of the most incredible, soothing, cathartic, relaxing, and erotic experiences ever. Sore feet can be the source of a great deal of pain and stress, especially if you spend a lot of your time standing or rushing around. Having someone lovingly massage your soles, toes, heels, and the aching muscles therein can be enough to bring you to tears of gratitude. If you can imagine having a foot massage that starts with someone doing it by hand, then transitioning to using his lips and tongue, well ladies, you've got yourself the ingredients of a bona fide foot-fetish fantasy!

Many keep this kind of fetish hidden until what feels like the appropriate moment, lest they be considered too fringe and freaky. Believe me, there is nothing freaky about literally loving to love feet. Nothing at all. There are plenty of men who become excited at the very idea of being given permission to let their appreciation for the exquisite architecture of the arch, toes, and a well-turned heel go wild. Why not let them? Ladies, if you've never had your toes sucked or sucked a toe, give it a try. You just might find that you have a knack for it. It could prove much more sensuous than you think.

If you, your husband, or both of you happen to have a thing for feet, then this is the perfect fantasy for you. Before we dive into this feetfirst (I couldn't resist), let's make sure those tootsies are in proper sucking order. **Clean and pretty feet are mandatory for this fantasy!**

Vixen Tip

A Good Pedi Is the Cure

Ladies, I shouldn't have to tell you this, but, well, nobody likes a crusty foot. There is no excuse for those callused heels you're running around with that are as rough as sandpaper. And for goodness' sake, do something about those corns! If you've been hiding your hideous kinkies inside sneakers, too-tight pumps, and house shoes (shame on you if you're running around in house shoes! shame on you!) just to keep them out of plain sight because you're embarrassed by the way they look, then it's time for a fix. If you've got no shame and your crusty heels and corny toes have been on display in strappy sandals and open-toed pumps...wow. Simply, wow. I have no more words for you about that one. It's time for an intervention on all counts. A foot fetish is a highly visual thing for men who harbor this obsession. They love the sight of pretty toes, the feel of soft heels, soles, and high, delicate arches. Even if you don't have small delicate feet and high arches, if your feet are super-size and flat, they can still be sexy and suitable for this fantasy, as long as you take the proper measures.

• **Seek the professionals.** While there is nothing wrong with do-it-yourself pedicures, especially in these frugal times, there is something to be said for leaving it to the experts. This is not just for the benefit of your feet. A pedicure can be a very soothing experience to help prepare you, body and soul, for a fun night ahead. There is nothing like having your heels sanded with a pumice stone, your cuticles pushed back and trimmed, your toenails shaped, and your soles massaged as your feet steep in warm-to-hot soapy, bubbling water.

• **Sit in the big chair.** If you can afford it, spring for a spa chair pedicure. They can be found at most nail salons around the country for an average starting price of twenty-five dollars, excluding tip. The lower part has a basin and faucets for the pedicure. The chair itself typically has massage zones from the neck area to the buttocks and is time-, temperature-, and zone-controlled by you via a handset attached to the chair. It is a perfect way to get your whole body in on this relaxing act.

• **Mix it up.** Many specialized salons take the pedicure experience to a whole other level, offering various types of scrubs and treatments based upon the one you choose. There are margarita pedicures where you are served a freshly made margarita to sip as essential oils, salt, lime, and sometimes sugar are scrubbed into your feet to exfoliate the skin, producing incredibly smooth results. There are mojito versions, done with limes and mint, or strawberry pedicures, even ones that use chocolate. For an even more exotic experience, fish pedicures have emerged on the American market, having made their way here from overseas, where your feet are placed into a tank filled with hundreds of tiny "doctor fish" (*Garra rufa*), which nibble away all the dead skin. Fans of this treatment swear by it, saying

Vixen Tip

it provides the smoothest pedicure they've ever experienced. If that floats your boat, give it a try. Just Google "doctor fish" or "fish pedicure" to locate spas in your area. Be forewarned: Some states have outlawed fish pedicures due to the fact that tools typically used for pedicures must be sterilized after each use. The "tools," in this instance, are living creatures. You can't sterilize the fish between treatments. So if you manage to find a spa that offers fish pedicures and decide to try it out, keep in mind that the same fish lips used to nosh on the crusty feet that came before yours will also be used to nosh on you.

• **Dip it low.** For even softer feet, get the paraffin dip. After the soaking, scrubbing, clipping, and massaging, just before your toes are painted, your feet are dipped into a warm wax bath that forms a soft-but-solid casing that is peeled off once it dries. Can you say "butter feet"? Your skin will be unbelievably supple, and paraffin dips are usually only five or ten dollars added to the cost of your pedicure.

• **Be colorful.** Pick a nail polish that brings out the sexy. Don't be afraid to be bold with black, gold, silver, blue, or whatever color matches and works with your lingerie. Even drawn-on designs are fine, if it works with the look you're going for that evening. Of course, freshly pedicured toenails painted in red are always the gold standard. Nothing beats a red-hot toe!

• ***Woooosah!*** This kind of thing is best experienced with a nonchatty technician, someone who just lets you lean back and enjoy the moment without distracting you with a litany of meaningless questions. ("You live around here?" "You work today?") You know the type. Not that there's anything wrong

Vixen Tip

with a little friendly conversation, but moments like this, when you're relaxing in the chair and being taken care of, are great to center yourself and prepare for the awesomeness that lies ahead between you and your man. If you must, discreetly inform the shop owner that you'd like a quiet pedicure so that you can unwind. In some instances you might get the stink eye, but trust me, if they want your money, they'll oblige!

Now that you've got pretty feet (and hopefully pretty hands to match), you're ready to get things going. **While sexy lingerie, hair, and makeup play important roles in this fantasy, your shoes will be the stage that allows you to perfectly spotlight your deliciously inviting feet.**

Vixen Tip

Shoe Me the Way

It's important to wear the right shoes for this particular fantasy. If you really know your husband, you know what kinds most turn him on. If you've never broached the subject with him (maybe he has kept his fetish to himself all this time), ask him. Your choice of shoe could run the gamut from expensive strappy five-inch heels to the standard-issue clear heels favored by porn stars and girls who work the stage at strip clubs. For most shoes, try websites like Zappos (www.zappos.com), which offer a wide selection, excellent prices, and free shipping. For clear heels, sites like Hot Stripper Shoes (surprised?) (www.hotstrippershoes.com/stripper-shoes-5.5-inch-heels.htm) and

Vixen Tip

Snaz75 (www.snaz75.com/clear.html) have a number of wickedly provocative shoes to choose from.

- **Practice makes perfect.** If you plan on donning very high heels, especially clear ones, but don't wear heels on a regular basis, please, ladies, I beg of you...practice, practice, practice before the big event! The last thing you want is to topple over, twist your ankle, or bust your ass as you're trying to entice your husband with your feet. Ending up in a cast is the ultimate fantasy killer...unless your man has a thing for casts. In which case, abandon this fantasy and Google the phrase "cast fetish." Trust me. You won't be disappointed. When I say everything is on the Internet, I mean *everything* is on the Internet.

If your husband is a true foot man, you can really blow his mind by taking things to the next level. Sure, sucking your toes and you rubbing your foot across his body may turn him on, but why not go one step further? **Become a master at the ultimate pedi-fetishist experience: giving good "foot."** It is like giving head, but using the opposite end of your body. Like fellatio, giving foot—for these purposes, let's call it "pedatio"—is not for the uninitiated. It is not just about putting your feet on your husband's dick and rubbing. There is a method to the act, an attention to detail that requires practice and focus to perfect what you're doing.

Not surprisingly, there are sites on the web that offer step-by-step instructions on how to do it. I found an excellent one on, of all places, eHow.com, called "How to Give a Foot Job." And this isn't the only place you might find such information. Oh, no! Not by far! Please, Google the terms "how to give" and "foot job," and you'll find more information than you'll be able to digest. The woman who wrote this particular article has contributed several sexual how-to articles to the site and is listed as an "authority." From the step-by-step detail she provides, it sure sounds like she knows her stuff.

By letting your feet do the talking, you and your husband can enter an exciting new realm. Who says hands and fingers should have all the fun? Toes are digits, too, you know. **Your husband's strategically placed and wiggled big toe can be just as stimulating for you as his finger or penis (depending on the size of his toe).** His heel, carefully planted, massaging your clitoris, can elicit outstanding results. Don't underestimate the power of your feet just because you're running around on them all day.

They just might take your relationship on a walk to remember!

Recap

- Feet, for some, are considered just as sensuous as more traditional erogenous zones, like the lips, neck, nipples, buttocks, and genitalia.

- Some men with hardcore foot fetishes love the natural aroma of toes fresh out of the shoes they've been tucked in all day.

- Clean and pretty feet are mandatory for this fantasy!

- While sexy lingerie, hair, and makeup play important roles in this fantasy, your shoes will be the stage that allows you to perfectly spotlight your deliciously inviting feet.

- Become a master at the ultimate pedi-fetishist experience: giving good "foot."

- Your husband's strategically placed and wiggled big toe can be just as stimulating for you as his finger or penis (depending on the size of his toe).

V-Log #12
It Must Be Toe Jam ('Cause Jelly Doesn't Stink)

Please tell me this V-Log isn't going to be what I think it's about. Tell me I'm not about to find out that you've just tried to do a foot fetish fantasy with crusty-ass feet. Please, please, say it ain't so. Oh my goodness! You did. Have you no shame?

And stop it with the . . . *but I was busy* crap. You read the chapter that came before this. I went into great detail about how to care for your feet, especially if you have a man who has a specific passion for them. You should be taking care of your feet anyway, for personal hygiene's sake. It shouldn't take your man having a thing about feet to make you take the time to care for them. Do it for you, not for him. Do it for your health, for the environment. Feet can get mad funky. Haven't you ever heard of toes that smell like Fritos?

Why would you even attempt this kind of erotic role-playing if you weren't going to do it right? Toe jam? For real? Seriously, who even has toe jam in this day and age? There's simply no reason for it. Pedicures are relatively inexpensive. Nail shops are as commonplace as air, found in practically every strip mall of practically every neighborhood in practically every city, village, and hamlet around the country. There are even nail shops for pets. That means right now, somewhere in America, a bulldog is walking around with better-cared-for feet than you. Think about that. A bulldog. Consider those words.

All right, let us examine how your misadventure went down, shall we?

So you order this book from Amazon.com after hearing one of your clients rave about all the sensuous stories and fantasies it details. She and her husband have already tried out the Video Voyeur and Self-Pleasure chapters, to great success. Those fantasies are now being incorporated into their regular sexual menu. She simply can't stop raving. You have to get in on all the action. Not their action, mind you. Some action of your own.

Yes, I know this is all rather meta. I'm writing a V-Log about you, even though I don't know you exist yet because I'm just writing this V-Log now. Oh, and your friend—the one who recommended this book to you—hasn't even read the book yet, even though you're in it. How could she? It's not out yet, because I'm just writing it. But wait, you're holding the book in your hands and reading this V-Log right now, so that means the book's out. And you're in it! Confusing? Of course it is. Meta stuff can be pretty hard to follow. But here's the thing: I already *knew* that you existed. Women like you always exist. You're that random chick—that's right, I said *chick*—who constantly needs to be checked for the simplest and most commonsense things, from the elements of basic grooming to inappropriate over-sharing in mixed company. Sure, you may look sharp and together on the surface, but underneath there's a whole lot of raggedy going on. You know who you are. You've long needed to learn this lesson, and it's high time someone sat you down and set you straight. Actually, you shouldn't have even jumped ahead and read this book first. You need to go back to square one and start with the book that precedes this one.

Toe jam. Man. I'm still reeling over the fact that I have to write about this.

What is most unfortunate is that you're the owner of a successful and lucrative business that allows you and your husband a certain level of financial freedom, so you really are savvy in that regard. Sadly, that has been your excuse for not taking care of the things you consider unimportant, like regularly shaving your underarms, waxing your lady parts, and taking note of the condition of your feet.

You are the master of covering things up, choosing to defer giving them attention rather than dealing with them on a regular basis. Your underarms are hidden under expensive blouses, which, in turn, are covered by well-tailored business suits. You eventually get around to shaving them, but go way more days without doing so than you should. Your rampant bush rages beneath dignified Spanx, covertly taunting all who would threaten to shear it. Worst of all, your hooves—your hideous hooves—are crammed into the most fashion-forward shoes on the market. Chanel. Gucci. Jimmy Choo. The ever-desired red-soled Louboutins. Shoe salesmen simultaneously love you and fear you. (Big commission! Frito funk!) Consequently, you've taken to ordering your shoes online, where there's no fancy-schmancy salesperson judging your feet. Women and men alike admire your shoe game, oblivious of the hideous humpbacked beasts lurking within. Discerning eyes sometimes notice a hint of bumpiness beneath the leather in the toe area, but most are so dazzled by the beautiful shoes, they somehow miss that telling detail. You don't go out enough to warrant anything strappy or open-toed, so your cringe-worthy digits remain cloaked from the world. Oprah once told Naomi Campbell that she was far too pretty on the outside to have her insides not match, or something like that. Well, girlfriend, the same thing goes for you and those beautiful shoes that you have cloaking those monstrous feet.

Anyway, I digress. Back to the fiasco that was your attempt at this fantasy.

Because you are so business-minded, you haven't really taken care of business where it counts. Your man, a stay-at-home husband, is devoted and loving, accepting of whatever it is you choose to throw his way. He doesn't complain about anything, often opting to keep his thoughts to himself just to maintain harmony at home. And while you're not cruel and unloving, you aren't exactly the most sensuous woman, either. You give him regular sex, but that's just how you do it . . . you give it to him. It's more surrender than lovemaking. There's nothing truly participatory about it. It's just something you allow him to do so that you can get it out of the way and move on to more pressing matters, like making money so your family can keep moving up the food chain. There's a McMansion you've had your eye on in a community just outside the city, and even though the economy has affected many of your friends, you and your family have been thriving—financially, anyway. Definitely not sexually. On the erotic front, you could use a stimulus check.

Sexually, you and your husband are stagnant. There has been absolutely no variety, not for years. Yours is an all-missionary diet, all the time. You've long realized this and may have even felt a tad bit of guilt for not being interested in doing more in bed. Just because your husband is stay-at-home doesn't mean he doesn't deserve special treatment. You need him, after all. Who's going to run the household and look after the kids? Not that that's his only usefulness. He's a man. He needs to feel like one.

You love him; very much so. But you need him at home so that you can focus on work, and the last thing you want is for him to develop a wandering eye while you're off making the proverbial bacon and doughnuts. Enter your friend raving about this book. Enter you reading the Foot Fetish chapter. It's a perfect match, so you think, especially since your shoe game is pretty on point. Just like that, in an instant, you decide (unfortunately, without your husband's input) that this will be the fantasy you introduce to kick up your sexual play.

You arrive home past eight that night (so typical), with making merry on your mind. Your husband, as is his usual fashion, is harried and tired, having cleaned the house, made dinner, helped the children with their homework, chased the baby around from room to room, and done the online banking and bill paying. After you've eaten and he washes, rinses, and puts away your dishes, you kindly tell him to have a seat and take a load off. You've got special plans for him. Your husband is astonished. You're doing something nice especially for him. What manner of trickery is this!

You run him a steaming hot bath, something you haven't done in a long time... years, even. You add fragrant, soothing oils to the water, then lead him into the bathroom. He's shocked, stunned, and immediately protests. No, he says, let him take care of *you*, you're the one who just returned from a long hard day at the office. He knows this because you constantly remind him of how you spend so many long hard days at the office. Still, you insist. His day was probably much harder than yours, you reply. Inside, of course, you don't really mean this. He's a freaking househusband, after all. You're the one who's on the phone all day negotiating deals, pursuing new business, steadily on the grind. You work hard for the money. So hard for it, honey. Your poor husband is so very grateful that you finally seem to understand how rough he has it at home—a truth that, sadly, you have yet to comprehend.

You undress him, surprised at his well-toned body. Was he always this fit? How had it slipped your notice? But then, you don't notice a lot of things because you're too busy *making that money*. Your husband, however, has always tried to remain sexy and appealing for you, so, unlike yourself, he takes time during the day to squeeze in a workout. Some of that money you make goes toward a membership at a twenty-four-hour gym. You both have memberships but, alas, he's the only one who makes the time to actually use it. He keeps his hair trimmed, his nails clipped, and his skin moisturized. He wishes you would do the same, but he's never exactly known how to say this to you. You're so damn touchy and resistant to criticism. He's actually relieved that you seem to be in such an upbeat mood tonight.

He slips into the steaming bathwater, hopeful that you are finally starting to pay attention to the things that really matter, like love, affection, and attention to your man. You kiss him as he settles into the water, exit the room, closing the door behind you, greet your parents at the door ten minutes later as they scoop up the baby and the kids, leaving you and your man free to enjoy this, literally, fantastic evening.

Once they're gone and your husband is still soaking in the tub, you change into something seductive—at least, the closest thing someone like you has to something seductive, which is a black teddy that you've owned for what seems like forever. You bought it during your college years to impress a boyfriend, and you graduated more than twelve years ago. The teddy is, admittedly, a little worn for wear, frayed around the edges, more grayish than black, a bit holey in the seat, but no matter. It works.

See, you don't consider lingerie that important. You never have. Spanx? Now, *those* are important. Gotta keep those emerging rolls around the middle under wraps. Business wear—suits, blouses, dresses, blazers, slacks—that stuff is important. Nice coats are important. So are cashmere capes with fur trim, and Hermès scarves, oh, oh, oh, and let's not forget the Tiffany necklaces and those blasted David Yurman bracelets you love so much. And expensive shoes. Those are definitely important. But lingerie? Meh. Not so much. That stuff is for women with too much time on their hands, women who prance around in garters, fuzzy slippers, and bustiers for someone else's amusement when they could be out making that dollar-dollar-bill, y'all. Unless they're hookers, call girls, and escorts. That's different. If lingerie is the tool necessary for a person to make money, then you understand. But it isn't your tool, so you don't bother.

As a result of this failure to realize the relevance of investing in a few nice pieces of La Perla, Agent Provocateur, a couple of Cosabella bras and panties, or hell, just some basic Victoria's Secret, now, in this moment when you actually need some, you don't have a thing. Nothing but cotton underwear and utilitarian bras—which in your mind should work just fine because this fetish is all about feet, not bras and panties, but, well, maybe you should at least put forth the effort.

So you reach for that ancient teddy. It's a little tight around the middle, but we knew that already, Spanx girl. Oh well. What can you do? So you squeeze into that ancient teddy and a fresh pair of sheer black hose. Your coarse, raggedy heels snag the hose as you pull them on, sending rivers of runs up the back of your right thigh. Fortunately, you keep lots of hose on hand, this being a familiar daily exercise for you. You'd rather stock up on extra hose than take the time to have your heels scraped. If that's not the laziest, most pathetic thing ever. How can you be so polished about so many other things, yet so wack about the basics? Ugh.

Finally, you pull out a pair of stunning, black strappy Louboutins, a six-inch pair you've kept hidden in the back of the closet, a treat for yourself from this season's new line. You had no idea if you would ever wear them, and buying them wasn't even about the wearing of them as much as it was the having. They are such gorgeous shoes. You must have been prescient when you bought them, though, because now, with this foot-fetish fantasy thingy, you finally have an excuse to put them on. You step into them, your craggy hose-covered bumpy toes and cracked heels hanging over the front and back. You ordered them online and when they arrived you realized that they ran a bit small, but you didn't want to send them back. You walk around in them now, familiarizing yourself with their shape and feel. You stop in front of a full-length mirror. *Nice, very nice*, you think as you fluff your hair. The teddy isn't that bad. Yeah, it's kind of tight, but your husband knows your body. He loves your body, so he says. You pull at the crotch from the back, moving a hole in the seat from view. There. That's better. Everything is perfect, except for…

What's that faint scent in the air? It's slightly familiar, yet not. You lift your pits, sniffing each one. Everything seems okay there. Your deodorant is one that brags about how it works overtime. Maybe it's nothing, you think. Just to be safe, you spritz on a smattering of perfume. That's right, there'll be no bath for you, no freshening up to present a clean canvas for your husband after sitting on your funky ass at work all day. You smell just fine as far as you're concerned. You took a shower this morning and you didn't do much running around at the office today. You've stewed in your juices all day, but it was a slow cook, not a boil, so I guess that makes it okay.

Sigh

Before I go any further, can I just say, um…*ew*? Like, super-ew? Über-ew? Ew to the infinity times forever? Yeah. That. Okay, back to this…

So you strut into the bathroom, you sexy vixen you. Wait. No. Let me take that back. I *refuse* to let you use the term *vixen* in your present state. You are not a vixen, honey. You are the anti-vixen right now. You're a *nixen*.

So you strut your nixen ass down the hall toward the bathroom. You fling open the bathroom door, completely disarming your half-sleeping husband. The poor thing was so exhausted, he drifted off in the bath. He rouses himself, believing he's dreaming, as you saunter over to the tub and sit down on the side.

"Wow, what's this?" he asks.

"A surprise," you reply.

"No kidding," he says, his nose unconsciously crinkling. "First a bath and now this? But what about the kids? Suppose they catch us?"

"Don't worry about them. They're with their grandparents for the rest of the night."

"Even the baby?" he says with slight concern.

"Even the baby. My mom is happy to spend some time with her."

"Nice," he says with a smile of relief, followed by a slight frown. "Do you smell something?" he asks.

You sniff the air, but all you get a whiff of is the extra layering of perfume you're drenched in.

"Something like what?" you ask. "I put lavender oil in your bathwater. Is that what you mean?"

"I don't know," your husband says. "No, I don't think that's what it is. It smells kinda strange. Almost like corn chips. Did you snack on some?

Are you still hungry, because I can make you something else to eat." He rises to get out of the tub, but you push him back down into the water.

"I'm fine," you say. "Just relax." You sniff the air again. Nada. You shake your head. "I don't smell any corn chips. You must be imagining things."

"Maybe," he says, returning his attention to you. "So get up and step back. Let me have a look at my sexy wife."

You oblige so that he can take you in, in all your old-college-teddy, unwashed, perfume-doused glory. As you do, one of your craggy nails snags the front of the hose. A run races up the front of your right thigh. His eyes follow the run as it rises higher and higher up your leg.

"Nice shoes," he says, being polite. He's been long disgusted by your unkempt feet. He's even tried to give you pedicures himself, but you always rebuff him, claiming you have work to finish and no time for silly distractions like foot care and whatnot.

You, of course, have no idea how much of a turn-off your hoofers are, so, in response to his compliment about your shoes, you dance your way over to him, placing one on the side of the tub, close to his face, so you can show off the spectacular Louboutins. He gets a full-on whiff of what he has been smelling all along. It hits him like a concrete wall as he realizes that, all this time, there really were corn chips right in the room.

"Baby!" he cries, unable to keep the ruse going. "Do you smell your feet?"

"What?" you exclaim. "What are you talking about?"

"Your feet," he says. "They smell like Fritos. No, like ass. How can you not smell that?"

You bend down and sniff, finally catching the funky breeze.

"Wow, I must have stepped in something."

You sit on the toilet and unfasten the shoes.

Oh. Do I even need to say that the fantasy's pretty much DOA at this point? Good. Then I won't.

But it is. Okay? Everybody's sex drive has been crushed at this point. His, yours, mine, the readers. Even the Frito-Lay company must be thinking about rebranding Fritos right about now.

So you unfasten the shoes. You remove the snagged hose. And there, between your rusty, crusty, corn-cobbed toes, is the most disgusting, unidentifiable dried goo-*cum*-dust-bunny-esque stuff—an erection and mood killer of epic, malodorous proportions. And it's just hanging out like it's always been there. Hanging out like that's where it belongs. Is it dead skin? Is it congealed lotion that you somehow, in your morning haste, failed to rub in all the way? What is that stuff?

It's toe jam. A thing once believed to be an urban myth, the Bigfoot of hygiene, oft spoken of but, really, who's ever actually seen toe jam on someone? You've gotta be some kind of lazy/filthy/McNasty to have goo jammed up between your toes. But you do. It's alive and well, rather, unwell. Right in your own and your husband's face.

This is beyond repugnant. You're lucky you don't get your lady-card revoked for this.

Okay, you guys, do I even need to address everything that is wrong here? That went wrong here? That shouldn't have gone wrong? Please don't make me do that. I can't. I just can't.

Whew! Thank you. Thank you for not making me go there again.

Let's all just agree that this woman—you, if it applies—didn't thoroughly read the prior chapter. You didn't read *The Vixen Manual: How to Find, Seduce & Keep the Man You Want.* You apparently were able to find and keep a man—how, I can't even begin to guess—but you definitely didn't do it via the art of seduction. Somehow in your life, you missed the good hygiene memo, too. You missed a lot. Too many things for me to list right now.

And I'm not just going to let your husband off the hook, either. He deserved that face full of corn-chipped, jammy toes you gave him. He should have long ago sat you down and given you a good talking-to about the state of your foot affairs. In my opinion, he is just as much a part of the problem as you. It takes two to tango, two to make toe jam. This was a joint effort. Shame on you both.

Aside from the fact that your husband should have said something about your bad feet long ago, you should have discussed with him beforehand your plan to implement the foot-fetish fantasy. It was highly unfair of you to spring it on him, particularly when your feet are in such a poor state. While it might seem like a good idea to surprise your man with one of the fantasies from this book, it's best that the two of you read it together, picking out something that mutually strikes your fancy. I can guarantee you that if you had mentioned to your man beforehand that you were going for the foot-fetish fantasy, he would have loudly protested and suggested the two of you try something else. Your husband knows the state of your feet. He knows the quickest way to kill the thrill in his pants is to shove those befunked crustables up in his face.

Ladies: Always, always, always take care of your bodies. Pay attention to grooming. And unless your husband likes a wee bit of stank on his woman as an aphrodisiac, please, take a hot bath before you even think about sexing him, especially after returning from a long hard day at work. That's not just good hygiene, that's courtesy, decency, dignity, respect. Come on, people, this isn't rocket science. It's everyday living. Wash your monkey. Take care of your feet. It's the right thing to do.

I'm so disgusted right now.

throws the mike down and exits the room

Epilogue

For Fuck's Sake

So there you have it. I don't know about you, but I could use a hot bath *and* a cold shower. Some of the things mentioned here are not for the faint of heart or the self-conscious. **However, everything in this book *is* for the adventurous and for couples who want more out of their intimate lives without having to venture outside their marriage.** My hope for this little morsel of sexual goodness is that it helps get your creative juices going and maybe, just maybe, ignites a spark in your relationship that neither of you was aware even existed.

Monogamous relationships can be the pits—the same damn thing, day in and day out, year after year after year. Like the song says: Forever? Forever ever? Forever ever? Forever is, indeed, a mighty long time to be doing the same thing the same way in bed all the time. He heaves himself on top of you with that same stroke and you lie there like a wet fish—maybe even a dry one, after all this time—moaning, halfway faking the funk, looking up at the ceiling, just wanting it to be over so you can get back to *Grey's Anatomy* or *Hoarders*. Ugh! Is *this* why the divorce rate is so high? It definitely has to be a major part of the equation.

So I wanted to put a little bit of something in this book for everyone. Even if you try just one thing, be proud—you have taken positive steps to invest in your marriage. **The word *fantasy* evokes such horror and dread in the minds of those women and men who feel as if their partners' fantasies couldn't possibly include them.** The natural assumption is that partners' fantasies are about some celebrity, a porn star, or, worst of all, a prior love. This book is proof that it doesn't have to be this way. I hope the chapters contained herein have hushed those evil voices in your head, the ones insisting that your partner needs or wants someone else to be and do all those things he imagines when he's alone in the bathroom touching himself.

I hope this book has helped you. God knows it has helped me. "How?" you ask? Well, for starters, *SatisFaction* has helped me realize how much I don't know about sex and how much of it lies in the mind and imagination. Everybody has their own thing that they're into, their own idea about the definition of *freaky* and what exactly constitutes a turn-on. And although I knew it already, I've learned on a much deeper level that while a thrilling sex life is a huge part of what keeps relationships together, it's still just a piece of a much larger puzzle. I believe any long-lasting relationship is built on genuine friendship, and unconditional love and trust, even in the face of the greatest adversities, even against the widest of odds. Clear, concise, and honest communication rounds out the list. **No matter what, you have to know how to talk to each other.**

The most surprising discovery in all of this is that I've learned sex actually makes me uncomfortable. I'm not talking about intimacy, nor do I mean that I'm uncomfortable doing it within the confines and safety of my marriage. It was the talking about it, over and over and over again; that one was a toughie for me. I feel as if I've been sucked into some sort of sexual vortex where, for the rest of my life, I will be expected to talk to you people about sex. Obligated, even. Much as I love giving advice, I must admit, a lot of the things in this book make me genuinely blush. Frankly, I'm not sure how Dr. Ruth does it!

As I live and breathe, writing some of the things in this book makes me feel like a literary whore. That's right, I said it. I am a woman expected to write about sex for money. I'm a hooker for hardbacks.

And I love it!

I hope you guys learned a lot and that this little book of mine has opened a series of discussions with your husbands, wives, and closest confidants. It was nearly impossible to put together, what with all the stopping for, ummm, intermittent sex breaks.

Now, this book, obviously, is not your mother's erotic fantasy how-to. No. And it's certainly not the sort of thing you bring to work or leave out on the coffee table for your children to happen upon! So please, do me a favor and keep this book safe from kids and bosses and those who would be mortified to know you would ever consider dressing up like a hooker and standing on street corners!

Thanks.

When my editor first suggested I write this book, I was mortified and, to be even more honest, I couldn't write it. I stared at my computer screen for six months and—nothing! But, just for you, I dug deep, and then my lover dug deeper, and voilà! Pure *SatisFaction*!

This book is très hot, so I'm pretty sure you've enjoyed reading it as much as I've enjoyed being forced to do the research... to say nothing of all the testing of the theories within its pages. Yes, I made the sacrifice. You can thank me later. And don't feel bad if you want to keep it to yourself for a while before sharing it with your spouse. There's some pretty heady stuff in here. The sexual fantasies in this book make great fodder for a little one-on-one time, if you know what I mean.

Um, or so I've heard.

So maybe you're like me. Maybe you were a little afraid before diving into *SatisFaction*, but warmed up to the idea after the first few pages of incorrigible sex talk. And maybe, like me, you've learned something about yourself in the process of feeding your sexual appetite. No matter what sort of sexual decisions you make, what's most important is that all of them are safe. For those of you in long-term, committed relationships, it is equally important that your sexual decisions are never made alone, but with the assistance and input of your partner. The *Oxford English Dictionary* defines a *fantasy* as: "a fanciful mental image, typically one in which a person dwells at length or repeatedly and which reflects their conscious and unconscious wishes." (Funny how similar that is to the definition of *stalking*, but I digress...) That definition says nothing about sneaking around, and it doesn't relate fantasies to shame or secrecy. Somehow along the way, fantasies got a bad rap and became this clandestine thing, something you kept to yourself for fear of discovery or judgment. It doesn't have to be like that. **Share those unconscious wishes once they become conscious and make sure to include your partner.** Invite your partner to share his or her own fantasies as well, and make this erotic exploration a part of your lives.

That's not to say you are expected to go to the extremes in this book every day or every time you have sex. That's way too much pressure for any relationship. (And, heaven forbid, what happens when you run through all the fantasies here? That leaves hundreds of days in the year that you have to come up with more. I can't even imagine the possibilities that lie out there beyond the ones laid out in this book. I don't want to imagine. I've already seen and heard too much.) Wanting to act out fantasies daily is an expectation that is unrealistic and unfair to your partner—heck, I'd go so far as to say that it's downright cruel. Your partner may eventually begin to feel like some sort of performing monkey, always expected to perform the extraordinary on command. Fantasies should be seen as treats... they are that exquisite dessert, a towering Death by Chocolate—layered with chocolate cake, chocolate ice cream, chocolate chunks, chocolate mousse, a chocolate brownie, then topped with whipped cream, chocolate sauce, crunchy almonds, and crumbled Snickers bars—that the two of you savor together at the end of a special meal on a special night out. It's decadent. It's delicious. It's out of the ordinary. You and your spouse couldn't eat a Death by Chocolate after dinner every night. I mean, you could, but you'd be as big as a proverbial house. Your arteries would clog. Soon enough you'd get sick of them. And if you kept going, insisting on eating them night after night, eventually that decadent, once-delicious dish would kill you.

Death by Chocolate, indeed.

That's not to say that too many fantasies will end you, but it might just put an end to your relationship. That's a helluva lot of expectation for two people to manage on a regular basis. We need treats to appreciate the routine. Mixing it up means just that: mixing up the typical pattern of your relationship, adding a zesty splash of excitement and adventure. It doesn't mean overkill. It shouldn't foster resentment and a feeling of begrudged obligation. Fantasies are meant to be fun. To turn them into the routine nullifies their very meaning. Once a fantasy loses its luster and allure, all the fun goes right out the window, and that was the whole reason for doing it in the first place.

Keep it special. Make it unique. Space them out. And be sure that whenever your partner wants to share a fantasy that has been lying dormant and unexplored in his or her head, you are open to it. At the very least, listen without judgment, even if the very idea of it leaves you wigging out a little on the inside. Even if it makes you wig out a lot, get over it. Just listen to what your partner has to say. Even if the fantasy is way out there, keep in mind that you know this person. This is the person you love.

And you'll also help ensure you won't be judged when you let your own freaky needs out of the proverbial closet. And heaven (or hell) only knows what kind of freaky needs you may be harboring. You are reading this book, after all, which means you've already got some kind of freaky rivers running deep. Freak.

Well, what else can I say? Thank you for reading and good luck in all your sexual endeavors. Close your blinds and keep this book in a super-secret place. If your kids discover it and ask if it's yours, act surprised, appalled even. Deny, deny, deny.

Just kidding. Pretend to be blind. Or make a big to-do and throw it in the trash. Dig it out later once they've gone to bed. And pick a better hiding place when you put it away again, ya big dummy. They shouldn't have found it in the first place.

There. That oughta do it. For freaks, you guys are pretty awesome.

Happy to have helped.